Lord of the Gallows

Lord of the Gallows

Tales of Terror and Strangeness

Jason C. Eckhardt

Sarnath Press ■ Seattle

Contents

Introduction

The stories collected here span a wide swath of time—almost forty years, from the early 1980s ("An Echo of Pipes") to the present day ("The Music of Your Life"). Looked at another way, they are representations of two-thirds of my life (I am sixty-three at this writing), and as such they represent the views and words of several different Jason C. Eckhardts. There is a great temptation to go back and "fix" what one's younger self has done, and I am not immune to such an impulse. But I am cautioned against such puttering through the example of other creative peoples, who sought to "fix" older works and thus ruined them (an anecdote about the painter Degas comes to mind).

Rereading these tales after many years, fortunately, I was very pleased to find that I did not feel any need to correct them. Oh, a misspelling here and a slight rearrangement of words there; but I have largely left these as my younger selves wrote them. Turns out they weren't bad scribblers after all!

Some comments on the stories themselves follow.

"The Hollow Sky" was one of my most ambitious stories to date. It, like "And the Sea Gave Up the Dead," "A Tale of a Lonely Island," and "The Silent Garden," was written specifically for an anthology or magazine. But its evolution started long before that.

In the late 1980s, I read an article about the hole in the ozone layer over Antarctica (you may recall it, and the effort to reduce the chlorofluorocarbons that helped create it). Scientists scrambled to discover what caused it. Being a die-hard Lovecraftian, I naturally thought, "It's *SHOGGOTHS!*" I cut the article out for later reference, but did nothing with it—I really did not know where to go with the idea. It took growth, the encouragement of my friend Sam Gafford, and the opportunity of writing for that anthology, to give me the added nudge to work on it. Once I did, it all flowed pretty naturally, with the occasional pause for reference to scientific tomes. By some miracle, I still had the clipping from the '80s, and, miracle of miracles, knew where it was.

"Lord of the Gallows" is just one of several stories built around Saxon pirate Ulle Ironkeel. As with "The Hollow Sky," the germ for this story goes back quite a few years. In the early 1980s I was in the throes of an Arthurian passion. I read much about "the Matter of Britain," including works by Malory, Mary Stewart, and others. But as much as I enjoyed them, I often wondered, "What about the Saxons?" At best they were portrayed as faceless "invaders"; at worst, bloodthirsty savages. This rankled a little. I knew that some of my ancestors were Saxon settlers along the south coast of Britain. Why not tell their story? As is often the case with me, an image came first. I drew it.

You will notice that I gave him the provisional identity of "Notfried, German mercenary on Hadrian's Wall." Name notwithstanding, the image stayed with me, evolving over the years. He became a Saxon, then a Saxon mariner fighting the Romans. A visit to the Portland Public Library in Portland, Maine, where I was then living, supplied me with an Anglo-Saxon/Modern English dictionary,

and an hour later, Notfried had a new name: Ulle ("owl"—I've always been partial to the old birds). Ironkeel, a likely sounding compound word, came later. But Ulle, like the Lovecraftian horrors behind the Hollow Sky, languished for long years, accruing traits and details as time passed, but never emerging as a whole person. Finally he sprang to life and demanded a chronicle of his adventures. Since then I've written several stories about him and the crew of his boat the Wave-cutter; perhaps that will be my next collection.

I drove a delivery van for wholesale florists for twenty years, and the experience helped inspire two stories assembled here, "Detachment" and "The Norther." The former I set in the lovely Oxford Hills region of Maine, one of my favorite routes, and the latter in the prairie lands northeast of Austin, Texas, another of my drives. I believe I have portrayed both areas faithfully, though the inhabitants of both are, as opposed to their fictional counterparts, some of the nicest folks on earth.

A lot of writing, I feel, comes from asking questions and then answering them. First of all, of course, is "What if?" With "The Walker in the Night," I asked myself how I could link two of the signal facts of Providence, R.I., during the twentieth century: H. P. Lovecraft and the Hurricane of 1938. Storms in general, and this storm in particular, have always fascinated me. I grew up with family stories about the Hurricane, which tore across New England like a wood-chipper, leaving 600 dead and incalculable damage. The storm was so strong that it set off seismographs hundreds of miles away, and blew salt sea-spray as far inland as Vermont. It rearranged parts of the Rhode Island coastline and flooded downtown Providence to a depth of eight feet; hence the Lovecraft connection. Lovecraft was already a year dead when the storm hit, but when has something as minor as death stood in the way of a good story? "Walker" is my favorite of the tales presented in this book. It was an experiment in a different voice and, in my estimation, worth the effort.

I have always had a love for the forest. "An Echo of Pipes" and "From the Realms of Glory" were both inspired by this feeling, although one tends toward fascination and the other to fear. For "An Echo," I recall that I was reading a lot of Algernon Blackwood in this period. Perhaps it shows. My birthday is Christmas, and that date has always held a semi-mystical meaning for me. This shaped "Realms" as much as any intended horror. I have no idea what it is that chases Roy through the woods, but it felt right at the time. Still does.

"A Tale of a Lonely Island" was born of my love of history and my former home of Portland, Maine. Similarly, "And the Sea Gave Up the Dead" was inspired by reading about the voyages of Captain James Cook. I was a history major in college, and my professors would probably have been horrified by these stories, and not for the reasons I intended.

"Sunderland House," "The Music of Your Life," and "Dry Spell" are all set in my fictional town of Pocasset, Rhode Island. It is my Arkham, a handy stage-set where I can inflict my fictions on my characters in a setting that I know well. I like to think that it is south of Little Compton (my hometown) and north of Tiverton (where I work in the public library), a geographical impossibility. John Annawan is not, by the way, the "last of the Pocassets"; that tribe is still vibrant and active, and has given its name to several locations in the area, though no towns at the present. "Sunderland" and "Music," I see in retrospect, were both also inspired by a rather eerie local legend as told in David Paten's book of reminiscences, *Three Sides to the Sea.*

Like "Lord of the Gallows," "Niddy Noddy" is one of a series of stories built around a central character: wandering Yankee Abra'm Symmes. I am a big fan of the tales of Robert E. Howard, and if Ulle Ironkeel is my pale version of Howard's Cormac mac Art, then Symmes is my Solomon Kane. Upon rereading "Niddy Noddy," I found that it also owes something to T. E. D. Klein's staggering tale "Petey," a far superior piece of writing. Look it up—you won't be disappointed.

I am indebted to S. T. Joshi for urging me to release this volume, and for his efforts in saving some of these stories from small-press oblivion. I have enjoyed myself immensely creating them, and hope that you may also find some pleasure in reading them.

JASON C. ECKHARDT

New Bedford, Mass.,
June 9, 2022.

The Hollow Sky

"The human race, then, is not alone in the universe. Though I am cut off from human beings, *I* am not alone."

—Adm. Richard E. Byrd, *Alone*

1

I am forced into speech because men of science have refused to follow my advice without knowing why.

Where have I read those words before? I know them well and see the rust of age upon letter and syllable. Yet they are pertinent still, eighty years on—or rather, they are applicable again. In this case, though, I am reversing the advice of my maligned predecessor: Where he sought to dissuade, I seek to encourage. Pray God, what God there may be, that these men of science heed me better than they did him.

Here I speak of "men of science" as beings apart when I am surely one myself. My name is Victor Hope Metcalfe, and I am professor of climatology at the University of Northern Rhode Island in Smithfield. My interest in science was born during field-trips with my father, a professor of physics at MIT, to the wealth of science museums near our home outside of Boston. I got to know the ancient glass specimen cases of the Peabody and Agassiz Museums of Harvard as well as my own room; and how I brimmed with excitement at the annual Christmas show at the Boston Museum of Science's Hayden Planetarium!

But I saved my most ardent enthusiasm for the Gilman Memorial Museum at Miskatonic University. All the way out to Arkham on the Fitchburg line I would daydream of the Gilman's dusty halls, its dioramas and its fossils. Of primary importance to me was the exhibit assembled around the university's ill-fated 1930–31 Antarctic Expedition. When you first enter the museum's classic granite building, you are presented with one of the expedition's huge Dornier Do-J "Wal" aircraft, suspended over the great hall in perpetual flight. Craning my neck, I could see the glint of the museum's lights off the plane's surfaces, still "bruised to a high polish" by the terrible Antarctic gale, as the writer H. P. Lovecraft put it. In the Antarctic Hall itself I half hesitated down its crepuscular length, both dreading and thrilling to the sight of the full-size reproduction of an "Old One." It hangs from the wall midway down the hall, the thing's pseudo-wings and tentacles spread in awful, ten-foot glory between a map of Antarctica circa 1930 and a blow-up photo of fur-clad explorers on a landscape of pure white. I had night-mares about it that I treasured.

By the age of ten I knew the whole tragic story of that voyage to the ends of the earth. The successful flight over the South Pole; the destruction of most of the expedition's company in a howling blizzard; the strange discoveries and Professor William Dyer's stranger revelations; and perhaps most tragic of all, the student Danforth's confinement to the Danvers Asylum upon his return to the States—all were chapter and verse to me. Later I would read Lovecraft's fictional treatment of the expedition, *At the Mountains of Madness;* and later still raged to discover how Dyer had entrusted Lovecraft with his notes, only to discover that Lovecraft had turned his learned dissertation into pulp fiction. Dyer was completely discredited. He had waited five years to publish his revelations, and the shock of Lovecraft's treatment of them helped kill him. He died of a stroke in August 1936, just four months after publication. If there was any justice, it was that Lovecraft followed him in March of the following year.

Of course, who would have believed Prof. Dyer's allegations of alien creatures, hidden antediluvian cities, and titan mountain chains anyway? The Starkweather–Moore Expedition of 1936–37 effectively quashed such wild rumors. There was a mountain chain, yes, but nothing to dwarf the Himalayas; and even the biologists of Miskatonic University itself, working from samples brought back by Dyer and Danforth, con-cluded that the "Old Ones," far from being extraterrestrial in origin, were almost certainly from a lost branch of the *Crinoidea* class of crea-tures—cousins to starfish and sea urchins. Monstrous, certainly, but well within the limits of sane biology. They belonged with the seven-toed lizard, the trilobite, and other dead-ends of evolution.

Yet, disaster or not, the Miskatonic Expedition exercised an inspiration over me. I resolved to make some branch of science my career. My second year at U. Mass. Amherst I was able to secure access to the papers of Professor Lyman Atwood, Miskatonic's Antarctic meteorologist, and it was these that inspired me to become a climatologist. It was through published papers of my own that I was invited to be part of this year's World Geophysical Society's Antarctic Symposium. Thus am I come full circle.

2

Some such thoughts as these ran through my mind as I sat in Logan Airport, awaiting the first of a series of flights that would take me halfway around the world to Antarctica. Outside the March sunshine was glittering off Boston Bay and melting the last of winter's snow, but I knew that where I was going the weather would be far less hospitable. March is the tail-end of Antarctic Autumn; it must truly be urgent for the WGS to beckon us to the bottom of the world at such a time, I reflected. But for the prestige of the gathering, my long-standing fascination with Antarctica—and the fact that the WGS was paying my way—I might have declined the invitation. Even then the whole southern continent was veering toward that months-long night when temperatures could drop as low as -90° F. All right then, I thought, taking a deep breath. You've always wanted to see True South—now is your chance. Brace up.

The theme of the symposium was kept something of a mystery. But being a climatologist and considering our destination I had brought all the information on polar climate that I could lay my hands on at short notice. A good thing, too; organizing this information and refreshing my memory on it occupied me on the interminable series of flights from Boston to New Zealand.

At last we raised the spires of Christchurch. More flying awaited me there, but at least I was given a couple days' hiatus while the organizers of the symposium waited for its last attendees. I made good use of the time by acquainting myself with my fellow scientists (I had little choice: we were secluded from the rest of society in a hotel close by Christchurch Airport). In particular I befriended a tart but brilliant biologist from Oxford, Thomas Spratt. A veteran of two seasons at the British Antarctic Survey's (BAS) Halley Station, Spratt had much to tell me about life on "the Ice." Spratt was exacting, acerbic, and uncompromising, but at the same time possessed of a wit that was as hilarious as it was unexpected. He was thin as a rail, and his short yellow hair never seemed to have known a comb. I liked him immediately.

Gathered here was the cream of intelligence in such fields as chemistry, biology, paleontology, physics, and geology. The place fairly sizzled with invention, but still no one was any wiser than I as to why we had been gathered. It was not until we were herded onto the massive C-130 aircraft for the actual flight to Antarctica (just another ragged band of tourists, to anyone looking) that we were given a presage of what awaited us. Each of us received a package that included polar-grade parka and snowpants (WGS stenciled in large black letters on the back of the orange parka—I felt like a convict wearing it); a manual on survival on the Ice; a set of earplugs and a pair of jet-black wraparound sunglasses; an entrenching tool that combined the virtues of a pick, shovel, and adze; and a hefty, ring-bound volume bearing the ominous title, INVESTIGATIONS INTO ULTRA-NORMAL PHENOMENAE ON EAST ANTARCTIC SHIELD. A computer disk in slipcase with the same Doomsday title on it was also included. No author was given, but glancing over the table of contents I was very surprised to see a section headed: "Miskatonic Expedition Findings—Dyer, Lovecraft, et al."

A tall, cultured-looking man in one of the symposium parkas (the phrase "a sheep in wolf's clothing" came to mind) appeared at the head of the cabin.

"If I may have your attention, please," he shouted. The C-130's four big engines were cycling up. "My name is Noel Personne, and it is my honor to welcome you here on behalf of the World Geophysical Society's Antarctic Symposium. Contained in the packets provided you will find several items essential to your participation in this event. The book—or CD, for those who have laptops—explains the background of the current emergency."

("Emergency"? I thought.)

"As our flight is long and the noise of the aircraft prevents any conversation, I strongly urge you to familiarize yourselves with the information contained therein. Its content will at first seem fantastic, but we rely upon the famous open-mindedness of your several disciplines to give it the consideration due to it.

"One more thing," he bellowed. The noise of the motors really was becoming deafening; the silvery chains holding down the luggage and supplies chimed. "You will find a pair of sunglasses in your kits. Put them on as soon as we arrive at McMurdo Station. The health of your eyes is at stake. Thank you."

Mr. Personne was right about the noise level in the plane at any rate. Even with the earplugs the din was terrific; and it was only due to its monotonous, unvarying nature that we were able to bear it for long.

But soon such considerations faded before the revelations held in the INVESTIGATIONS. Its full content and scientific proofs would be tiresome or at least confusing to most laymen, so I will omit them here. But in essence what it said was this:

What the Miskatonic Expedition of 1930–31 purportedly found, as reported by William Dyer, was real. There *were* two titanic mountain chains stretched across East Antarctica, and nestled against the lesser group was a sprawling city of pre-human origin. The creatures that had built it were "not dinosaurs, but far worse," the text quoted Lovecraft (whose fictional treatment, we were informed, was in all essentials correct)—the star-headed "Old Ones," interstellar entities of pentamerous symmetry and astounding intelligence. For the past eighty years, since the confirmation supplied by the Starkweather–Moore Expedition, a curtain of secrecy had been drawn around that entire section of Antarctica, and a select group of scientists, linguists, and researchers had been studying it all. Since the discoverers had been American but the actual territory involved was Australian, the two governments had cooperated in the largest conspiracy of silence the world had ever seen. Security, for example, was handled by a largely Australian force with the colorful name of the Ice Shadow Army. The plot was aided by the region's near-inaccessibility and later by events in the human sphere. What with depressions, a world war, and a cold war, who had time for a chain of hills in the coldest place on the planet?

There were some close calls in all that time, of course. In 1956 two Soviet destroyers vanished when they approached the seaward end of the larger mountain chain on the Wilhelm II Coast—not sunk, not destroyed, just *vanished.* Scientists at Australia's Mawson Station reported an eerie light high up in the south about this time; at first thought to be a rising planet but later identified with the "beacon" from that unholy mountain range which Dyer had seen in the distance. At first the Soviets had blamed "capitalist aggression" for the loss, but there was no proof. No Western craft were anywhere in the area at the time. There is a sense of high-level meetings in large, dark rooms in Washington and Moscow; and the whole incident faded amidst official declarations of the bravery of the People's Navy. And, it seemed, the Russians were brought into the fold.

The conspiracy's second big concern came with the advent of satellites. Nothing, it seemed, could prevent any nation with satellite technology from peering down from on high on the hidden mountains. But here it developed that the mountains and their enclosed superplateau had a property that blocked electronic images. To all the circling mechanical eyes the region presented a satisfyingly white blank.

In the meantime, the investigators at the base of the Mountains of Madness had not been idle. Linguists attacked the dot-groupings that had served the Old Ones as writing, and after decades of toil had begun to decipher them. Comparing dot-texts with adjacent sculpture-bands in the Old Ones' buildings, recognizing repeated patterns and drawing analogies from human languages by computer programs, the linguists had determined that the Old Ones' writing was very like musical notation. Meaning and context were changed by tonal variations, much as in Chinese and Vietnamese. All this fit in precisely with Dyer's descriptions of the Old Ones' "musical piping over a wide range."

Many of Dyer's other observations were also verified or revised in the light of later science. For example, carbon-14 dating of the petrified shutters in the Old Ones' very oldest buildings had confirmed Dyer's proposed age of +-50 million years (a figure so staggering that the test had been repeated seven times to ensure accuracy; all results were identical). Dyer had also speculated that the Old Ones had used their wings to navigate interstellar "ether," a concept since destroyed by Einstein; but later discoveries of solar winds and "dark energy" have given the scientists further food for thought. Even in minor details Dyer's conclusions were being borne out. The "vast-winged pterodactyls of a species heretofore unknown to paleontology" that the Old Ones had employed to build their taller structures were almost certainly examples of the mighty *Quetzalcoatlus*, whose wingspans could reach fifteen meters (a re-creation of one may be seen today in the Texas Memorial Museum in Austin).

And what of Dyer? He was clearly vindicated, and within the confines of Lake City (the research station established at the foot of the Mountains of Madness) venerated. But in the greater world he must, for the time being, remain discredited. As for fantasy writer Howard Phillips Lovecraft, his role in Dyer's downfall takes on darker overtones. It was never stated explicitly in the INVESTIGATIONS that Lovecraft was part of the grand conspiracy of deception; but it was never denied either, and certain hints as to the source of some of his "revision" payments were ambiguous at best. Then, too, what were we to make of the fact that he died on March 15, 1937, just a week after the return of the Starkweather–Moore Expedition?

I took off my glasses—rubbed my eyes. It was all too much at once. I felt a nudge at my arm and opened my eyes and saw a blurry hand holding out a blurry pad and pencil. Replacing my glasses I could see written on the pad in Tom Spratt's frantic handwriting:

do you buy this?

I considered a moment, then took the pad and pencil.

I'm not sure [I wrote]. *The evidence is daunting, but I need more. And you?*

He took the pad, scribbled furiously on it, and tossed it back. It read:

bloody tripe

To break up the strain of reading this remarkable document, I would turn and gaze out the window to the sea below. Once we had cleared New Zealand's beautiful South Island we were above the "Roaring Forties," that belt of raging sea below 40 degrees south which had been the terror of mariners for centuries. From our breathless height it was an endless expanse of gray streaked with white. Antarctica rings itself in concentric defenses of which the "Roaring Forties" was only the first. Later we saw white flecks upon the Southern Ocean that were the outliers of the great Antarctic pack ice. These increased in size and number, ice floes, icebergs, ice-shelf, and ice-barrier, until a terrible vastness of white ate away the entire southern horizon.

The one small break in this world of white came as we circled down to land at McMurdo Station on Ross Island. The worn buildings along the torn, brown streets of the settlement looked like a giant child's forgotten blocks. Here we were to change planes, and here we first tried out our black sunglasses. Although the sun was low it burned with a pure, pale intensity, and I was glad of the protection.

After the crushing din of the C-130, the smaller Baslers to which we transferred seemed blessedly quiet. But they soon filled with the excited chatter of scientists, pent up after the six-hour flight from New Zealand, as we debated the content of the INVESTIGATIONS. Outside the white walls of our little aircraft the short Antarctic day declined slowly, the dull sun eroding by degrees into the flat horizon. It spread a golden splendor across the endless snows. Finally its last blinding arc slunk under the horizon and was gone. The purple of the zenith deepened into an inarguable black, and stars blazed forth with mad intensity. Still we flew on.

Later, people spoke quietly in pairs or not at all; a few slept. Tom and I debated the possible double meanings of a quotation from *Alone,* Admiral Byrd's account of a winter spent alone on the Ice: "The human race, then, is not alone in the universe. Though I am cut off from human beings, *I* am not alone." I was flipping through my copy of the book, looking for a retort to Tom's latest argument, when he softly said, "Good God."

I turned to look at him. He was staring stock still out the airplane window. I unclicked my safety belt and leaned over him toward the window. Other belts were clicking open, and a mixed rumble of moving bodies and hushed voices signaled that others had seen what Tom had seen. Past the straight orange edge of the airplane's wing; beyond countless leagues of flatness dimming to blue in the evening; in the nexus between earth and sky at the horizon's rim, an ominous purple line of sharp-edged peaks arose. The haze of distance hid their bases but the afterglow picked out their summits in sharp contrast, like the bared teeth of a mouth ready to swallow the world. It became very quiet in the airplane.

3

Lake City lay scattered like bright beads at the base of the Mountains' foothills. For the past hour we had been watching those Mountains of Madness swell and grow into the northwestern sky until they seemed to claw at the very zenith. Then we saw the tiny array of lights of the station and the neat double row that guided us to our landing strip on the ice, and down we glided.

The silence that had invaded the cabin of the plane swelled a thousandfold when we disembarked. It wasn't as though there were no sound at all, for audible even miles above we could hear the high, mindless screaming of the wind among the peaks. Rather it was a silence of the soul; a weight of Presence and a reverence that quashed all mere human utterance. Anything you could think of to say seemed inane. Grand and awesome and terrible towered those mountains, purple-black against the indigo sky, and all other features of the world felt far away and insignificant.

It was here, too, that I got my first real taste of true Antarctic cold. Our brief sojourn at McMurdo Base had exposed me to some bitter cold, but nothing I had not seen in New England. Here the cold gripped you and held you, pierced you and crushed you. Here, too, we were high above sea level. I breathed in short, painful gasps. I was relieved, therefore, to see our transportation nearly to the plane when we arrived. Two enormous Kharkovchanka tracked vehicles awaited us, growling and steaming in the polar twilight.

The main building of Lake City stood above the snowpack like a big black shoebox on short pillars. A line of yellow-filled windows dotted and dashed down the side of it. At one end a cylindrical tower stuck up an added two stories above the main structure—"the Silo"—and, I later learned, extended two stories into the ground below. Another building had been erected over the site of Lake's first excavation (Pabodie Depth 2, in local jargon), and the lights of this glowed in the blue distance. Other buildings bulked close by—service sheds, garages, the army barracks.

Our hosts ushered us into Lake Central, the outpost's main building. After stopping at our dorm rooms to leave our luggage, we had a quick meal in the station cafeteria. Then we were led to a long meeting room with a bank of windows looking out on the mountains. A screen stood against the wall opposite the entrance. Five men—four in the heavy pants, boots, sweater, and beard that were the unofficial uniform of Lake City, and one in army fatigues—stood by an open laptop and projector at that end of the table. The men looked as though they hadn't slept in days.

When we were all seated the eldest of these men stepped forward to the laptop and began speaking.

"Good evening," he said in a deep voice. "I am Doctor Dubchenko of the St. Petersburg Institute. I will be facilitator of this symposium.

"I wish I could say it was my pleasure to welcome you all here, but we are met in the face of crisis. We are working under the twin constraints of secrecy and urgency. Therefore I will dispense with niceties and proceed to the matter at hand.

"All of you, I'm sure, and our distinguished climatologists especially, will remember the 'ozone-hole crisis' of the 1980s. It was, in fact, only the most public phase of a story that began in the '70s and continues today with the monitoring of human-based production of the chlorofluorocarbons thought to be responsible for the hole."

A susurrus of shifting moved through the room. I could pick out my fellow climatologists by their reactions to this statement: "human-based"? "thought to be responsible"?

"For the benefit of all here," Dubchenko continued, "I will give a brief summary of this story.

"Beginning in the 1970s scientists began noticing an alarming reduction in the ozone in the stratosphere over the Antarctic continent. The damage was such that between 1975 and 1994 the ozone level here dropped from 300 DUs to 150 DUs—a reduction by half."

"'DUs'?" Spratt whispered to me.

"Dobson Units," I said. "Used to measure ozone concentrations."

"Thank God," Spratt said, sitting back. "I thought it was a form of DTs."

I covered a smile with my hand.

"The causes for this drop," said Dubchenko, "were found to be the man-made trace gases chlorofluorocarbons—CFCs—produced for aerosol cans and air-conditioning units, as well as aircraft exhaust and nitrous oxide from fertilizers, among others. Fortunately, the efforts of developed nations through such agreements as the '89 Montreal Protocol have effectively eliminated many of these sources. We were encouraged by a noticeable recovery of the ozone layer and a reduction of the so-called 'ozone-hole. ' CFC concentrations peaked in 2002 and have been dropping ever since.

"However, more recent measurements have painted a different picture."

He touched a couple of keys on the laptop, and an image blossomed upon the screen behind him. It was an image I knew well: the 2006 satellite photo of the Southern Hemisphere, showing the ozone hole at its largest. The globe was false-colored in areas of greens, blue, purple, and black, indicating progressively lesser concentrations of ozone. The purple and black areas covered most of Antarctica.

"This shows the ozone levels for Antarctic Spring of 2006," Dubchenko said, waving at the screen. "Although impressive, it did not worry us at the time. The hole fluctuates naturally with the seasons, swelling in the spring months of September and October. Also, halocarbons such as CFCs last a long time in the stratosphere, so we expected a delayed event such as this.

"What we didn't expect was this."

Another couple of taps to the computer, and the image changed. Again the Earth appeared in false-color glory; but now the black and purple nearly covered the entire globe, extending well into the lower tips of South America and Africa.

"This was taken in February of this year," Dubchenko said.

The chatter the picture had generated now exploded into exclamations and oaths. One big, bearded man across from me jumped to his feet and blurted, "Im*poss*ible!" My own heart sank within me.

Tom was looking left and right and finally caught my eye.

"What's going on?" he said.

"It's not so much that it's bigger," I said, shaking my head; "it's the timing. Under ultraviolet radiation halocarbons release chlorine and bromine atoms, which catalyze with ozone to break it down. These atoms get bound up in stratospheric clouds during the Antarctic winter, but are released when the atmosphere warms up. Then, too, ozone breaks down naturally in light wavelengths under 1,200 nanometers, so the worst damage tends to come in September and October with the return of the sun." I swallowed, staring back at the screen. "If it was that bad in February, it will be catastrophic come October."

"How catastrophic?"

"Rule of thumb is a one per cent increase in ozone depletion equals a two per cent increase in UV reaching the earth," I said, "which in turn translates into a four to ten per cent increase in the incidence of squamous cell skin cancer. You're the biologist—you tell me."

Tom blew out his cheeks and slumped back in his seat.

Dubchenko was trying to speak above the clamor. "You will understand now the urgency of bringing you all here," he called as the other voices died down. "Ultraviolet radiation levels have already been recorded in the 240 to 300 nanometer range across the continent. We are on the verge of a global disaster, and we need all your help to avert it."

A heavy, pretty woman with dark hair raised her hand down front.

"Del Rio, UT, San Anton'," she said in the gentle sway of central Texas. "The Montreal Protocol has loopholes for some developing countries, but I find it hard to believe that any country could produce such an effect in so short a time."

"You are correct, Professor Del Rio," Dubchenko responded. "No country, indeed, no group of countries could produce so drastic an effect in the time indicated. In fact, no *human* technology is capable of doing so. That is why we are meeting here," and he swept his arm to indicate the bank of windows, beyond which the mountains loomed in indigo sleep. "At this point I must turn you over to our head of security, Colonel Mooney."

Dubchenko stepped back, and the stocky man in fatigues—the head of the Ice Shadow Army—took his place. The fluorescents in the room glinted off his hair's silver bristle, and his wide-set, sleepy blue eyes scanned across us all sitting there. I had the feeling that the sleepy look was deceptive and that Colonel Mooney could be a very dangerous man.

"You have read the INVESTIGATIONS," he said in an Australian drawl, "so I don't have to tell you the history of this locale. We are in the presence of very cunning and very lethal entities, and it is They who are behind this alteration to our environment."

"Wait a minute," Tom said, raising his hand. When Mooney gave him a cold look, he put in, "Spratt, Oxford. Biology." (Secretly I wished I could blurt out credentials so impressive, but somehow "Metcalfe, University of Northern Rhode Island, Climatology" didn't have that same sharp tang to it.) "Are we speaking of the 'Old Ones,' then?"

Mooney continued his icy stare, but Tom was unimpressed.

"No," Mooney finally said. "All indications are that the interstellar crinoids have been thoroughly neutralized. We believe that the crinoids' Artificial Utility Entities are behind these actions."

Tom was rubbing his temples and in a low voice he said, "'Neutralize,' 'Artificial Utility Gizmos'—Christ, why can't you just speak the fucking language?" In a louder voice he said, "Shoggoths, you mean?"

Mooney looked at Dubchenko, who gave him the tiniest of nods.

"Yes," the colonel said, "shoggoths. And to judge from Dyer's report, shoggoths of a greatly increased mental capacity."

"D'you know what you're saying?" Tom said. "A fifteen-foot blob of protoplasm, able to sprout any number of limbs and organs at will? It sounds like an amoeba to me, Colonel. Do you know what an amoeba is, then? It's a single-cell organism—*single cell.* You can't have a fifteen-foot single-cell, Colonel, I'm sorry. It just doesn't *work.*"

"I beg to differ with you, Mr. Spratt—"

"*Professor* Spratt," Tom interrupted, "Colonel."

"At any rate," Mooney sighed heavily, "the AUEs exist, whether you believe in them or not."

"You've seen them, then."

"Myself personally, no."

"Others, perhaps?"

"Others, most certainly. We have sent several recon as well as combat units into their tunnels."

"And?"

"They never came back."

Silence descended.

"We do, however," Colonel Mooney continued after a pause that seemed to stretch for days, "have this clip extracted from a remote motion detector-activated video camera, installed in Tunnel G-12. It is an older tape, so I apologise in advance for the poor quality. Still, I think you will find it instructive."

Mooney took his turn at the laptop. The ozone hole-blighted Earth vanished and was replaced by a grainy image of a stone-walled space. It was filmed at an angle from some high point with the exaggerated perspective of a fish-eye lens. At the lower right corner was the date 20 AUG 85, and a digital clock ticked away from 02:20:06. The floor and the stone wall opposite stretched back into the darkness at the upper right of the picture and, just discernible along the wall's length, a carven band. A chill ran up my back as I realized that I was looking at one of the reliefs created by the Old Ones—or by their rebellious creatures, the shoggoths. Even as I thought this Something came up out of the darkness at the right of the image, swept up with incredible speed, and filled the screen. The image suddenly turned to static.

People around me cried out in alarm. I probably did, too—it all happened so quickly that it was only in retrospect that I recalled the flashing lights in the Thing, and the awful hand that sprouted out of nothing to envelop the video camera. It was all the more terrible for being utterly *silent.*

Mooney turned from the screen toward us.

"Over the past forty years," he intoned, "we have lost one hundred and seventy-eight men to these things. I know damned well they exist and you had better, too. Since Dyer's time they have extended their network of tunnels into the foothills—at least. From these the AUEs have dug vertical wells to the surface. At first we thought these wells were fumaroles, gas-vents of volcanic origin. But," he added quickly as several geologists poised to argue, "we quickly recognized that this region is sedimentary in origin. That was, in fact, what clued us in to the vents' provenance. It is from these wells that they are propelling halocarbons into the atmosphere."

"Then why don't you just block them up?" cried a bespectacled man who looked close to hysterics.

"That we have," said Mooney, "and bombed them. But as soon as one is taken care of, two more appear elsewhere. Some are easy to detect. The big ones can be fifty, sixty feet across and lined with masonry stolen from the Old Ones' city—'cauldrons' we call these. But we didn't catch on to the false fumaroles until many were established. Even with our best detection equipment and echo-sounding they succeed in creating more."

I thought of the plumes of moisture Dyer had seen coming off the mountains in '31. How far had they gotten since then?

"And how are they effecting this pollution?" asked an engineer in heavy horn-rims.

"We don't know," said Mooney. "Mics put down the holes get what might be the sound of machinery, but probes have never found the bottom of these pits."

The hole too deep for any line to sound, Lovecraft whispered in my mind.

"The thing is this," Dubchenko said, stepping forward. "The ozone crisis is not wholly the shoggoths' doing. We don't get off the hook that easily. But the shoggoths have recognized the long-term effects of ultraviolet radiation on the planet and have been exploiting and exacerbating it for years."

"To what end?" This from Professor Del Rio. She pronounced the last word like *ind*.

Mooney, Dubchenko, and their three companions traded weary looks. Finally Dubchenko faced us again.

"We don't know that either," he said slowly. "But we can guess. You have all probably heard the term 'terraforming.'"

"Bloody science fiction," Tom muttered none too quietly.

"Yes," Dubchenko answered, "maybe for us but maybe not for them. All we can think of is that the AUEs are trying to—to get rid of us, *all* of us, humans, birds, and beasts. To make a *tabula rasa,* a clean slate upon which to start anew."

In the humming quiet that followed, the words of poor, doomed Lake—the same Lake for whom this outpost of humanity was named—came back to me: ". . . Elder Things supposed to have created all earth-life as jest or mistake." And now the shoggoths were attempting to rectify that mistake.

4

In the following days we were split up into groups according to our disciplines. I was fortunate in that we climatologists and meteorologists were given the top floor of the Silo attached to Lake Central, as the main building was called. I believe the thinking was to get us closer to the weather we were to predict and, it was hoped, prevent. Poor Spratt and his fellow biologists were consigned to an odiferous lab one level below the ground, which they promptly dubbed "the Dungeon" (only the geologists were buried deeper—appropriately enough). I liked my co-workers and we worked well together. Still, I sought out Spratt's company as often as I could. The man made me laugh, and laughter was at a premium in that place.

One day, after a week's worth of hard work, we managed to rendez-vous at the cafeteria. Unlike the labs, this room had no popular nickname. It was officially "The William P. Dyer Memorial Refectory," probably the only place outside of Miskatonic University that still honored his name. Tom, however, in his inimitable fashion, had dubbed it "The Crinoid Arms," and such it has remained in my memory.

We were sitting there over two glasses of "homer," the homebrew our Aussie soldiers concocted in the barracks and called "beer." I had arrived late and had found Tom already keeping company with two empty glasses. After a preliminary sip of my first I turned to him.

"So how goes it in the Dungeon?" I asked.

"Just peachy, Carnahan. Living cheek by jowl with a mob of geologists is a never-ending source of wonder." He suddenly cradled his beer glass in both hands, gawped at it round-eyed, and said, in his best American accent, "Look, guys, it's a ROCK!"

I was halfway through my next sip and I snorted a laugh that brought beer into my nose. I set the glass down and, wiping my face with a napkin, said, "I'm so glad you're fitting in, Tom. But I really meant about your work."

Tom Spratt always had the good grace never to laugh at his own jokes. In addition, his normal expression was one of thin-lipped annoyance at the world; but the gloom that clouded his face now was something I had not yet seen. It brought age into his face, and I suddenly noticed the shadows under his eyes. He looked down at his glass.

"Bad," he said, "bad. And the science is sound. Some of my BAS mates at Halley sent some of it. The ultraviolet let in by the ozone hole is hitting the wildlife hard."

"I remember reports from the '80s of penguins and sheep in Patagonia blinded by overexposure," I said.

"Well, this is a tad more serious than seeing-eye penguins in Ray-Bans and white canes," he said after another pull at the homer. "We're sorting reports now of mass die-offs of phytoplankton in the Ross and Weddell Seas, even up into the South Atlantic as far as South Georgia, and *that* is serious, mate. If you and I and all our big-brained friends disappeared it'd be a quiet couple Sundays in the park. But phytoplankton . . . Jesus, where do I begin? They're a major consumer of carbon dioxide, so without them we're further along the road to a steamy new Jurassic. Never mind the fact they're at the base of one of the bigger food-chains in the neighborhood—no phytoplankton, no prawns. No prawns, no little fish. No little fish, no big fish, la de da de da, and eventually, no *us*."

He poured the rest of his homer down his gulping throat, licked his lips, and pointed at me. "I'll give 'em this," he said, his Cockney coming out as the alcohol took effect. "Bleeding shoggoths, man, thought of everything. This is like burning the foundations of the House of Life."

Then his expression brightened. "Now the shog's masters," he said, "there's another story. Talk about smart . . . did you know they still have a couple Old Ones here, I mean *here?"* He tapped the table for emphasis.

"No, I didn't," I replied.

"Yes they do, and they let us take a swipe at 'em with the scalpel." He shook his head slowly, his eyes focused on something wonderful in his memory. "Amazing. They could out-think us, outrun us, and out-fart us, even wiv all five tentacles tied behind their backs—if they had backs, that is. I still don't know why they're not still running the show. They make the zoologists run around on the ceiling—'Are they animal? Are they vegetable?' Who the Christ cares? Make us look like the apes we are. Just amazing."

He sighed. "So what about you, mate? What're you lot going to do about the weather?"

I took a long breath. "There's talk," I began, "of reseeding the stratosphere with ozone."

"Oh, that's great. And how d'you keep it from falling back to earth where we *don't* want it? That's right brilliant, that is."

"It's better than what Smith from Harvard proposed. He wants to set off a bomb in the ozone hole to 're-encourage ozone propagation.'"

Tom scrunched up his face and stared at me. "And he's from Harvard?" he said. "God help us." It came out like *gorelpas.*

Before we could settle into an inescapable funk, McCracken, an Aussie sergeant we had befriended, bustled up to our table. He scraped over a chair, sat, and leaned cross-armed on the table.

"'Release McCracken!'" quoted Tom and raised his glass.

"Evenin', gents," McCracken said, his big face grinning closely at us. "Fancy a jolly up to Spookytown?"

"Spookytown" was what the locals had taken to calling the Old Ones' city. In all the panic over the environment we had nearly forgotten it. In those brief moments when we could gaze out the windows at the mountains there had been scant time even to consider a trip there. Now we huddled close to McCracken, eager for what he had to tell.

"I have here," he almost whispered, looking around the room, "the list for a flight to take place in two days." He pulled a folded sheet from his fatigues and palmed it flat on the table. "Brass are limiting it to twenty, and I thought you blokes . . ."

"Where do we sign?" Tom pulled a pen from his pocket.

5

The next two days passed slowly. It's funny how the mixed dread and excitement over seeing the Old Ones' city made time drag, when previous days had all seemed too short for the tasks at hand.

But there was plenty yet to fill them. We busied ourselves creating computer models of present and future climates based upon 10%, 50%, and 75% reductions in the ozone layer, and they were all depressingly consistent. Projected increases of UV-B and the far more harmful UV-C ultraviolet radiations were off the charts; and in collaboration with Tom's biology crew we predicted widespread incidences—*pandemics*—of blindness and skin cancer, massive phytoplankton die-offs, and destruction of coral reefs across the globe. The sequel to this list of disasters hardly bore thinking about: the ripples through the food chains Tom had mentioned, crop failures, long-term DNA damage . . . We now understood why the WGS had insisted we wear those sunglasses.

So suffice it to say that we were more than ready for our little holiday in the mountains. One of the Ice Shadow Army's camo Hägglunds—odd two-car tractors—came to bear us to the plane; and by nine A.M. we were airborne. While we had been at work the Antarctic day had shrunk. The sun now scraped along the southern horizon for only a couple of hours, so we had to take what advantage of it we could.

What words can describe that flight? I could resort to Dyer/Lovecraft's logorrhea, but to me the very massiveness of the landscape demanded sparseness, simplicity. Stark. Colossal. Barren. White of snow and black of bare rock. Seared by rays from the hollow sky, the mountains heaved their titan shoulders to bar our way.

McCracken was there, of course, the one smiling face in all Lake City. He squatted down by Tom's and my seats, and we chatted about his army. When we asked about the army's efforts to fight the shoggoths, he shook his head. No one knew for sure, but it certainly appeared that conventional weapons, and even such things as flamethrowers, were ineffectual against the "shogs," as he called them.

"Like sticking pins in Jell-O," he said. "How can you kill it if you don't even know where its heart is?"

"Or if it even has a heart," interjected Tom.

"Or if it can grow a new heart even if you hit the first one," I added.

But the engineers were working closely with the linguists to recreate the "curious weapons of molecular disturbance" (Dyer) used by the Old Ones to combat the shoggoths, and McCracken was optimistic.

"Well, that makes one of us," Tom said with a thin smile.

The mountains had grown until they blocked out most of our sky. We could now see the cube-like buildings and snaking fortifications built by the Old Ones on the precipitous slopes, and I felt again that shiver of discovery. To our left was Mt. Gedney, highest of the chain, its 36,000-foot peak razor-sharp against the navy blue sky; to the right, Mt. Carroll. Straight ahead the pass through which we were to fly gradually widened. Everyone was now at a window.

Dyer was again vindicated. The panorama beyond the mountains burst upon our sight all in a rush, and several of us gasped. There was the Old Ones' city, Spookytown, the oldest settlement on the planet by a factor of thousands. Just its sheer size, a giant's labyrinth running to left and right as far as you could see, stopped your breath. The pilot flew us across the city toward those other peaks, invisible in haze, until the city dwindled away in isolated ruins. Banking back, he gave us a heart-stopping vista of the city sprawled along the line of black mountains, silhouetted by the weak glow of dying Antarctic day.

The plane landed on a cleared stretch between the mountains' foothills and the city. We synchronized our watches and put on our oxygen masks; then they released us upon the city.

Again I come to a place where words escape me. Even with all our briefing we were dumbfounded. How must Dyer and Danforth have felt! We have their account—or Lovecraft's version of it—but having actually been there I find their words pale and inadequate. We staggered down the slight slope to the dark ruins, feeling their dim weight upon our eyes and souls. When at last we could touch the ancient walls, I cried aloud. Tom and I wandered together through room after Cyclopean room, our heads tilted back and staring like the most callow of sightseers. We found one room that still retained its roof and was lit by a row of shaded lights installed by the army. By their soft glow we examined some of the carven bands Dyer had described. The roof had protected these specimens from the worst of weathering, and we thrilled at the skilled depictions of the Old Ones and the contemporary flora and fauna of millions of years ago—*done from life*. Here were giant *Magolodon* sharks, *eohippi*, gigantic *Indricotherica,* and the humble *Moeritherium*. And here too were hairy, prognathous *Australopithecenes* whose descendants we were. At one point I turned to look at Tom and could see through his goggles how his eyes were alight with childlike joy.

And of course there were the Old Ones themselves. Perhaps one of the most jarring things for me was to see those alien, starfish-headed non-animals doing things once thought the exclusive province of man, and doing them in a natural fashion the ancient artists captured all too well. I am no artist myself, but have no qualms in saying that the unhuman artists who created these reliefs must rank among the finest this planet has ever produced.

Our time in the ruins felt frightfully short. In fact, it was far shorter than we were supposed to have had. While we pored over the antediluvian artwork a soldier came to get us. His mask and goggles hid his features, but with urgent signs he indicated that we had to go and had to go now. Reluctantly we left the megalithic ruins and trudged after the soldier as fast as our bulky clothing would permit us.

Inside the plane all was loud confusion. It was all the more disorienting after the eon-long silence of the ruins, but we soon discovered what was happening. McCracken was hunched over the radio set in the cabin. He had one-half of a pair of headphones pressed to his right ear, and his normally cheery face was crumpled with worry and alarm. After a few moments of extreme concentration he set down the headphones and stood up to greet us.

"Bloody blizz static," he muttered. "Can't make out half of what they said, but seems a blow has come off the mountains and they want us back at base ASAP."

He slid past us and stalked down the plane's center aisle.

"Best buckle up, ladies and gents," he bellowed. "We're in for a ride and there's no mistake."

And ride it was. Once we cleared the pass the wind hit us hard and seemingly from every direction. I could have wished for a larger plane as we were buffeted, tossed, rattled, and jolted. Outside our windows the magnificent scenery had faded behind a hellish streaking chaos of flying snow. I wondered how our pilot could tell where we were.

But see he somehow did, and he guided us down to the hazy twin lines of lights that outlined the runway. We thudded down, and the plane sledded to a long, hissing stop. McCracken was already up before half of us had unbuckled our seatbelts.

"Keep your seats, ladies and gents," he said, motioning us back down. "No rush until the Hägglund gets here." His smile had returned, but the eyes he turned to peer out the windows showed a little too much white.

"What's happening, Sergeant?" asked an academic-looking Indian man up front.

"Nothing to worry about, nothing at all," McCracken responded. I started to worry.

I saw the lights of the Hägglund roll up past the plane. We all pulled the hoods of our parkas up over our heads, rose, and began shuffling for the exit of the plane. The driver had brought the Hägglund close to the airplane staircase, and we were soon all crowded inside. I had barely gotten seated when the driver engaged the tracks and swung us around toward Lake City. He seemed to be driving pretty fast for the near-blind conditions, but I didn't feel it was my place to criticize.

McCracken was sitting up front beside the driver, and he leaned over to speak with him. I'm sure he thought they were inaudible to the rest of us, but I caught enough to start the alarm bells ringing in my heart.

"How many are there, Davis?"

". . . know, Sergeant, but they've taken Pabodie."

"Shit. Where's . . ."

". . . last time we heard . . . radioed Code Black, all personnel . . ."

An explosion sounded in the blizzard—more a vibration in the gut than a sound.

"What was that, Sergeant?" came a querulous voice from the back.

"Just routine," McCracken said. "Probably just setting some cauldron to rights."

I leaned forward and peered around McCracken's broad back. All was a dizzying race of snow past the windshields. I was never as relieved as when I descried the lights of Lake Central glowing like unearthly chrysanthemums in the blue blizzard ahead. McCracken turned to address us.

"All right," he bawled. "We are approaching the main building. When we get there we go straight into the building; we do not, I repeat, do *not* dawdle. Captain Urquart and Doctor Dubchenko will be on hand to—"

There was a loud *crack,* and the whole front car of the vehicle lurched forward and down. The four of us sitting in back were tossed forward onto the others. A man screamed. Snow rattled against the tractor's windows.

"What's happening, Private?" McCracken boomed, heaving himself upright.

"Crevasse more than likely, Sergeant. I'll see what I can do to get us out."

"See that you do, Private."

The driver hooked his right arm over the back of his seat and turned his face toward us. Blood ran down from his nose in a wide, red stripe to his chin, but aside from this he had the casual attitude of someone trying to back into a parking place. We heard the tracks under the floorboards whizzing over the snow, but it was no good. The Hägglund was stuck.

McCracken threw open the front hatch and leapt out into the blast. A puff of snow blew in past him like diamond dust. We could see him limned starkly in the lights of the tractor, first looking over the damage, then grasping the front fender and trying to heave the vehicle out. Tom and I were about to join him when he came back in. He was breathing hard.

"No use," he gasped. "Got . . . try another way."

He opened a locker by the dashboard and pulled out a coil of rope.

"Take this, all of you," he said, feeding it out to each of us. "Stay in line and don't let go of the rope. The last one passes it on to the lot from the back car. If you get separated from the rest of us, make for those lights." And he pointed at the lights of Lake Central.

The sergeant gave us a minute to secure our clothing, then led us out of the wrecked tractor and into the storm. It was roaring, freight-training down off the mountains as if it would clear away the whole surface of the planet. Even through our protective clothing we could feel the wind-driven snow pummeling us, pelting us as if to pierce us in its fury. One or two of our smaller companions were blown off their feet, and the rest of us had to lean far into the wind, making as small a target for its violence as we could.

We were trudging along like this for I don't know how long—time itself seemed to have been carried away on the demon wind—when I bumped up against the person in front of me. I had been so intent on just keeping my feet that I hadn't seen that the others had stopped. I looked up now and saw we were all backed up in a crouched mass behind the slightly taller form of Sergeant McCracken. He appeared to be looking hard ahead of us; his left hand was cupped around the side of his face to block the snow. Following his gaze I saw the great, dim bulk of Lake Central on its stubby pillars, perhaps not twenty meters away. Even as I looked a prolonged metallic groaning came to us through the wind; and to my horror I saw the Silo on the end of the building tip, lean, and carried by the wind plummet to the ground. It blew up a vast cloud of powder that the storm tore away, and we felt the concussion through the soles of our boots.

Then the lights went out.

Lake Central shifted on its foundations. It leaned away from us, poised at a twisted angle like a huge insect considering its next step. This was too much for some of my companions. Several broke from the line and careened windmilling and slipping and falling into the snow until they vanished. McCracken tried to grab them, but they scattered like chaff in the wind. The rest of us clung to the rope like men overboard, huddled into the hurricane with no clear idea what to do and no way to communicate it to each other.

Then I noticed the army. They passed singly and in groups, on fast machine-gun–mounted snowmobiles stitching the air with yellow fire and in hulking armored vehicles. They were hurrying past the ruined main building toward Pabodie Depth 2 (". . . they've taken Pabodie . . ."). I felt another explosion rumble through the air and this time saw an orange-yellow glow swell off in that same direction.

McCracken seemed to have made a decision and was pulling us forward again. We hadn't gone ten arduous steps, though, when the earth some thirty meters to our left—toward the unseen mountains—burst up in a flying spray of rock and dirt and ice. We cowered lower and put our arms over our heads to shield us from the wind-blown debris. When I looked up again I thought I was hallucinating. Something like a giant black hand with three long fingers had risen up out of the hole the blast had created. Across the gleaming surface of this devil's claw, lights of blue and yellow and green blinked on and off and branching patterns of light ran like lightning. Several soldiers who had been running past now stopped and raised their rifles toward it. We could see the star-flashes as they fired away at it, and we saw the thing arch like a black wave and crash down upon them, obliterating them entirely.

That was the last straw for McCracken. He threw down his end of the rope (the driver, behind him, reached out a pleading hand) and ran into the teeth of the storm. I had always regarded the sergeant as an affable, slightly goofy figure; but anyone who could run into that insanity of wind commanded my complete respect. My respect grew further as I watched him unlimber the rifle slung over his back, crouch to a shooting stance, and carefully and with deadly, unerring effect fire into the rising monster. *Pop pop pop*—each shot destroyed one of the proto-eyes on the thing's swelling front. McCracken was now near one of the massive Kharkovchanka vehicles, and as he pushed toward it he continued his lethal marksmanship. "Like sticking pins in Jell-O"? Maybe. But Sergeant McCracken knew just where to stick those pins. I hunched with my fellows as the snow drifted up around our legs and the wind screamed about our ears, and in my heart I cheered that intrepid Aussie onward. The thing—shoggoth, blob, AUE—hesitated in its assault on the world. And in that moment McCracken reached the Kharkovchanka, tossed away his rifle, and swung himself up to the hatch. In a second he was in; in a trice he had it running; and in a moment twin geysers of snow fanned out from the back of the treads as he pushed it into full-throttle. The shoggoth again gathered itself like a wave; new eyes appeared to replace those shot out. The big tractor gathered speed and plowed straight into it, catching it just as it rose, the thing's sudden tentacles and feelers and flaps wrapping around it, enveloping it. I saw one tentacle punch through a window of the tractor, and I'm sure others did as well. But the machine bullied on. It swept the thing off the snow, back, back, and in its impetus over the edge and into the hole whence it had come. The last we saw of the Kharkovchanka was its tail-lights tipping to the sky as it bore its awful burden down to hell. Then it was gone.

Now it was my turn to panic. Without the fascination of the battle before me anymore, something snapped. I don't remember dropping the rope, only a headlong rush out into the polar dusk. The wind was at my back and carried me pelting onward. Sometimes I felt as if I were flying—perhaps I was. A high keening sounded in my ears, and after several seconds I identified it as my own voice as the panic exploded in my mind. I had no idea where I was going, only that I had to get away from what I had seen. But night was falling, it was fifty below zero and dropping, and I was alone in a blizzard in the most desolate place on earth. In reality I was running toward certain death.

My keening had died away as I tried to screech the air into my overworked lungs. Still my legs hammered on into the twilight. Then my right foot punched down through the ice. My left knee banged painfully down, too, and broke through. Suddenly I was thrown flat on the ice, my legs pedaling madly in nothingness. I had hit a crevasse. Just when you thought things couldn't get worse, I thought, and wheezed out a laugh.

Then things did get worse. I had no purchase at all on the ice and began sliding back into the hole my legs had made. At last I was left hanging by my mittened fingers, and that is when the ice snapped from under them.

In truth, it was this slow slide down that saved me. Because I was stretched my full length—and the length of my arms—when I fell, I reduced the distance I fell by a good seven feet. For a breathless second I dropped—then my feet struck ice. I crumpled to reduce the shock of the fall, then picked myself up to see what new predicament I had gotten into.

I had been wrong—it was not a crevasse. Crevasses were not this regular. I was in a tunnel, a very long, straight tunnel about fifteen feet in diameter hollowed out of the ice. In the twilight it glowed a luminous royal blue; snow sifted silently down from the hole. Out of the storm, which I could hear howling above me at having been cheated of its prey, it was even a beautiful place. The tunnel was an almost perfectly round cylinder with just a slight, rounded ribbing. I wondered what kind of machine could excavate such a structure. Then I knew, and started looking for a way out.

I briefly considered following the tunnel to either of its termini, but thought better of it. I had no idea where they went, nor what I might meet before I found a way out. But climbing back out the hole I had made, which beckoned only fifteen feet above, seemed impossible. The walls of the tunnel swept up in smooth arcs, barren of any handholds. At least it's warmer, I thought. A mild air was moving from the left, from that dark hint of earth. Far, far away down there, in the heart of the blackness the tunnel dwindled into, something glinted, and suddenly it was far more urgent that I find a way out.

Desperately I looked around me and noticed a couple places where the tunnel had intersected smaller gaps in the ice. None of these was big enough to admit me, but some four feet up one side was a dark oval in the ice that seemed to indicate a closed space. I reached back and unclipped the entrenching tool from my belt; folded the blade to its pickaxe position and locked it; and laid into the ice.

I was in luck: the axe bit through into space on the first swing. Hurriedly I hacked at the ice, the chips and splinters flashing around me. Down the tunnel was a growing rumor like that of a crowd. I swung harder, faster. The moving air had increased to a breeze, a wind. Lights flashed in the distant darkness. The ice flew—just a little more . . . a fluting, a high whistling like *"tekeli-li!"* echoed down the icy tube. The next few seconds saw me through the ice and into a smooth bubble just big enough for me to wedge myself into.

None too soon. The onrushing air, pushed by a body I scarce dared think about, became a gale, and fast on its heels came the shoggoth. And like Lot's wife, like Orpheus—like Dyer and Danforth and every other doomed, curious soul in history—I had to look. I only had a second to peep as it shot from one unholy errand to another, but in that second I saw the evolving eyes, the inchoate organs and gaping mouths; the pseudopods and pseudolimbs reaching for definition. And across the whole, bulging, rushing surface, the blue lighting of synapses of a mind we cannot even begin to comprehend.

And I had one more impression before I thrust my face deep into my arms. It was the cacophony of *sounds* coming from it. From Dyer's report I had been warned to listen for the eerie *"tekeli-li!"* But as the thing swept past, so close, *so close* that a twitch of my shoulder would have put me in contact with it, I heard a multitude of voices. Human voices, the voices of today and the voices of the past; English, French, Russian, Chinese, and I don't know how many more; the legacy of a century of explorers and radio messages. The shoggoths had found new "masters" to imitate.

And crowded amongst all that jumble of voices, did I hear the Down Under accents of Sergeant Abel McCracken? I like to think I did; I like to think that, in some terrible, ironic, yet fitting way, his words live on somewhere under the Ice he fought so hard to defend.

I waited a good two minutes in my hideaway before I came out. Even then it was only because I heard another voice—Tom Spratt's voice.

"Vic! Vic! For Christ's sake, Vic, are you there?"

I unfolded myself from the hole and hobbled, stiff in every limb, to the spot where I had fallen. Looking up, I was greeted by the sight of Tom Spratt leaning down like some maned gargoyle in his parka hood.

"Hullo, Tom," I said.

"Hullo your own mad self. What're you doing down there—waiting for the Tube?"

"Just missed it," I shrugged.

Tom had seen me bolt from the guide-rope and with the four remaining others had followed. I had been moving pretty fast, he later told me, and they lost sight of me at first. My footprints were swept away almost as quickly as I made them, but they found the hole—and they had had the presence of mind to bring the rope.

Once they had hoisted me out of the tunnel, we worked our way back toward Lake City. The lights in the buildings were all out, of course, but those lining the runway still burned. There was also the occasional explosion to help guide us, but by the time we reached the runway those had all ceased. The storm screeched over a vastness terribly still.

Stumbling to the runway ended up being the best of all possible fates. The plane we had taken across the mountains was not yet completely cold; and Tom had flying experience from his days with the BAS. I sat up front with him and watched the runway lights click by faster and faster—and suddenly wink out.

"Bollocks," Tom muttered, but by then our skis were off the ice. We had a generous tail-wind, too, and soon we were climbing into the dim sky.

6

The rest is quickly told. We aimed for Russia's Vostok Station, three hundred miles south. It was a toss-up whether that or some of the coastal stations were closer, but the coastal stations would have required us crossing those Mountains of Madness again, and not one of us was willing to do that.

In the event it was a near thing. Tom had just made out Vostok's red metal drilling tower, its most obvious landmark, when the engines sputtered and died. We had run completely out of fuel and coasted down in silence to the featureless ice dome. Tom had already contacted Vostok by radio, though, and we didn't have long to wait before they rolled up in a tractor to rescue us.

The *Vostochniki* were hospitality itself. There was some initial tension when we told them what had happened and where we had come from. They thought it was a problem in translation when it was simply that they knew nothing about Lake City, the mountains, or any of it. At last one fellow with a stupendous black beard came in, patted the translator on the shoulder, and sent him away. He turned a chair around and sat backwards on it, leaning on the back, staring at us silently for a minute. Then he said, "Gone."

We nodded.

"And Dubchenko?"

We shook our heads. He bowed his own head in silence. Then, "You are welcome to all we have. As soon as we can, we will get plane in to take you home." And they did.

It is hard to write of these things and believe them, when the young leaves are out and flitting dizzy shadows across this page as I write. Sometimes I take out my "souvenirs" of that time—a bit of fossil coral given me by "Del Rio, San Anton'" (I hope she went quickly—she was not on the plane); a paper cup lettered "Crinoid Arms" in ballpoint, with Tom's cartoon of a smiling Old One; the entrenching tool that saved my life—and hold them and remind myself that it all really happened. Then I get on the phone or on the computer and beg, urge, plead, and demand that government agencies take action against something that threatens not some, not most, but all of us. And then I wait for responses from people who are "unacquainted" with any polar station at Latitude 76°, 15′ South, Longitude 113°, 10′ East. The great secret has been kept too well.

And as often as I can I call and e-mail Tom Spratt. He too saved my life, but it is painful speaking to him. He drinks a lot now. Can't say as I blame him. But I keep calling and keep hoping that somehow it will keep him from descending further into that deep tunnel of his own he has fallen into; that tunnel where things gibber and things race on missions known only to themselves.

Detachment

There was one stop left to go and Jimmy was ahead of schedule. At this rate, he thought, checking the mirrors, I'll be in Portland before three. Everyone had been cooperative along the route, helping to unload the big, anonymous boxes from the back of the van and even amicably accepting the bills. That had happened in three places so far—the checks were neatly folded in half to fit exactly in Jimmy's left breast pocket. If I wanted to, Jimmy mused, I could take these checks and head for Canada. Those three checks alone would keep him in Nova Scotia lox and furs for a year. Nothing was ever itemized on the distribution company's bills, and Jimmy got the feeling that the items were different at each stop. But two things were clear: the cargo was expensive and heavy. He supposed that he wasn't being paid to think, only to drive, but he couldn't help wondering about the boxes and the unmarked, prefabricated warehouses to which he delivered them.

The van bucked and swayed dizzily over the roads in its lightened condition. Jimmy wasn't too sure where he was just then. He'd passed through West Paris almost an hour before, but had seen no more of the white, vertical-looking town-line signs since then. He hadn't been doing the route for very long, and this part of Maine was still something of a mystery to him. He glanced over to the other seat, where a tattered copy of the Maine Atlas lay curled back. Let's see, he thought, say I was doing about forty average, accounting for the stops and some of the worse roads—But it wasn't any use. He was doing sixty miles per hour now, on a road unsuited to forty. Even his direction of travel was unclear: a uniform wrinkling of grey hid the sun and what had started out as a clear October day. He was all turned around. At least it was a pretty ride, the countless hills humped up one behind another like bouquets of warm flowers, the infrequent houses and trailers like dark boxes half-hidden among them. A stretch of field, a glimpse of silver river—yuh, a pretty ride.

He saw the little girl twirling out in front of his van only peripherally, only momentarily. He reacted like a shot, but it wasn't fast enough. The horrible "thump" against the van seemed to cut him loose from reality. His foot, at first, had snapped from the gas pedal to brake, slipped off of that, got caught underneath and had to be yanked free with enough force to tear the rubber toe from his sneaker. All this was within a second; but after feeling his truck strike, Jimmy let it be. He wasn't on the road anymore—he was somewhere between the dismal sky and the bright-patched hills up ahead. He was anywhere but here. The van had almost coasted to a stop before he thought to try the brake again. He came back to reality numbly, stupidly, and he shut off the engine with care. It took a bit of conscious effort to unlock his left fist from the steering wheel, the one thing that had kept him on the road.

Jimmy opened the door and slid out and down. The door buzzer sounded irritatingly at his back, and a light breeze swept leaf-rustlings and rich spice of autumn past him. People were running down the road toward him. He tried to put together a coherent sentence, something to say everything—"I'm sorry, I didn't see her—she ran right out—" but then he realized. They weren't running to him; the little girl must've got caught under the van. He backed up against the van's dirty white metal and sank miserably to the ground, all strength gone.

He stood back up when the children started staring at him. The fat, pink, dirty faces watched him emptily and thick hands wiped absently on threadbare corduroys. Not daring to look back at the van, Jimmy focused on the boy in front of him. The boy's colourless belly hung out from beneath a too-small black T-shirt and its brightly coloured rock 'n' roll cartoon, cracked and faded beyond legibility. His sneakers, sans laces, covered feet of shockingly uneven sizes. The boy looked up at Jimmy and one eyelid fluttered down and back up under a fringe of red bangs. Jimmy reached out a shaking hand, said "Excuse me" and pushed away from the van.

The adults were gathered on the passenger side, and some of the men were gingerly lifting something from behind the front right tire as Jimmy came around. His hand went involuntarily to his mouth, a move of horror, sorrow, disgust. The whole operation was dreadfully silent. Two women, both in a tired limbo between seventeen and forty, stood on the road's shoulder, and Jimmy tried vainly to guess which was the mother. He dreaded meeting her most of all—the world couldn't contain enough words to explain himself to her. But whoever the mother was, she evidently wasn't one of these two. They watched the men and their grim labour with a positive lack of emotion, except for a possible trace of curiosity. One chewed gum. Jimmy looked back at the men, who were, thankfully, just finishing wrapping the little body in a green army blanket. They stood and turned as one, and Jimmy tensed for a curse or a punch. But none came. He watched the gaunt, unshaven, dispassionate faces moving by him without a flicker of interest in him. He turned to the last man, a man of about thirty with drooping features and unevenly cut blond mustache.

"It—what can I—" Jimmy managed before the man said, "It's all right. C'mon inside." One of his eyelids trembled down and up, but he kept his gaze on Jimmy.

They walked him to an old and ramshackle house, undiscernible from hundreds of others in the hills, and sat him down at a very old, very shaky table in what must have once been a kitchen. What it was now wasn't very clear; cardboard boxes crowded firewood where ancient, paint-stripped chairs didn't clutter up to the ceiling. The floor probably hadn't been swept in a hundred years, but the boards under the filth were wide and solid. Jimmy noticed an aged cast-iron stove squatting under the boxes, and not all the wooden "gingerbread" had been knocked out of the hall doorway. He sipped the coffee they'd handed him and looked at the doughnut with one bite taken out of it in his hand. There was no telephone in this house or, apparently, in its odd collection of outbuildings, so a skinny teenage boy had been dispatched to get a doctor. Jimmy was actually glad for the lack; it delayed the eventual call to his boss. The twitch-eyed man had sent the boy and now sat opposite Jimmy in what little clear space there was. Through a window past the man's dirty blond hair, Jimmy could see the reassuring white of the van. Someone had moved it there off the road sometime in the last half-hour or so, parking it close to the several cars and partial cars in the dirt by the house. Jimmy looked out at it once in a while, just to be sure. Occasionally a small blond head would race by the window and eclipse the van, making him look again. With no phone and apparently no other working vehicle nearby, Jimmy didn't care to lose sight of it. The feeling of detachment there was overpowering. The remove from the comforts of the city was bad enough, but Jimmy couldn't get over the group's personal detachment. Their apathy over the injured girl made no sense at all to him. It was like the cliché New England stoicism taken to an absurd extreme, and it bothered him.

The watery eyes beneath the drooping lids couldn't help but notice Jimmy's nervousness, but the other man didn't say a thing. Jimmy made an effort to drink his coffee but quickly gave it up. He tried looking around the room for distraction, but found nothing to interest him. Then he noticed the man's hands: there were bandages wrapped tightly around three of the fingers and two more had obviously been badly hurt. White scars crossed them like crude rings against the pink flesh. Jimmy stared at the bandages, their browns of old blood and dirt, the green of grass. He looked up at the other's face and realized that he'd been staring.

"Oh," Jimmy said. "Uh, I'm sorry. Your hands, I was—"

"Chainsaw," the other said. He rubbed his hands together gently. "Cuttin' wood a few months back."

Jimmy thought to say something, but thought better of it and just nodded.

An old man wobbled into view from behind the separating wall to the parlour, his mouth open in a stiff pucker from which the lower row of teeth rose up like a rotting picket fence. His eyes were moist and moved nervously around in their loose collars of flesh, and one stiff hand maneuvered a cane as he walked. His left leg was wrapped, knee to toe, in a length of sheet. The eyes continued their panicked search of the kitchen.

"Is that," the old one said, "what is that, is it—What time *is* it?"

The younger man finally pulled his sad gaze from Jimmy and turned halfway around in his chair.

"Not yet, Thomas," he said in a voice that was startlingly firm. The old man shut his shrunken mouth abruptly and turned away. The drooping eyes turned back.

The old man had shambled out of sight (or else become one with the omnipresent clutter) a seemingly long time ago, and Jimmy felt he'd had enough. He got up and put the unfinished coffee and doughnut down on the nearest level surface, and mumbled something about seeing to his truck. The other nodded and got up too.

The truck was fine, only a shallow dent just above the bumper to show where the little head had struck. Jimmy moved his finger over the dent slowly and felt himself beginning to shake again. Looking away, he noticed the license plates on the ruined cars nearby—Massachusetts, New Jersey, Rhode Island . . . where were these people from? They sounded like Mainers; to look at their home, you'd think they'd been there forever. Jimmy moved away from the van to where the sad-eyed man stood surveying the patchwork sheds, running children and tall woods.

"Is the doctor far?" Jimmy asked, and simultaneously realized that he could've driven the child there in his truck. This waiting around for the doctor to come back was stupid, though he felt stupider for not having thought of the truck before. The other man pushed his lower lip up and slowly shook his head.

"No, not far. Not too far," he said.

Jimmy looked at the bewildering patterns of tree and leaf for a minute before speaking again.

"Look," he said, "if you tell me where he is, I can drive the girl there." Silence. "Really, I'd like to, I want—You can come, if you—"

"We shouldn't move her." That killed the question. Jimmy thought of an argument or two against that, but nothing seemed worth saying. All right, he thought, drawing a deep breath. This is your turf, it's your rules. He wandered away from the man toward the nearest shacks. Several miserable-looking hens strutted in a wire box at one side; a dog of untraceable parentage and uncertain colour pawed a hole under a plank wall. Coming clear of one shed to his right, the one directly behind the house, Jimmy saw three boys leaning against the wall, trying to smother laughter. One of them, in denim jacket and a jungle-like mass of black hair, should've been on his way to the doctor. The eyes looking out from behind the hair were calm and amused as they met Jimmy's, but the boy clamped his lips between his teeth to keep from laughing.

"Hey!" Jimmy stepped toward the group with growing anger in him. The other two boys looked around, a little embarrassed, but they too were laughing. One tipped a soda bottle to his lips and raised fresh, unrestrained laughter when the soda burst from his nose. "Hey, *you!*" He pointed at the black-haired boy. "What's going—" He heard a loud, dull thump, a star blazed before him and then faded into blackness.

When Jimmy awoke he had enough room to reach up and rub the

lump on the back of his head, but no more. He was looking at hardware cloth closely from ground level, and his first thought was the chicken cage. But this cage had firmer restraints, bars of metal cut, it looked, from pieces of cars. Above him was a sheet of plywood, greyed with weathering and also reinforced with metal. Then he noticed that his legs were freer than the rest of him, and looking back over his shoulder saw that they extended through a square hole cut into the side of one of the shacks. He looked a little to his right and saw the rest of the building, all tar-paper and mismatched boards, beyond and uphill from which were several rotting cars. And beyond those was his van. The sight of it filled him with a desperate reassurance. How was he to get to it? What was going on, anyway? With some contorting he reached back and checked for his wallet—which was there. This was a strange robbery, at any rate. From another point of view it might even be funny: the simple coun-tryfolk not knowing enough to take the city man's money. From Jimmy's cramped point of view, it was confusing, and very scary. He heard a grinding moaning nearby and managed (with minimal pain to his head) to look around to his left. What he saw only served to confuse him more. Seven or so feet away was a structure much like his own, replete with an inmate. It was the nature of this fellow prisoner that baffled him; for it looked like a man, but only the head and one leg projected from its filthy T-shirt. The face, streaked with oily, grey strands of hair running down from a mostly bald pate, was that of a man in his fifties. Grey and blond beard hairs were thick with what looked like manure and black soil. An oak leaf stuck ridiculously to one side. The little loll of a mouth moaned some more coarse sounds, and the eyes looked out with an expression of dumb pain. When they alighted on Jimmy, the sounds became louder, and coherence seemed just beyond reach. Jimmy stared, frozen, at the prisoner. Then he caught movement in the left corner of his eye, and looked further. Again there was a wire cage and again a prisoner. This one was a woman, and she watched Jimmy with one terrified eye. A hand with two fingers pushed the bushy hair out of the other blank, gaping socket. She steadied herself on an elbow that went nowhere. Jimmy began to see other things, too, like the bandaged hands, the old man's wrapped leg, odd proportions in the children. . . . His hands began to shake again, unstoppably, and mewing noises came from behind his clenched lips. A light, lopsided skip approached, and Jimmy snapped his head around to see bright curls and a flouncy dress hopping closer. The dress had a tear all down one side and was smeared with blood, and the curls were all pushed violently to the left, but Jimmy had no trouble in recognizing the little girl. Her apple cheeks blossomed as she smiled, cracking the little streams of dried blood on them.

"Hey, y'know what?" she said. Jimmy mouthed, No, what? The fat little hands twisted a blade of grass. For a second her heavy lower lip drooped and her eyes stared. Then: "The doctor's comin'!" Then she turned and skipped her lopsided way back up the hill. Beyond her cheerful shape the sad-eyed man directed the removal of the boxes from the van. One of the teenagers was inspecting something from one of them: an automatic rifle.

The Walker in the Night

Say, boy, I'll take one of those.

Buster Weeden digs into his pocket, withdraws a handful of tinkling coins; picks out a nickel with thumb and forefinger and hands it to the waiting newsboy. Keep the change, kid. The boy pockets the nickel, hands Weeden today's Providence Journal. Pinches the brim of his cap and walks off down Exchange Place bawling headlines.

Weeden snaps open the Journal and gives it the once over. Depression's still on—no news there, just ask any Joe on the street—and the Germans are at it again in Europe. But when are they not? Forecast: Rain, probably heavy today and tomorrow, cooler. Well, they missed the boat on that one. Warm and sunny this last day of summer, 1938, in the good city of Providence, State of Rhode Island and Providence Plantations. Too warm for the jacket looped over Weeden's arm. A few horsetails blowing up from the south and a funny yellow tinge to the sky, but no rain, nossuh. The Industrial Trust Building (still tallest in New England, so *there*, Boston) stands out against that sallow sky like a gigantic, black tombstone. Howard hated that *Art Deco nightmare*, but he'd have liked that effect. Of course, Howard's been cold in the ground in Swan Point this past year and some. But still, he would have liked it.

Exiting Exchange Place on Fulton Weeden crosses the river over the Crawford Street Bridge. Off to the left the open space of Memorial Square with its seventy-five foot column to the dead of the Great War— Suicide Circle to the locals, cars whipping around it like maddened bees. College Hill rises before him in the heavy green shades of late summer; gables and steeples peep out of the trees like shy giants. Cars purr, hoot, spin past. Weeden ignores them. As he always does he looks right down the River to the harbor. Not that there's anything new there, either— same old steamers, tugs, fishing boats, the antique white bulk of the sidewheeler *Annawan*. The harbor is as still as glass—flat as a mill-pond, his mother would have said. The wide reaches of Narragansett Bay beyond to the south, too. Boats slice across it in the silence of distance and the Vs of their wakes fade as quickly as they form. And over it all, that queer yellow sky. Weeden thinks, Maybe the paper got it right after all. I'm no weatherman, nor mariner (his father, God bless him, knows that, after all those frustrating hours out on the Bay in a catboat when Buster was a boy). But even I know this *bodes ill.* There's Howard again, no doubt. Weeden doesn't talk like that. Only Howard Lovecraft would come out with a gem like that these days—and now even he's gone. Sure gonna miss that old ghoul, Weeden thinks as he cuts right down South Water Street. How that man could talk.

Weeden reaches the E-Z Lunch just before two. He walks in, smiles at the regulars at the counter, slings his hat and coat on the coat-tree. Steps around the counter, drops the paper by the shabby gent on the end. He picks up an apron and ties it on just as Rocco takes his off— two gears in the same little machine. Weeden glances around to make sure no ladies are present, says Hey you wop bastard, how's the trade.

Rocco shrugs, waggles his hand. Slow, Bustah, slow. Rocco scoops his hat off the coat-tree and onto his black pomade in one smooth motion. In another he exits the diner and is gone. Weeden turns to the grill, shaves an epidermis of crisped grease off it with his spatula. Turns back to the afternoon trade at the counter. Usual suspects: that hand from the *Annawan,* Mr. Arnold from the bank on his two-hour lunch (doesn't he know there's a Depression on?), some 'bo down from the India Street railyards, no doubt. This last is carefully counting his pennies on the counter. Even through the grease-and-burger atmosphere Weeden can smell the guy. Christ, why doesn't he spend the dough on a bath instead of a sandwich? But Weeden's polite, asks the guy What'll you have? The 'bo looks up from his pennies as if from the grave of his best friend.

Ham sandwich.

Coffee.

Please.

Weeden pivots back to his grill and Coldspot Super Six refrigerator (that cost a pretty penny but worth it) and starts assembling a ham sandwich. Gonna be a long evening, he thinks. Same old crowd, same old conversations. Not even conversations, really. Lectures. Soliloquies— now *there's* a good Lovecraft word for you. Soliloquies about what a jerk the mate aboard the *Annawan* is, what the stock market is doing (as if anybody has two dimes to rub together, never mind invest), where's the best place in town to get a haircut. Weeden could write it out, word for word. Not like talking to Lovecraft—or even just listening to him. Better'n a radio play, and always something new. Guy knew local history as if he'd lived it, and he could tell it so that you felt as if *you* had lived it, too. Red heels and periwigs on Benefit Street, patriots in tricorns marching off to burn the *Gaspee,* the Great Gale of 1815 that carried away the Great Bridge and drove ships up as far as the Market House. And his own stories—Christ. Howard gave Weeden a couple to read—one about some octopus-thing out to destroy the world—Kooloo? Cathuly? And a novel about a wizard right here in Providence. That one even had a character named Weeden in it.

That's right, Weeden thinks, turning to hand the ham sandwich to the tramp. That's how we got to talking. Me, I was working the graveyard shift, and in walks this fella, middle of the night, and him dressed to the nines. Takes off his hat—a grey Homburg, Weeden remembers—hangs it carefully on the coat-tree. Sits on the stool like he's sitting down to dinner at the Biltmore. A coffee, if you will—a real gent. Weeden brings him the java. Guy pours in a measure of cream and spoons in five, count 'em, five sugars. Takes a sip.

He's staring at something over Weeden's shoulder—the E-Z Lunch's license from the City of Providence hanging by the Coldspot.

Are you Mr. Weeden, the guy asks.

Folks call me Buster, Weeden says, offers his hand. Guy takes it. His grip is soft to Weeden's calluses.

My name is Lovecraft, he says, Howard Lovecraft. I am a writer. He says this as if it explains everything, the high, quiet voice, the intense brown eyes, his presence in a waterfront greasy-spoon at one A.M.

And in a way, it does. He walks at night to think, he says, get ideas for his stories.

Ever been published? Lovecraft smiles demurely (definitely a Lovecraft word)—Here and there, he says. I beg your pardon (he goes on) if I was forward in asking about your patronymic.

My what? Weeden frowns.

Your name, Lovecraft explains. It is a fine old Yankee name, extending back to the gracious days of the Colony.

And just like that they start talking. That first night it's easy—Lovecraft's the only customer—and they cover a lot of ground. Turns out they're both native Providence boys (though Howard grew up on the East Side and Buster down off Smith Hill), even know a couple of the same folks. But aside from that they don't really have a lot in common. Buster gets the feeling that this strange, brilliant man is lonely. Why else would he be talking to a jamoke like him? Maybe he just doesn't have many people to talk to, Weeden thinks, and pours Lovecraft another cup of coffee.

Lovecraft visits often after that. Not every night, but two-three times a week. Sometimes it's in the afternoon, coming back from one of his epic walks. Guy even walks to Lincoln and Johnston, for cripe's sake. Did the man never hear of buses? Cuts through Federal Hill and even the guineas don't give him a hassle. Weeden has seen Lovecraft go off down the street and doesn't think he'd bother him, either. There's a restless, burning energy to the man, a regular dynamo in a blue suit. Can barely sit still. That same electricity fires his walking. Tall, thin, intense, Lovecraft strides through the everyday *like a Pharaoh out of Antient Egypt* (way he said it, you could even hear the funny spelling, Weeden smiles and shakes his head). He walks—walked, Weeden sadly corrects himself—as if he was on some kind of mission.

And really, how many times could you walk over the same old streets? One night after they had gotten to know each other a little better, Howard has an answer for that:

I'm making sure everything is in its place.

As if things would fall apart without his supervision. And he made that odd, bound-up smile of his. Other times he'd gas on and on about the in-born connexion of a soul to its native soil, of the almost mystical linkage of the Yankee to the rock-ribbed hills and gambrel-roofed cottages of New England, his by tradition –buttressed birthright, blah blah blah. But it was that first answer that stuck with Weeden:

I'm making sure everything is in its place.

And what are we to do now, Howard? Now that you're gone, who will make sure it all holds together?

And Weeden has seen the end coming, though at the time he refused to admit it to himself. It was that fall of '36, and Howard was coming around less and less often. When he did it was obvious that something was wrong. His endurance was slipping, for one thing. He came back from a jaunt to Neutaconkanut Hill in Johnston positively winded. Yet he kept walking. His appetite, usually so robust, was off, too. Indigestion, he said primly, putting a hand to his belly. Weeden offered him a bicarbonate of soda, but Howard politely declined. Another cup of your excellent coffee, Buster, five sugars, please.

And he kept walking.

Yet when the end came, Buster didn't even know about it. It was at the tail-end of winter, '37, a season Howard hated anyway so Buster wasn't even looking for him. It had been weeks—months?—since he'd come in, and in stray moments Weeden hoped he was all right.

Then he opened up the Journal one day in March and there it was: Local writer dead at 46. Cancer, it said. Hell of a way to go. Eaten alive, and all the time Howard thought it was just indigestion. It made Weeden sad in a slow, undefined way. He couldn't really say he was Howard's friend—could he? Certainly not as close as some of the correspondents Howard used to speak so warmly of in Texas or Wisconsin or God-knew-where-else. Still, the news punched a hole in Weeden's life. He caught himself looking up the street nights, expecting that swift-legged scarecrow to appear. For him the loss of Howard Lovecraft was like a spoke missing from a great wheel: Every now and then it came back around and you wondered how the damned thing could keep turning without it.

Sorry?

Weeden swings from the grill where he had been cooking some-one—*someone*—a hamburger. Who asked for the burger? And who was just talking to me? He looks to the counter. Now there are four customers. A middle-aged woman in a black summer-dress is sitting between Mr. Arnold and the bum. A little closer to the banker. Did she order it?

I said, wind's picking up.

It's the hand from the *Annawan*. He's sitting all the way to the right where he can look out the side window at the harbor. Then Weeden hears it—a wind like a moan of pain. It makes the small hairs on the back of his neck bristle.

Sounds like it, Weeden says, and goes back to his burger. The hand shifts on his stool as if he's sitting on a hot-plate.

It's like them rats, he says, d'joo see them rats?

No, Weeden says (the rats, the rats in the walls, Howard whispers to him).

All them rats leavin' the waterfront, says the hand, headed inland, uphill. He is wringing his cap between his hands. When I come over earlier, I seen them rats. Damnedest thing.

Sir, says Mr. Arnold, motioning towards the woman.

Beg pardon, ma'am, says the hand. And suddenly he's up, off the stool as if flung off. Gotta scram, he says, scattering coins across the counter and turning to run out the door. Chief'll want me to batten down the tub. All of youse oughta think about leavin', too. The last thing they hear of him is the one word: *Bad.*

The door slaps shut. Weeden stares at where the sailor had been a second before. The banker pushes the scattered coins into neat piles which Weeden sweeps off into his apron with his hand. The bum watches, fascinated.

What about my hamburger, young man. It's the lady in the black dress—so that's who ordered the burger. Weeden scoops the burger off the grill with his spatula, drops it onto an open bun on a plate (guess I set that up, but damned if I can remember it). Slides the plate, bun and all across to the lady. It's then he notices it's getting dark. What time is it, anyway, six? No, the clock over the Coldspot reads 3:40. Rain hits the window like bird-shot.

I think I should be getting back, says Mr. Arnold. He pulls his billfold from an inner jacket pocket and selects a new one-dollar greenback to lay upon the counter. When Weeden turns to the register to get him change Arnold holds up his hand. That's fine, Buster, thank you, Buster, goodbye.

The lady pats her mouth with a napkin and gets up, too. The burger is half-eaten upon the plate, a crescent Moon of bread. Don't you want—starts Weeden.

Thank you, no, young man, it was very good. She turns to Mr. Arnold. If you'd be so kind…

I'd be delighted, and they go out the door arm in arm. Wind howls into the diner when they get the door open. Mr. Arnold grips the door and it yaws wide and almost throws him. Both his and the lady's hats vanish off their heads. Slowly Mr. Arnold pushes the door to until it latches. Then the pair of them huddle into each other and shuffle down

South Water Street in the direction of downtown. Rain lashes them like whips and their coats slap about them like black wings.

Whatcha gonna do with that? It's the bum and he's pointing an alcohol-palsied finger at the half-eaten burger.

Help yourself. Weeden watches the 'bo eat the burger. Takes all of five seconds. Weeden looks down at the lady's napkin where a perfect lipstick smile puckers up at him.

The gale swells. It muscles the little building around, creaking and cracking. But the E-Z is solid on its blocks and pilings, right?

Right?

While Buster busies himself at his cleaning the tramp pages through the Journal Weeden bought. The two men trade comments—Where you from?

Rochester, New York, says the 'bo, but pronounces it like RAH-chister, NerYerk. Know a good place to get a haircut?

Weeden grins at the stove-top. Yeah, he says, and a bath, too. That shuts him up.

Rain slaps sheets against the walls. Maybe I should close early, Weeden thinks. Give Mabel a jingle, see if she wants to take in a show at the RKO Albee. A look out the harbor-side window shows the water's up, but it's getting on towards high tide anyway. Even Buster the Landlubber knows that. But the water has an ugly cast to it, a weird, pale, milky green color Weeden has never seen before. The wind tears it into strips of foam and spume. Good day to stay inside, he thinks. On the South Water Street side out through the door and front plate windows, rainwater pours down the alleys connecting to South Main and the vertical slopes of College Hill beyond. The wind is constant now. Its moaning rises and falls like a madman's keening.

It gets darker.

Weeden snaps on the diner's lights and stands by the door a minute, watching the freshets galloping down the alleys. Checks the clock—4:15.

Walking back around the counter he says to the bum, You want anything?

The 'bo slowly reaches back and down towards a non-existent wallet, but Weeden stops him. No, on the house. The bum smiles, sunrise through the undergrowth of his whiskers.

Why sure, pal, he says. You're all right.

Weeden goes to the Coldspot and takes out two eggs and a butcher-paper full of bacon. He lays four strips of bacon out on the grill in careful, parallel lines (the rain hammers the walls), cracks the eggs with one hand and drops the liquid onto the hot metal (the wind bellows destruction), tosses the eggshells into the trash and fiddles with the cooking meat.

All at once there is a metal screech from overhead and a gang of boys playing kick-the-can across the roof. Turns out it's the stove's metal flue, now sailing north towards Woonsocket at seventy miles an hour. Within seconds a stream of rainwater pours out of the hood over the grill. It hits the hot, greasy stove and explodes into a cloud of steam shot with grease spatters. The bum barks something he probably wouldn't have said if the lady were still there (probably), and Weeden jerks back hard against the counter, covering his face with his apron. He darts a hand under the steam and turns off the gas feeding the grill. Rainwater continues to stream in—steam billows up to the ceiling.

Well, Weeden says with a lopsided grin, dinner's off. The bum licks his flaking lips, stares at the ruins of bacon and eggs floating in a pool of oily water. Just then the E-Z Lunch gives a shrug like a fat man shifting in his sleep and the bum is up, tipping his fedora and saying, So long, pal, and he trots to the door.

Weeden says, Where you gonna go? Look at it out there.

The bum hesitates with his hand on the doorknob. Looks out at the streets running water; looks at the diner full of steam.

Somewhere else, he says, and yanks the door open. Wind yells in triumph and tears the door out of the bum's hand. The door slams into the front wall of the E-Z Lunch and cracks the left-hand plate window. Weeden runs to pull the door shut. The 'bo, hat clamped to his head with one hand, is hunched shuffling through the ankle-deep water up (where else?) South Water Street like an enormous beetle pushed on by the gale. The water is almost up to the top of the diner's front step, and in the time that it takes Weeden to manhandle the door shut the water rises over the step and fans out across the diner's floor.

Buster stares out the windows, panting. Licks a rill of rainwater out of the corner of his mouth. Outside the world he knows is disappearing. The flying wrack is so thick he can barely see the brick warehouses across the street. Beyond them College Hill is just a dream Howard

Lovecraft once had—gone. As Weeden stands there the little diner gives another heave *and shifts three feet to the left.* Weeden can't know that exactly, of course, but damned if he didn't feel it. He remembers the deckhand's parting word—*Bad.* Bad, my foot, he thinks, this is terrible. His feet turn cold and he looks down to see the water has covered the entire floor and is inching up his shoes. Releasing the door (his hand has gone numb) he backs away from it to the middle of the room.

He stands there alone.

Thinks, I should get the mop, push this wet out of here. Then thinks, You idiot, the street's full of water. He sloshes to the harbor-side window, water to his ankles, looks out at a scene he does not recognize. The downtown side of the River is gone behind rain and spray; the harbor itself littered with junk, boards, crates, a life-preserver, a dead dog, a rocking chair? It all races up the current towards the bridges, downtown. And Weeden realizes with a shock that the water in the street outside—the water that is filling his precious little restaurant—isn't rainwater. It's Narragansett Bay.

For a full minute he stands frozen at the window. What do I do— *what do I do?* Through the roar of the wind he hears wood crackling, glass bursting. A wall of bricks falls out of nowhere to splash thunderously into the rising water and dash spray onto the window in front of Weeden's face.

That breaks the spell. In three slogging strides he is at the cash register. Punches SALE and the drawer shoots open with a musical *ding.* Ones, fives, tens (not too many of those), a handful of quarters. Leave the small change for the storm. Stuffs the dough in his pocket. He rounds the counter one last time, pushing through the knee-high water towards the front door—and stops. Looks around. I can't leave, he thinks. I built this place, for Pete's sake. Put ten years of my life into it. I'll be God-damned if I let a rainstorm drive me out. *Dumb, pig-headed Yankee,* says a voice in his head. *You stay here, you'll die.*

But he does stay. He backs up to the counter, heaves himself up to sit on it, sopping feet resting on one of the stools. It's high tide, he tells himself, that's all it is. A lot higher'n usual, but just high tide. It'll crest soon, then drop, same as always. He twists around to look at the white idiot face of the clock—5:05. Won't be long now. Claps his hands once, twice. Shifts his feet on the stool. Not long now. The wind screams.

At 5:15 the lights go out. Weeden cranes around to stare at the clock in the gloom in the little diner where it will be 5:15 forever. The water now laps at the red vinyl seats of the stools, and the coat-tree, buoyed up by the water, nods drunkenly and falls with a splash, taking Weeden's hat and coat with it. He is staring stupidly at the weird little circular boat his hat has become when the harbor-side window explodes inward and glass and rain spray everywhere and that same voice in his head is loud now and it says GO.

Weeden shoves himself off the counter, plunges feet-first into the flood. Up to his groin now, rising as fast as you could run water from a spigot into a glass. Harder to slog through. Harder, too, to get that damned door open, but here for once the wind helps him and he's dragged out into the storm with the door.

Outside there is nothing but storm. The gale—a full hurricane now—rampages over the earth, races and roars in its mad circle as if it never had to stop. It scours the planet like a rasp, tearing up anything and everything and hurling it all through the air like some insane giant child in a tantrum. It has cut the world loose from its moorings and sent it spinning.

The wind shoves Weeden down into the salty water. He pushes himself back up into a crouch but he can't think, can barely see. The gale tears his shirt away like a magic-trick—presto, now you see it, now you don't. The air is so thick with spray it is neither air nor water, both, and riven with flying shingles and shirts and glass like crazy chimes down the wind and a sign that reads E-Z LUNCH *Quality Meals At Old-Fashioned Prices.* Squinting into the blast Weeden thinks, Maybe make it up to South Main, up the Hill to high ground. Somewhere under the green water his legs start working slowly, painfully. A piece of something metal—rain gutter? hubcap?—slashes down the wind and opens up a gash across his shoulders. He pushes on.

And then he gets one of those idiotic little ideas that won't let men sleep nights and send them off on tangents they can't imagine:

Did I shut the door?

It's stupid, trivial, what will it matter? But it won't let him go. It's only a few steps back—better make sure. So he turns and gropes back and the Bay water bullies him downstream and the storm flings leaves and newspapers and pillows and flagpoles overhead. Weeden reels to the door—which is open. Knucklehead. He grips the edge and tries to push it shut but it's like pushing a bag of wet sand.

It is then that he hears it. Different people will later describe it in different ways—a waterfall, a locomotive, a boiler-factory—but to Buster Weeden it sounds like God taking a deep breath before delivering the loudest, yelling-est lecture in the Universe. He looks up.

Towering over him, over the E-Z Lunch like a monument, is the bow of the *Annawan*. Weeden barely registers the vast, green wall of water it is riding as the 200-foot side-wheeler heaves up—and down. It hits the E-Z Lunch and folds it up like wet cardboard. The next second everything disappears.

He is pinwheeling through salt water. At the very last second he gulped air and shut his eyes. Now he opens them, but all he sees is that sickish green of roiling water boiling with swarms of bubbles. The water is cold and the bubbles would tickle his bare skin, but Weeden feels nothing. He is in shock from the impact of the tidal wave. A blessing, really. For several moments he has no idea where he is and doesn't even care. The hurricane has shoved the waters of Narragansett Bay up the Providence River as if into a funnel. Later records will show that the wave swelled the River thirteen feet above mean water. Which puts Buster Weeden about five feet under the surface at this moment. But he still has no idea where he is, and with returning consciousness comes the panic understanding that *he does not even know which way is up*. He thrusts arms and legs in all directions, reaching for solid ground, air, blessed air. He kicks out (one shoe is gone, he won't even know it until he steps on dry ground much later) and by a miracle drives his head above the flood. Nothing but that flying soup of atomized spray but he manages to gasp in several lungfuls. A glance down College Street to where Canal Street ought to be shows a flotilla of refrigerators sailing by, bobbing like giant cakes of soap on the tide. A man sits on the foremost, wet, disheveled, aghast. (Say, buddy, show you how to sail that thing? I'm no good at catboats but I'm aces with a Coldspot).

Under again. Weeden is being carried up South Main Street past the new Court House, the What Cheer Building, the Rhode Island School of Design. Weeden blinks into the murk ahead of him—lights. Pairs of lights. Headlights, he thinks. An underwater funeral cortege of cars caught in the flood. And a noise:

aaaaaaaaaaaaaaaaaaaaaaaaaaaaaaaaaaaaaaaaaaaaaaaaaaaaaaaaaaaanh

The floodwaters have shorted the cars' circuits and their horns blare endlessly. Closer now, and the dark bulks of the cars resolve themselves. The first one's a Chevrolet—see the long-cross symbol on the grill?—the second a Dodge. The third car Weeden can't identify because he's looking at the man's face and hands pressed against the driver's-side window, eyes staring in horror at his own drowning. In the back of the car a little pair of chubby legs and the hem of a frilly dress dangle from up under the roof. Weeden doesn't look any more.

Up again and there's the First Baptist Church, Finest Georgian Steeple in America, as Howard used to like to say (shut *up*, Howard, can't you see I'm drowning?) But the light is wrong. The normally bone-white steeple is now a black knife against the flying wrack. And the business blocks along South Main rise black and sheer as cliffs—no windows, no doors. Other structures hump up the hill like outgrowths of stone. Where is the Art Club, where the old mansions? All is strange and Weeden feels a dizziness of strangeness come over him. Like the E-Z Lunch, everything feels knocked three feet to the left.

Down he goes again, his head still spinning. Torrents of rain gush down what should have been Waterman and Thomas Streets to feed the flood. The currents become confused, angry, grab at Weeden, buffet him, tug him and twist him in several directions at once. He knows that he is near where the Moshassuck and Woonasquatucket Rivers join to make the Providence River. The City long ago filled in the Cove (Remember the Cove, his grandmother would say, wistful smile, remember the Promenade?) and buried the rivers under Memorial Square. If Weeden gets sucked into the Moshassuck's stone canal he'll be dragged into the tunnels under the Square and drowned for sure.

When he breaks the surface again he's sure he is in the canal. He's pressed against dressed stone by the current. No, not the canal, this stone stands up out of the water. The railroad viaduct over North Main? He pushes away from the stone to get a better look up—and up. It's a stone tower, a rough triangle a hundred feet high—*on North Main?* It is slick and black with slime and festooned (thank you, Howard) with seaweed. The blocks that make it up are not cut square but at every angle imaginable. Weeden can see no cement between them—how do they even hold together? Looking around him through the dimness he sees other, similar towers standing up out of the waters. They loom and fade and loom and fade as squalls blow past them. They lean and droop as if tired out by the weight of a thousand years—a million? There is nothing of Providence in sight, not the First Baptist, not the Court House, not the River. Nothing. A cold not from the water sinks through Weeden's body. Where *am* I? He feels the water beneath him drop into unfathomed nothingness—*black seas of infinity*. Got that one right, Howard. Did he know this place? Did he fear it? Weeden digs his fingers into the seam between two stone blocks and holds on, shivering. Waves slap him into the hard stone but he holds on, dear God, holds on.

Finally a wave larger than the rest comes along and sweeps Weeden off the strange tower. He scrabbles wildly at it but the wave bears him away.

And under. Currents whirl him and toss him and his air is running out, his chest locked tight with bands of pressure and panic. But when he finally claws to the surface again it is in the Providence he knows. He gapes at the old familiar buildings as greedily as he gasps in air, thank God thank God thank God. The storm still rages but the wave has crested. Now, he thinks, it will start withdrawing, dragging all with it back to sea. Got to get a-holt of something, get out. With the water poised in equilibrium between flood and ebb, Weeden swims as hard as he can towards the side of the street. Grabs hold of a railing and hauls himself up and out of the greedy waters. Crawls hand over bleeding hand up a cobblestone lane—South Court Street, there's the Old State House, wouldn't Lovecraft be delighted. Weeden is shaking with cold, exhaustion, pain. The salt water has gotten into the cut on his back and set it afire. But he is alive, thank God, and pulls onward ten, twenty feet up from the terrible waters, to the side of this building, that's enough, and collapses.

———————

When he wakes up it is to a darkness Providence has not known for three centuries. Here and there windows flicker with the unsteady yellow glow of candles. Above downtown, blue-white shafts of antiaircraft spotlights probe the torn skies. Weeden pushes himself up off the pavement, stumbles back down to North Main. The flood is gone, most of the wind, too. But the stately old trees of College Hill are stripped down to mere sticks and Weeden hugs himself against a new chill. It is suddenly, brutally, autumn.

He turns left on North Main, right on Steeple. Glass crunches underfoot with every step. It is then that Weeden discovers he has lost his left shoe. Finds another, two sizes too big but he straps it onto his foot with a strip of wet bedding. The flood has left all its broken toys behind. Weeden steps around bricks and lumber and chunks of concrete; over cornices and banisters, gas-cans, books, a Victrola, a body; past cars and boats and bait shacks. A wing-chair full of dead fish. Here's Memorial Square and its granite monument. Was this what I saw in the flood, he wonders. But he knows it is not. The city looks like something out of a war movie. And it *was* a war, wasn't it? What on earth—if of earth—hit us?

A radio sitting on the square and plugged into nothing drones on. Sorry, Mister, you can't go downtown. Weeden looks up. A Guardsman appears out of the gloom, bayoneted rifle in one hand, blanket in the other. Off limits, he says. Martial law. Here, have a blanket. Weeden takes the blanket. It's damp but still dryer than he is and he wraps it tightly around himself.

The Guardsman vanishes—Weeden walks on. It is so very quiet but for a few last shreds of wind up amongst the black towers of Exchange Place. Here's a boat, the *Lochinvar* out of Portsmouth. A car folded in half by a falling chimney—bricks everywhere. Glass everywhere. And everything's wet. What he wouldn't give for a hot cup of coffee and a dry couch to lie down on. But not now. Sometime he'll go down and see what's left of the E-Z, too—but not now. Now he wanders. He sees the Market House, built 1773, windows blown out but still standing. And looming behind it, white as ever, the First Baptist's stubborn Yankee steeple. A spotlight glances off the Industrial Trust Building, flashing into startled existence—good. Still there. He walks on. Up the Hill stand the Athenaeum, the Unitarian Church, John Brown House, the Christian Science dome. If he starts walking now he can see them all before daylight.

An Echo of Pipes

The woods shifted above and around Kris as he walked through them; yellow to green to dark green, their canopies veined with black branches. The grass was soft under his feet, where it wasn't hidden beneath countless layers of leaves, and he was glad for having left his shoes at home. Beyond the leaf-pennants overhead, infrequent clouds passed, huge and swelling and shining, and birds chattered, unseen. A lone leaf flirted in front of him on its descent to the ground, and he paused to watch it fall.

He was far into the woods but, though he had left the path, was unconcerned about finding his way back. He knew, regardless of the many turns and explorations he made, that the route home would be damnably easy to find; yet he could still hope. Echoing quietly in his mind were irritating reminders—"The woods end at Tower Road—they only extend so far, there are only two ponds in them, the path leads away to the right, beyond the boulders"—all these things and countless other intimacies of the forest he knew, but he kept to his determination. He *would* get lost in these woods, he *would*. Once, in a blizzard one December, the path had dimmed to nothing in the snow, the trees had stood, rank on rank, identical, and he had lost his way, reveling in the omniscience of the snow and the quiet it brought, and the illusion of endless hills and hollows of trees. Soon, however, familiarity returned; first a stand of birch, almost invisible in the downfall, then a huddle of boulders, and soon the entire forest regrouped around him, suddenly dull in its precise arrangement. He trudged home that day, saddened and wearied by the presence of well-known and often-traveled roads and paths.

But this day was right, Kris knew. He wouldn't need the curtain of snow today, nor dusk, for the presence of the forest was huge upon him, and he could hear a sound as of multitudes cheering in the swaying of bright tree, for miles and miles. He'd conquer that dullness, for he recognized it as within himself. There was nothing dull in the woods themselves, and only association made them seem that way. The most important thing was to relax, as he had, and to let the rolling hills and his feet take him where habit and reason could not. And, like currents beneath a glittering sea, the land was taking him.

The last familiar thing he had seen had been a huge, flat, lichen-spotted rock he called "the Wolf's Seat," even though there had not been wolves in the area for many years; the name just seemed to fit. Having passed it only minutes before, he decided to walk back and rest on it for a minute or two. However, after topping a familiar-looking rise and surveying the hollow before him, he couldn't see it. At first doubting the very familiarity he had wished to lose, he ran to the opposite ridge, thinking he hadn't gone back far enough. But the rock wasn't there either. At the hollow's bottom were a stand of elm, some stunted blueberry bushes, and a still puddle; nothing more. He ran back to the other ridge and looked beyond it at the long slope, ending in a stream he had leapt only minutes before. It was familiar, but only from the recent past, and he realized, as he ran to the stream, that had beaten the memories. He was lost.

The stream was far behind him, in what direction he neither knew nor cared. On every hand rose trees, spreading into brilliance above, fading into uniform green on the hills in the hazy distance. The forest flooded his senses in a total seduction to which he surrendered himself; he smelled the scents of leaves spread in the sun, the damp ground, and strangely alluring pollens, tinged with omnipresent decay; to his ears came myriad choruses of crescendo and retreat in the forest ceiling overhead; and color vied with color in the brilliance all around him—sullen greys of boulders, yellow and green and black, and infinite shades between them, flashing from the trees; and beyond everything loomed the almost twilight-blue of the limitless heavens, electric and alive. Here, nature was in full festival, and Kris felt more alive by its very presence.

Once, the land dipped steeply and rose even more so, and Kris climbed the slope to a thinly-wooded crest. Standing straight with his hands on his hips and breathing deeply from the effort of climbing, he scanned the treetops. His breathing slowed to almost nothing and he felt his gaze drawn deeply into the spaces around him; for look as he might, he could not see an end to the wilderness around him, in any direction. He shaded his eyes and the smile slipped from his face; he couldn't see any houses, nor any regular breaks in the trees, as of roads, not even the steeple of the white church in town, which he knew to be visible from his house, across the woods from it. He marveled at the trick geography had played on him, in hiding all traces of man, and tried to guess in what direction the church would lie, if he could see it. However, even this seemed futile, for the arrangement of hills resembled nothing he remembered seeing in the area. Looking to the sun gained him only frustration, for it burned noncommittally in the heavens' center—a Summer noon. Kris guessed that he was headed North, but couldn't be sure of this, either, because looking up from the promontory made his head swim, as though he would fall endlessly over the earth, and he could get no bearing on the horizon. And when he started to descend, his anger was complete; for in his confusion, he couldn't remember which side of the hill he had climbed. Randomly choosing a side, he left the summit quickly. The sky had been too overwhelming there, and had only served to make him dizzy and confused.

He walked onward, but his spirit was dampened by his failure to orient himself . The woods now pressed a little too insistently on him, the trees becoming monotonous in their sheer numbers and the silence too complete. The wind had died, he realized suddenly, but he could not recall when. Surely it was blowing when he was on the hilltop, for he remembered its tugging at his clothes there. The quiet drew his thoughts out of his anger, just as the sky tugged at his gaze, and he felt again a returning peace. It was changed, however, from his earlier impression. With the stilling of the wind had come a tranquility and a solemnity which sharply contrasted with the trees' former festive attitude. Kris was standing very still now, and could hear only a single cicada, singing softly from the trees to his right. He looked intently around him, as expectant as the forest seemed to be, and noted the thinning of the trees ahead and to his right. He walked slowly, unconsciously quieting his steps over the leaves and twigs and stones. He had just discerned something peculiar up ahead, when he felt the cushion of moss under his hesitant feet, and he looked down at it. Reassured that it was just moss, he had started to raise his eyes when he saw prints in the soft growth. He knelt down and inspected them; the prints were sharp and deep, and had the telltale cleft of a grazing animal. Kris searched his memory for reports of deer in the area, but couldn't recall any. Still, that didn't mean much, considering the strange area he was in, and the difference between this print and that of a deer. Not only was the print itself unlike a deer's, but the arrangement struck him as peculiar. The grouping of prints was unlike any he had seen either in books or in the wild, although the print itself seemed vaguely familiar. He puzzled over it for a few seconds more, and then rose and walked toward the white objects in the clearing.

Had his feeling of strangeness about the area not been complete, his inspection of the clearing would have completed it. The white shapes turned out to be stone, unpolished marble that reminded Kris of century-old gravestones in the cemetery in town, and they were carven and some had weathered hints of writing on them. They appeared, at first glance, to have no order; but Kris walked to the right of the clearing and looked again, and found them to be scattered from one central mound of stones, as though a building had once stood there and had thrown the carven blocks around it in collapsing. Looking again at the tumbled blocks, he was sure of it, for the patterns on them could easily be connected from one stone to another, several feet away. The central group of stones disclosed that the building must have been circular, and the bases of pillars could be discerned from the rest. Whatever kind of edifice it once was, that had been long ago. Most of the blocks were half-buried, grass growing from splits in them; lichens brightly spotted their every surface. Kris was sure that no one had seen the ruin in a long time, perhaps since its destruction, for he could recall no mention of such a thing from any person or source in town. Certainly, a structure such a this would have been big news in a town as small as his, considering the ancient aspect of it. The mystery fascinated, yet frustrated him; he was somehow angry with himself for not knowing more answers. The very writing on the stones was frustrating, for while some letters were familiar, others completely baffled him. Tiring of the confusion, he walked across the clearing to a rock outcropping and lay down to rest, shielding his eyes from the sun with his arm.

He opened his eyes and sat up, surveying the clearing. He was a little groggy and hoped that he hadn't slept; without any way to tell time, he could not be sure about the lateness of the day. The sun, however, had moved behind some branches and no longer shone in his eyes, and he thought it wise to try to find his way again. As he stretched and brushed leaves from his arms, he tried to remember what had awakened him. He remembered only that something from the outer world had penetrated his resting, something like a warning or premonition of an impending event of importance, and even as he wondered, he noticed that the woods had become absolutely quiet. Although they had been still before, they felt now as if there had never been life, or wind, or sound in them. He sat back down on the warm stone, watching as intently as the skies beyond the trees seemed to be.

For a few endless minutes, the world stayed absolutely still, and then two things happened, almost simultaneously. The wind returned, gently at first, then swelling majestically, and Kris, looking around at the animated trees, noticed something new in the darkness across the clearing, beyond the ruins.

Almost invisible in the surrounding greenery was a face. It was a bearded man, as far as Kris could tell, its eyes dark and trained towards him, although the changing shadows made it difficult to discern details. A surge of the wind cleared the shadows from the face for a moment, and Kris was stunned by the expression on it; a mood of tranquility and confidence that was deeper than any expression on any other face he'd seen. The intensity of it so hit Kris that he felt himself drawn into it, relaxing from the first shock of seeing it and forgetting all else. He might have thought he was being hypnotized, but he still heard his thoughts running in his head, even noting the details of the face itself, mostly the large, tilted, placid eyes, He might have kept gazing at the face, except that the wind turned and the shadows slipped back over it. Kris blinked and looked around, as if to find people watching him, but he was alone. No, that wasn't entirely true; the woods were there. He shook his head at his not noticing before: there was a consciousness in the shining wilderness around him, a soul that was older than mankind and complete without him, but there if one looked for it. Its presence pervaded everything in sight; a quiet exuberance and victoriousness in the bright leaves, the fallow grass, the sullen rocks and the ponderously swaying tree-trunks, and Kris ached to be part of it, There must be a compromise between man and nature. At that moment, he was pulled from his thoughts by movement in the far trees. Between two ancient, twisted trunks, stray sunlight had sifted down, held as if by amber in the dusty air. A figure trotted through the bars of light—it was there and then gone, but in that moment Kris recognized it as the owner of the strange face, running half-naked in the soft light. He ran awkwardly, and Kris was puzzled that the man should wear dark pants and narrow boots, but no shirt. Kris walked carefully to the arch between the trees, but the figure was long gone. A cricket or cicada piped in the columned shade, and Kris turned to find his way home.

He remembered the point where he had come into the clearing, but little else. The sun was now noticeably lowering into the west and Kris decided that his way led to the south, although even this detail was mostly unconscious. His conscious thoughts were taken with contemplating the scenery around him. In and out of the slanting, yellow light he wandered, realizing that, ironically, now that he no longer cared about it, the path was plain to him and already under his feet, natural to his direction. It was leading home and thus was one less thing to distract him from admiring the landscape settling down for the approaching dusk. He'd keep to the path, watching the woods through which he passed on his way, content with his place therein.

On his way, he ascended a rise, taking in the tranquil panorama around. Whether it was the same hill he had climbed before, he couldn't tell, although he doubted it; for due west, beyond the forested hills and occasional houses, all bright in the reddening sunlight, the church was plainly visible, the white blade of its steeple thrust coldly into the sky.

Kris knew that he would probably never find the ruins again. Still, he didn't care, for he felt that they and the naked figure that lived among them shouldn't be frightened away. That the creature had indeed been totally naked was clear to Kris now, as clear as the meaning of the temple's ruins. Even the meaning of some of the alien, carven letters was known to him now, even before he walked the long, pine-shadowed road back to his house, took down several books on mythology from their shelves, and spread one open on the table. There, the twilight showed dimly the ancient Greek letters for the name "Pan," letters already familiar to Kris. Beyond the window, in the advancing darkness, the woods would always be there.

A Tale of a Lonely Island

The Casco Islands Historical House was a straight-backed three-story brick building on the highest point of Brackett Island. From its eight-paned windows one hundred and fifty years of inhabitants had watched the city of Portland grow across the water; once they'd seen it burn down. That was westward. To the east, north and south could be seen the broad, blue sprawl of Casco Bay and the sheer tree walls of the other islands. In summer, bright sail triangles floated by or crowded around the one, state-owned dock. In winter only the ferry came out, and that half as frequently as in summer. The island's other houses were all half a century younger than the Historical House, and looked up to it on its prominence as children to a story-teller.

But such niceties were lost on Mr. Milton Twitchell. He was an historian and his interest lay in documents, not in scenery. His path that morning had been a straight one: from Silver Street apartment to ferry terminal, from terminal to Brackett Island dock, from dock to Historical House, from front door to favorite table. He'd made the trip innumerable times in his long years of research, and whatever charm the accompanying views may have once held for him was long since faded by routine. This day in particular, bright and gusty as it often gets in October, Mr. Twitchell had hardly glanced up from his reading matter the whole way.

The object of this consuming interest was the history of a certain Colonial-era family, the Winfields. They had been five—father Abraham, mother Susan, sons Isaac and Thomas, and daughter Elizabeth—refugees from an intolerant England and later a scarcely less restrictive Massachusetts Bay Colony. The mother, in particular, interested Mr. Twitchell, for it appeared to have been she who decided (or precipitated) the family's moves. Tall, cow-boned, plain-spoken and persistent, Susan (Digby) Winfield was reminiscent of other women whom the Salem authorities would see fit to hang under the guise of witchcraft. But Susan had been wise enough to leave Salem in 1641, long before the witchcraft madness began, and all accounts record that she and her family were welcomed by the independent souls of the northern wilderness. Oddly, the Winfields declined offers of land on the Neck (as Portland's peninsula was then known), settling instead on the same island that now boasted the Historical House. Abraham set up his fishing trade with the merchants on Richmond Island, down the coast. Susan and her three offspring tilled the land they'd cleared, churned the butter, set preserves and kept the house warm and righteous for father's return. It must have been lonely, and terribly hard during the Maine winters, but it was the life they chose. Carrington Tanner, a resident of the Neck, wrote to his son in 1660 that the Winfields were "a good people, but solitary & not given to much intercourse with our community, tho' Winfield's Island [i.e., Brackett Island] was only a short distance away." In general, the townsfolk liked Abraham and respected Susan. There was no question that Mrs. Winfield ran house and island.

Be that as it may, none could blame Mr. Winfield for deferring to his strong-willed and practical wife. This arrangement, accepted by all, might have continued over the space of a natural lifetime, but for the hand of tragedy. On March 5, 1642, Susan Winfield sailed her husband's modest fishing boat to the landing on Falmouth Neck. To see this woman on shore at all, much less alone, was cause for interest in the small community, so Mr. Twitchell had little difficulty finding corroborative accounts of what followed. Mrs. Winfield was terribly upset—another surprise from the granite-hard woman—and her plain dress was dotted with blood. Mr. Winfield's prize musket lay in the water sloshing in the bottom of the boat. As the men helped Susan from the boat, her hands shook, and her normally booming voice was drained of power as she began to speak. Indians had visited Winfield's Island, and their trade had not been friendly. A boat and several men armed with muskets were readied even before Susan revealed that she was the only Winfield left alive.

Once again, Carrington Tanner picked up the tale. He had been a young man then and was in the party that landed on that horribly silent island. The Winfields were indeed dead, *very* dead. As used as the Englishmen were becoming to Indian raids, they were stopped cold by what they found near the Winfields' home. Mr. Winfield lay face down in the snow by the garden, several vicious-looking gashes in his back and a musket-ball in the brain. The sons, teenage Isaac and ten-year-old Thomas, had gone down fighting; the older boy's beheaded and mutilated form sprawled across his father's fowling piece, and his brother's nearly severed arm still held a club. Tanner would not dwell on little Elizabeth's fate. The reader was left with the pathetic image of a small bed soaked in blood. The little house itself was in shambles, and the party wondered how Mrs. Winfield had gotten out alive.

Then something was spotted near the shore, downhill from the eastern field: the bodies of two Indians. Their canoe was there too, pulled up on the smooth stones and lined with fish. Had this been it, then? Had the Winfields been massacred for a day's catch? The Winfield boy must have gotten off a lucky shot before he'd gone down, for one of the bodies bore a neat hole in its throat. The other's cause of death was less apparent until the white men prodded the body and the head rolled into an impossible position. Poor Abraham must have gone at this attacker with his bare hands, snapping his neck in his rage and frustration. The investigation done, the Winfield family was set in the cellar of their house, the ground still being frozen. The Indians were put back into their canoe and set adrift, a toy for the cold Atlantic.

Back ashore, Susan had given as good an account as she was able. She had been in the dirt cellar when the Indians arrived. It had all happened so fast—two of her children were dead before she'd scrambled out of the earth, and she had listened in horror as her baby was slaughtered in her own home. Before the Indians had emerged from their work, Susan had run to her husband's side—he was badly wounded but just alive—and gotten his rifle from him. The first Indian to emerge received a musket-ball to the throat (he was, then, the Indian found by the water), but there were still three others inside. Susan, practical even in the midst of the horror, knew she could do no more; and ran to the landing where her husband kept his boat. She looked back once, and saw the remaining murderers emerge cautiously from her house. One put the barrel of his musket to Abraham's head and pulled the trigger. Abraham's gun was useless, its one shot spent; but the fleeing Susan dared not part with it.

Grown men had cried upon hearing the tale, but the effect on Mr. Twitchell was rather less. He closed the manila envelope over the account's antique pages and rubbed his eyes. He knew the story already;

the Englishmen formed a deputation which eventually found the murderers hiding by the banks of the Presumpscot River. The three, who never offered an explanation for their cold-bloodedness, were hanged from a tree located near the modern-day intersection of India and Congress Streets. The Aucocisco, the tribe to which the killers had belonged, were furious over what they saw as the groundless murder of three of *their* number, until "persuaded by God's own Truth, which cannot be polluted nor made unclear," but possibly aided by superior firepower. Mr. Twitchell had read it and reread it in at least three different versions, and was resigned to reading it in three more versions, if necessary. *On a Troubled Bay: Colonial Life on the Islands of Maine* would be perfect; Milton Twitchell's first book would have no errors. But at the moment he wasn't certain that he hadn't made some.

He couldn't understand why the surviving Indians had left two of their dead and a boatload of fish on the island. The English had put it down to "Native barbarism and stupidity," but that was just white prejudice. It would have been highly atypical—worse, it was wasteful, a cardinal sin for Yankees and Indians alike. Mr. Twitchell wondered if perhaps the Indians had been in a hurry to evade capture, knowing that Mrs. Winfield had gone for help; but he still couldn't believe that they would leave their dead. Had the other three Indians even *been* there? Had Mrs. Winfield lied about them, knowing that *some* Indians would hang, in revenge for her murdered family? That, too, was unlikely. It was unfortunate—and possibly tragic—that the accused had remained tight-lipped to the end of the rope. But if there was another side to the story, Mr. Twitchell was determined to ferret it out.

A glance at his watch showed that only half an hour remained before the closing time of five o'clock. Mr. Twitchell groaned and looked at the historical mess he'd assembled on the table. In the midst of it, still untouched, was the bundle donated by a Winfield relative only a week before. When the librarian, Miss Turner, came by again, he asked whether he might stay a while after closing.

"It's unusual," she said, and frowned at the books and papers in front of him, "but I suppose so." Then she looked at her watch: "Oh dear, I have to be in town in an hour and the ferry's at 5:10 . . . Well, all right, Mr. Twitchell. We know you pretty well, I think." The two exchanged inexpert smiles. "Be sure to lock up when you leave," she said, and placed a small ring of keys on the table. "This is for the front door and that's for the alarm. I'll be here until five, if you have any other questions."

Mr. Twitchell looked around and realized that he'd been the only guest there for hours. Satisfied with his solitude, he pushed his glasses down from his forehead back to the bridge of his nose, and reopened the file.

He didn't notice Miss Turner leave, nor the fall of night. His usual supper-time came and went unheeded, too, and still the scholar bent his balding head over his papers. The pile of notes he'd started that morning had grown to rival that of the documents, a mound of papers at each hand. But for the whisper of his pen on paper and the turning of pages, the old house was still. Vagrant winds came, to rattle the windows, but finding no entrance passed away. Through the glass, twilight's exquisite purple had deepened into a star-tipped black; Portland's many lights sent wiggling reflections of yellow and blue and white across the water towards the islands. In a pause of the wind, by some trick of atmospherics, the sound of City Hall's bell winged over the bay and into the pale-walled room. It chimed clearly, gently, eight times. Mr. Twitchell looked up and said, "Hmm?" For a moment he thought a question had been put to him. Then he pulled back his sleeve and stared at the watch-face there. It didn't seem possible, but there it was: he'd been there almost twelve hours. The collection of notes seemed ridiculously small for such effort and he decided that it was the end of the day's work. He was only part-way through the new file, but it would be there tomorrow. Let the guilty rest another day. Besides, if the documents continued on in the same vein, he probably wouldn't find what he wanted anyway. Mr. Twitchell produced a slim yellow piece of folded paper from his jacket pocket, unfolded it and ran his finger down the list of times on it. If he hurried he could make the 8:10 ferry back to the city. A little late for dinner, perhaps, but some place would be open. Then he turned the schedule over and saw the words SUMMER 1984 printed upon it.

"Oh, hell," he said. Not only was the schedule for the wrong season—it wasn't even for the current year. "That'll teach me not to clean out my pockets," he muttered as he buttoned up his jacket. He'd have to take his chances on there being a boat soon; and if not, there was an inn by the landing. As he pushed the papers into neater, different piles, he kept out one particular book and opened it to a place kept by a bookmark. On the page was a portrait of Mrs. Winfield, done thirty years after the tragedy on the island. As in life, her portrait was the only likeness of the family to survive. Mr. Twitchell looked deeply at the reproduction; at the time it was done, Susan Winfield had become Susan Welch, was the mother of four more children (plus stepmother to two), and hadn't left Falmouth Neck in all those thirty years. She never went back to the island, and when Asa Brackett resettled it in 1710, only a shallow depression in the dirt and some rotting boards were left of the Winfield homestead. Susan herself survived one more Indian attack. In 1678, when the local tribes rose up during King Philip's War and burned Falmouth to the ground, Susan, then close to seventy, defended her home with an iron bar. She "did the Heathens most serious hurt" before being dragged off to the boat for evacuation. In 1690 the French and Indians returned, and Susan Winfield's luck ran out. The French recorded that, like her young sons years before, she went down fighting. She, along with the rest of the dead, were left to rot in the sun.

She had been a singular woman, and Milton Twitchell found himself acquiring some of the respect for her that her contemporaries had had. Having witnessed the murder of her family, she had picked up and gone on and rebuilt her life. Her bravery in the face of deprivations and the recurring nightmare of Indian raids was phenomenal. Mr. Twitchell could think of only one other Colonial-era woman of such strength; of modern women, none. He wouldn't quite admit it to himself, but the old bachelor was rather taken with his subject. She deserved, at the very least, a clarification of her story.

"You've kept me up late enough, madam," he said, and shut the book. He looked up from it and Susan Winfield looked back from the window. It gave him a shock, but it was only an afterimage on his eye. It was, anyway, until it raised a calloused hand and tapped the window. Mr. Twitchell took in a long, silent breath and held it. The woman's eyes pleaded with him but she remained silent. Mr. Twitchell had pushed his chair back against the wall and was trying to push it further. Just a coincidence, he thought, just some local woman wondering why the lights are still on. He let go of the chair, smiled weakly and held up his finger to indicate that the woman should wait. He shook his head as he strode to the door, thinking what a fool he must have looked. She did look like old Susan, though, right down to the stiff collar and grey bonnet. . . . Something was wrong with this picture, he realized, and stopped short of the door. Looking over, he saw that the woman had gone from the window. Am I just tired? Mr. Twitchell thought. He stood, irresolute, for a long moment, then went back to the table. He grabbed the keys Miss Turner had left, walked back to the broad, brown, paneled door and locked it. At any moment, he thought, she'll knock and ask to be let in—but she didn't. When nothing happened after two or three minutes, he shut off the lights and backed away from the door. A bit of light caught the edge of his eye and turning he saw that the woman was back at the window. Now he *knew* something was wrong; for her face shone as distinctly in the dark as it had when the lights were on. Mr. Twitchell had long ago acknowledged that he wasn't a brave man; so rules of conduct didn't restrain him from finding the deepest, most secure closet in the house, and putting himself in it, before the woman at the window had a chance to repeat her tapping.

Even so, it was a very embarrassed man who opened the door to Judith Turner the following morning. Her expression was one of anger and shock, her mouth hanging open and her brown eyes wide. The tangle the wind had made of her long, gray hair added to an overall look of bewilderment.

"Mr. Twitchell," she said, after an interval to allow him to be completely humiliated, "what—what is going on here?"

Mr. Twitchell tried a laugh that came out dreadfully. "Oh, I'm truly *very* sorry about this, Miss Turner. I—I, uh, I fell asleep, it got so late . . ." All the excuses he'd cooked up in the long, black hours dissolved in the light. Miss Turner turned violently away.

"The door is ruined!" she exclaimed. "This is terrible! I can't believe—" Words failed her and she faced Mr. Twitchell again. "How did this happen, Mr. Twitchell? Do you know who would have done this? Did you see them?"

She was holding the door part-way open so that he could see the front of it. It looked as though someone had gone at it with an ax; long gashes crisscrossed it over most of its surface. The door was, luckily, thick; but even so two of the panels were split all the way through. The brass facing around the knob was torn entirely away and the white door frame bore several ugly cuts. Brick chips littered the threshold, fallen from white scars in the wall by the door. Mr. Twitchell was dumb-founded.

"I . . . honestly, I don't know." And he really didn't know, that is, how this had occurred without his hearing it. He let this stand as his answer to Miss Turner's question, though, because he had his own idea about who had done it. On this point he felt it better not to add insult to the librarian's injury.

After reshelving his materials and answering a few questions for the tired-looking island constable, Mr. Twitchell walked to the dock and waited there an hour until the next ferry arrived. There was no reading today; the image of the shattered door persistently crowded his mind. When the door faded, he imagined Susan Winfield, fighting off the Indians her whole life, then persecuted even past the grave. Why hadn't he let her in last night? *Could* he have let her in? Was the whole business as real as the gashes in the Historical House's door? All he could be fairly certain of was that the wrong Indians had been hanged and that Mrs. Winfield had let them be hanged. Mr. Twitchell saw a mad chase down the echoing corridors of centuries, and the vision chilled him.

It was several days later before he worked up enough courage to return to Brackett Island. He delayed it as long as he could, but the deadlines of the book and a nagging need to clear up the three century old questions sent him back. The day was iron-gray and rain-swept, and it made his spirits sag. Still, he kept to his resolve. He went early in order not to be caught on the island after dusk, but circumstance played against him. The Welch/Marsden File, the one just recently acquired, had been taken by another scholar before Mr. Twitchell had arrived, and he had to content himself with rechecking other chapters of his book. The morning ticked by on the polished mahogany clock on the mantle, and still the file was in use. Mr. Twitchell took a long lunch at the dusty restaurant by the landing, in order to give the other scholar time to finish; but in vain. It was two before Miss Turner, casting worried glances at Mr. Twitchell, came by to tell him that the file was available.

He found what he wanted—though not what he had expected—after another hour and a half of searching. It was a letter from a Constance Welch, Mrs. Winfield's stepdaughter, written to a friend in Cape Elizabeth, Maine. Dated December 17, 1669, it described how Constance had taken care of her stepmother during an illness, and how the older woman had sometimes raved when the fever set in. The substance of her ravings had frightened the young woman, but it set in place the last piece of Mr. Twitchell's puzzle. It fit with a terrible certainty. Milton Twitchell, dumbstruck again and (it must be admitted) a little heartbroken, couldn't deny the evidence. His heroine had turned harpy in the space of a page.

But Mr. Twitchell wasn't about to be defeated. After a minute's reflection, as quickly as love can become hate, he turned disappointment into victory. He recognized the value of his latest revelation and determined to exploit it. It wasn't a major change in history, it's true; but its appearance in his book would help establish him as an authority. The casual observer might think that there was also a little revenge behind Mr. Twitchell's decision—but that would surely be doing him a disservice.

As far as he knew he was the first to see the Constance Welch letter—but what of that other scholar, who had the file that morning? There was no way of knowing, short of asking him, which he dared not do without revealing his secret discovery. Well, he couldn't alter the past (too well he knew!), but he *could* control the present. No one else must see that letter. When he was confident that no one was watching, he slipped the brown parchment sheet into the middle of his own file folder.

He made himself work right up to five o'clock, closing time, before bringing the Welch/Marsden file up to Miss Turner's desk. That way she had time for only a cursory look at it before putting it on the to-be-filed cart. Mr. Twitchell wished her a smug and empty "good-night," to which she responded with a nod and a wary look.

The ten-minute walk to the dock was miserable. Rain had set in and thickened the advance of twilight. Mr. Twitchell's right hand felt highly sensitive to the weight of the folder it held, and he kept looking behind him for pursuers in the gloom. It would be good to be off of the island, good to be back in his own rooms with a cup of tea. For the moment it was enough to arrive at the dock unmolested and to find the Abenaki nosing up to the dock, her motor gurgling and her lights mellow as darkness fell.

The ride home gave Mr. Twitchell some time to reflect. The rushing and researching was done for now; all that remained was a big, grim "Why?" He summoned up the image of Susan Winfield again, deeply set eyes and solid, sweeping jawbone—the great, stoic heroine of the Islands. What twists of reason she and her family had fled in Salem had been nothing compared to the gloom they had brought with them to Maine. The months of toil on a wretched scrap of land in a godless country; a weak and unambitious husband and three sombre children to feed, day after night after day after night; swarms of insects in summer, and incredibly brutal cold in winter, the wind coming through gaps in the walls like long nails into the skin. . . . And over it all hung the Puritan God, like a giant in black, half as mad as Susan Winfield herself. It wasn't so hard to understand. Maybe it was simply a lack of comfort, an aching memory of how it once had been back in England. Mr. Twitchell felt badly for the Indians, too, who had probably just stopped by to trade stories, and instead had walked into the white man's Hell. The three on the mainland had done nothing, hadn't even been there, and were hanged merely out of convenience.

The throb of the Abenaki's engines and the rocking of the rough water eased Mr. Twitchell's thoughts along. Turning and looking out the windows to his back, he saw the yellow rectangles of windows on Brackett Island's dark hump. Through the windows to his right he spied a sail, dim and pale, rocking wildly over the Bay. It, too, was headed into Portland harbor through the cold drizzle, and the scholar wondered what brave soul would be on the water on such a night.

The rain made the sound of many fingers tapping, and the bricks in the sidewalk glistened by street light. Mr. Twitchell hurried up from the Casco Bay terminal to his apartment on Silver Street; unlocked the ground floor door, ran up three flights of stairs and let himself into his own apartment. As he shed his wet coat and hat, he noticed that the radiators were making a new sound that night—somewhere between a thump and a gasp. The book will bring me a place with *quiet* radiators, he thought, putting water on to boil. As he waited for it, he withdrew the Welch letter from his folder and studied it by the lamp in the living room. It wasn't as though he'd stolen it, really. As soon as his studies were done, he'd slip it back into its proper place, where it could be found to verify his results. (The noise from the radiators was really getting annoying; he *must* talk to the landlord the next day.)

He walked to his window and stared out over Portland's sharp roofs toward the rainy blackness of the Bay. He idly ran his finger down the grooves of mortar in the exposed bricks of the wall. The building dated from around 1870, made of bricks from a brickworks that once stood right in Portland. He laughed at his musings—he couldn't escape history! For all he knew, the crumbled bones of old Susan Winfield had been mixed in with the very clay that housed him. When he turned back toward the room, a pair of arms emerged from the wall opposite him. He couldn't breathe or move—all thought stopped. The arms were strong and lean under the gray of the sleeves, and the calloused hands looked all too familiar. The nail of the right-hand thumb was blackened as from a blow. The arms faded into the bricks at the elbows, and when Mr. Twitchell looked up to the appropriate height, sure enough, there was a face. It was an odd thing, but pits and bumps that had always been in the masonry fit perfectly into those stern features. Behind his recognition of those features, Mr. Twitchell was vaguely aware that the noises he had attributed to the radiators were taking on disturbing forms. The eyes in the wall, that Mr. Twitchell once recalled as pleading, now demanded. The rough hands jerked suddenly towards him. He flinched back and involuntarily wheezed out a plea. The thumping now had a sickeningly liquescent quality to it, and the gasps had turned into screams in the distance. The hands stayed rigidly out, the eyes in the brick were tight-rimmed with fury, soft whistles preceded every thump/chop, louder and louder, and children screamed for their mother, *to* their mother. . . . Mr. Twitchell had stepped forward and dropped the letter into those merciless hands before he realized that he'd done so. The rawboned hands closed around the papers and withdrew into the wall. The awful face was gone, too, but a high scream continued to rise in the stuffy air. Mr. Twitchell let himself down to a crumpled position on the rug, and didn't get up until long after the screaming had spent itself, and the teapot that had caused it had melted through.

Milton Twitchell now lives in New York and does something that has nothing whatever to do with history.

From the Realms of Glory

"You travel fast?" said Scrooge.

"On the wings of the wind," replied the Ghost.—Dickens

The meal was done, the coffee poured, and chairs were pulled close to the fire. A man, his wife, and their guest sat in those chairs and kept the ancient winter's night vigil. The moving yellow light shone on hands folded in thought and sleep-lidded eyes, and glittered on empty coffee cups; it was the only light in the room. In the quiet spaces between conversation, the wind could be heard testing the old panes of the windows. Following one of these lulls, the guest set his cup down gently on its saucer and said, with finality: "Well."

His host nodded in reply, his eyes never turning from the fire. He waited a respectful moment, let the fire have its crackling say, and spoke.

"Sure you don't want a ride?" he said. "Listen to that wind." As though on cue, the narrow panes rattled in their frames.

"No," replied the guest, and looped his scarf around his neck. "But thank you, anyway. I walked up—I'll walk back. It'll do me good. This time of year is always so hectic—I could use a little quiet by myself."

The host was watching him now, and an odd look came into his long, intellectual face. At first the guest wondered whether he'd said something wrong; but he was misinterpreting the look. What he'd taken for annoyance was merely a disturbed thoughtfulness, though its tensed lines remained on the host's face when he turned back to stare at the flames.

"It's certainly the right place for quiet," he said after a long sigh and a shiver. "I guess I'm still a city-boy at heart, but sometimes it really gets to me. Some nights it just seems to leak in around the doors and windows. I don't suppose you really feel it, having lived around here all these years . . . ?"

"Mm." The guest shrugged.

"Hard to put into words," continued the host, "but very real, for all that." He paused. "It's like—like walking into a church when a service is in progress. Something sacred, I don't know. You feel intrusive, out of place . . . I do, anyway. I keep catching myself tiptoeing around the snow so I don't make any noise." He looked at his wife, who was curled in a warm ball in her big chair, and he raised his eyebrows. "I'm running on at the mouth, aren't I?"

She looked at him languidly and smiled. He smiled back, took her hand and said, "Thought so."

The guest, a little embarrassed, resumed arranging his clothes for the walk home. Colder'n hell out there, he thought, but continued dressing. He wouldn't impose on his host further by asking for that ride; one doesn't repay dinner and coffee that way. Besides, he was a fast walker, and he didn't really care to hear more about the host's impressions of a lack of noise.

The host and his wife saw him to the door with wishes for a merry Christmas for all the guest's family "Tell Joan 'hello' for us," said the wife. There were promises for future dinners at both the host's house and the guest's. Then the door was open, and winter came in with a bluster and a sparkling of ice dust, pinching the trio's faces. An image of a warm automobile interior and a brief ride home flashed through the guest's mind, but he kept to his resolve. He shook hands with his friends and stepped carefully down the ice-glazed front steps.

Several yards from the house the guest caught a fragment of the host's voice before it was snatched away on the wind. *Why is he worried about snow,* he thought. He looked back and saw the host standing in the light of the yellow outdoor lamp, arms folded, looking up at the night sky. Following his gaze, the guest scanned the sharp-starred blackness above. To the west the sky faded to a white-pure blue behind the peaked silhouette of the old house and spears of pine woods; to the east, above the gloom that held home for the traveler, clouds had risen to fill half the sky. To the guest they looked like nothing so much as giant handfuls of snow pressed against heaven. *I'll be walking into the face of it,* he thought. Oh well. With a final wave to his host, the guest turned and tramped across the driveway toward the woods.

The forest pillars parted to let him pass. His feet punched neat holes in the smooth surface of the old snow, and he started looking for the gaps between the trees that would betray the path to him. In summer the path was plain, winding among the low blueberry bushes and tree trunks; but the guest found he had to rely upon memory as much as sight to put his feet upon it now. It wasn't long before he found it; yet already the host's outside light had dwindled to a mere dot among the trees and blackness. Another few yards on and it was lost from sight altogether.

For several minutes the path paralleled the road that went past the host's driveway. The guest, alone with the sound of his boots chomping the snow, had lost himself in that quiet that his host seemed to dislike so. It was quiet, he had to admit. It didn't bother him as it had his friend, but he could feel it pressing with cold, cunningly delicate pressure against his ears. The winds that had played so persistently about the house must have stayed near it, for only the slightest, distant gasps of them could be heard now, high up among the pinetops. The guest was thinking about how long the walk would take him and when he would get home. It was after nine, he knew, though not exactly how long after, and the walk would take him no more than twenty minutes. The kids'll be in bed; Santa won't have any problem putting up stockings this year.

And then there came out of the night to his right a sharp, uneven clanging and a growing fan of light, and for a second the guest had the absurd notion that the real Santa Claus was coming to punish him for his planned imposture. The light grew into a long, sideways cone behind the black trunks, and the jingling and clanging rose in volume. Finally the cone ended in two headlights, and the clanging, now mixed with scraping sounds, crescendoed and began to diminish quickly. Just a car; sparks jumped from beneath it as the dragging muffler banged over the road. The guest watched the apparition go with a little embarrassed re-lief. Tree trunks beside the unseen road, like supports of an endless tun-nel, flashed into view and flashed out as the car sped away. The guest watched until noise and lights alike were gone. Then he turned back to the path.

The snow began to fall. The guest, his eyes to the uneven ground, was unaware of it until a flake settled on his nose. He rubbed it away and looked up to see hundreds, thousands of the fragile things drifting down the hollows between the trees. For some reason he couldn't place, with a surety he couldn't explain, the sight of the snowfall made him nervous. It wasn't as though he'd never been out in snow. As a child they couldn't keep him away from it; and more times than he could recall the fall of night and snow had found him walking alone, pondering one or another of a young man's problems. The woods, too, were as familiar to him as family furniture would be to another man But there it was. The back of his head felt sensitive, as though someone watched him from hiding—he consciously stopped his breathing to listen. And behind this nervousness was the thought that he was acting foolishly, though he couldn't help it. He'd stopped walking, too, and with a more careful tread he began again.

The woods grayed and began to fade with the strange, confusing glow of snowstorms. The guest pushed his hands deeper into his pockets and pulled his head down into his coat collar; and all the while he watched the many-alleyed woods for something he couldn't name and could not even acknowledge as real. He began to watch the snow, too, as it fell and swirled and filled the hidden places of the darkness. He had little use for idle imaginings—his friend the host would have described him, accurately, as "earthy"—but the mood of the night had infected him. The storm was thickening and overspreading the land, and in his mind he saw its invasion. He saw the woods and empty fields, miles upon miles of gentle stillness beneath the somber skies; small towns wrapped in a sense of their own warmth and hominess, a few yellow windows blinking timidly at the titanic majesty of winter; even the great cities hushed, and the wild flakes flowing down to fill their chasms, their fine, wide boulevards, deserted parks, the streets and alleys, the left-open doors and glassless windows. Beyond the cities wide vortices of snow were spiraling down to disappear on the gray waste of ocean, and single specks clung to the eyelashes and beards of fishermen as they hauled up their heavy nets. In iron-fenced yards the whiteness drifted wistfully against gravestones. They would keep each other company, for no feet would print this snow tonight. He saw the world stretching out from the forest in all directions, desolate, snowbound, and silent. The image was a strong and a new one for the practical guest. He shivered to think of it.

His ruminations had taken his attention away from the way he went. With his gaze on the snow just in front of him, he was off the path and into a gentle-sided depression without knowing he'd strayed. Abruptly his lead foot pressed down through the snow and smashed through an underlying layer of ice. It threw him off balance, and he jerked his hands out of his pockets and forward to catch himself before his face hit. His hands also plunged into the snow and through thin ice into water. The cold of the water gripped the guest's hands through his gloves, and began to insinuate itself through his rubber boots and heavy socks. The edge of the ice cut at his ankle, and for a moment he couldn't push himself upright.

"Damn."

And with that said he suddenly realized just how quiet it was out there. The forest stillness was immense. Memories of the evening's social visit came to him now in jangling, deafening tones. Again, though he was panting with surprise, he hushed himself. It was very easy now to understand the feelings his host had mentioned. The guest felt ashamed, contrite at his exclamation in a quiet so *sacred*.

But even as he thought this, bent over with three limbs in the freezing water, his ears wide to the ageless quiet, another sound broke in the distances of the storm. It clanged along some road out of sight, and faint and brief though it was the guest was glad for it. The sound roused him from his thoughts and he pushed himself upright, twisting the water out of his wool gloves and stepping away from the dark holes he'd broken in the snow. The clanging had recalled the real world: the imagined sanctity of the woods had lifted. *It's just trees,* the guest thought, *trees and some snow, that's all.*

The trees, however, weren't familiar. The guest knew that all he had to do to regain the path was follow his own footprints back until he found something familiar, but he resisted the idea. He had walked these woods forever and he could certainly find the path again without backtracking. It couldn't be far. The guest looked back once to check the direction he'd come from and started off at angles to it.

The storm brooded. Steadily the snow deepened in every quarter of the forest. The lone guest toiled through it as quickly as he could, more and more conscious that his choice of direction had been a mistake. He didn't find the path, and every turn he made, certain that it would bring him to familiar places, seemed only to mislead him more thoroughly. The rises and hollows, stands of proud pine, leafless, snake-branched oaks and elms, low areas with ranks of dead yellow weed bayoneting up from the snow—all began to look alike, but none was familiar. Buried blueberry bushes and dead branches grabbed at his feet. It was as though the guest had stumbled into another forest entirely—and that he was trespassing. The guest was no longer welcome.

He was beginning to get angry with himself, and only a strong sense of common sense and dignity in his character kept him from running headlong through the darkness. As lost as he was, though, he still refused to follow his tracks backwards. Every hilltop promised to reveal the old woods, lovely and calm in the falling flakes; not these stern trunks, not this bewildering swirl of light and dark. At this point he wondered whether his footprints weren't already filled with snow anyhow. He even doubted that, were they clear, they'd lead him back to familiar land.

Then he did top a hill, and just visible behind the maze of distant black branches was the snow-blurred glow of a window. It had to be his own house. His was the nearest to that side of the forest, and it brought a smile to his face to think that his wife was probably reading the paper somewhere inside that light. The guest tromped resolutely down the hillside, and all at once began to discern familiar details in the landscape. This tree ought to be farther to the left, but that's certainly the right tree. And here's the path after all. The path led him up a small slope and onto a level area between two stately rows of towering pines. The effect of this double colonnade, its thick, spiny overhang almost lost in the night and downfall far overhead, and the broad path down its center, was not lost on the guest. For several moments the long-absent wind returned and soared through the tree-tops with the sound of a multitude sighing. It was a beautiful place, but a strange one. The guest's doubts began to return—he knew that he couldn't have forgotten a spot like this, especially so close to home. He stopped and blinked snowflakes from his eyelashes. One of his heavy socks had slipped down inside the boot, and he stooped down to pull it up. *Can't even get a pair of boots in the right size,* he thought. A rattling jangling rang out somewhere in the woods, and the guest straightened up sharply. He might be lost, but that couldn't have come from the road. If it came from anywhere, it was back along the way he'd come. With a shiver that chattered his teeth, he realized that the sound was closer to him than it had been before, and he disliked the idea that he'd left a trail of bootprints behind him in the night.

The guest moved alone briskly, raising his feet high to clear the deep holes they made in the snow. The situation was unnerving, but he was close to home now. The yellow light had resolved itself into a square, and now two other squares, less brightly lit, had appeared beside it. Beyond the grand corridor of pines the forest pulled back a little to leave a broad, irregularly shaped open space before the house. Unfiltered by the trees the snow fell more thickly there, and a gust of powder obscured the lighted windows again. The guest fairly ran across this space in his anxiety to get home. Now the roof, a long, pale, snow-covered parallelogram, materialized above the windows. The ground rose slowly toward the house, and the guest, in spite of himself, had to slow down. He was watching the ground again to be sure of his footing; thus he was very near the house before he realized that something was wrong. When he finally looked up he saw that the door, previously hidden by a stand of trees, was open. Worse, it wasn't his door. This doorway was arched and looked wide enough to admit his pickup truck, while the door itself looked to be about a foot and a half thick. A wan, flickering light, evidently the same one that lit the windows down at the other end, showed an interior wall of huge, split logs. There was one end of a table visible around the edge of the doorway, with stout branch legs and a top scarcely less thick than the door. It looked like a table, anyway, except that this table had a back to it. Its position relative to the door called to mind the picture of someone pushing back their chair and leaving in a hurry . . . Far away, but not too far, something clanged and rattled along the upper air.

The falling snow blew into his face with a thousand tiny, icy touches as he ran, his legs pumping furiously to lift him above and through the rolling drifts. He fell several times and his collar and boots were becoming jammed full of snow. The melting snow on his face and neck made the skin ache, and the effort of running was feeding sharp cramps in his thighs; but on he ran into the gloom. His gasps for breath seemed to bring in as much snow as air: he wheezed terribly. It was a blind flight, the headlong run he'd denied himself before. He had no eyes for familiar sights now, only for the easiest way; and what clear thoughts he had were mostly regret for turning down a ride home in a warm car. Drumlins and ditches, hummocks, hillsides, tree trunks, streams, and boulders presented themselves to him, and he tumbled and bruised himself purple hurling himself over them. Behind it all, around him and through the patient trees for miles and miles, there reigned a great quiet.

Out of this crazed rush the guest came floundering to an ungraceful halt. There was a light burning in the trees ahead. It was impossible; he had run wildly but not, oh God, not in a circle . . . When he'd caught his breath he realized that it wasn't the same light after all, and very possibly it was the light of his own house. He lurched up and plowed toward it. There was an especially large pine to his right that looked familiar; and there could be no mistaking the dead, silvery, burrow-ridden trunk just a little past it. With a gasp of hope he realized that he was back in the old woods and that his house was scarcely two minutes away.

He came out into the thinner woods that bordered his property and pounded furiously for the light. Barely a hundred feet separated him from the house now. Maddeningly, he remembered crossing that space among summer's greens and yellows in a few seconds. This winter's night, his legs churned with the futility of running in a dream. The flying snow lashed into his face. The roof of his house emerged dimly from the darkness, angling toward heaven. Now the door was visible, and the three cement stairs leading to it. Another few yards and the clapboards materialized. The snow yanked one of the guest's boots off his foot and he struggled on. A shadow with its hair pulled up in a bun eclipsed the lighted window for a second. The guest's wife's name came rushing to his lips—but before he could call out there came a long, ringing clanging from somewhere above and behind him. Then he was across the last remaining yards, up the steps and pushing through the doorway. He was through and slammed it shut, and he stayed with cheek and hand pressed against it.

"Roy?" his wife's voice called warily from the other room. She came in, hugging her quilted housedress to herself and shuffling in her slippers. "God, Roy, you made such a racket—What on earth—"

The guest had no idea what a picture he presented. His cap was gone and snow and sweat had strung wet strands of hair across his forehead; the rest of it curled wildly up over his scarf and in all directions, and was peppered with snowflakes. Coat, shirt, and pants were patched with white. From the knees down the pants were soaked through and ringed with melting ice from the tops of the boots. He stood in a small puddle of melt, his unbooted sock dragging ridiculously. Shivering a little, he listened through the door as the wind began moaning again, but there was nothing else to hear.

"Roy," his wife said more softly, "what is it?" Behind her in the small kitchen, a clock struck, softly, impossibly, midnight. The guest turned dazed eves to her.

"It's Christmas, Joan. Christmas."

The next morning the children had their stockings and there was the annual pandemonium around the festive tree. Daddy looked a little tired but did his share of opening gifts and eating candy. When it was over and the children preoccupied with their new toys, the guest put on a pair of work-boots and went out to retrieve the boot he'd dropped the night before. The snow was deep and blindingly white in the new sun. The boot was almost buried, and not a foot to the left of it, in an unerringly straight line from house to woods and paralleling his own tracks, were several furrows in the snow. It looked as though long robes and heavy chains had been dragged by in great haste. The guest followed this track a hundred yards back into the woods, to where the storm had erased it completely.

Lord of the Gallows

The wind roared against the mead-hall walls. Earlier, cold rain had pelted down with the sound of mad horses galloping over the roof; but the frost-giants were abroad, and it had turned to snow, and now it was silent without, but for the wind. A fire burned on the hearth before us, a great Yule-clog that had taken the brawn of four burly men to carry in. It was the warmth-giver, the light-giver on this awful night, and we crowded it close, hungry for its heat. At our backs, stray wraiths of frost slipped through the chinked walls. They chilled our backs like the subtle voice of Death, saying, *You may be warm now, but one day you will be mine and cold forever.* We huddled closer to the flames.

There were few of us left this Yuletide night to keep vigil for the Sun. Oh, at first the hall rang to the revelry of Festival, was bustling and bursting at its seams with thegns and their ladies, warriors and their women; slaves carrying trenchers heavy with the slaughtered boar and horns brimming with mead; and the tow-headed and rust-headed brats of Saxonland, running between our legs and acting out the raids they would one day lead.

But Night, this Night, this Longest of All Nights, wore on into the small hours; and wearied with food and ale and celebrating, many had slumped off to sleep the Night away in their own cots. There remained only we eight to keep the vigil: our great King Godric, and his queen, Wealtheouw: one of the King's thegns, and a slave-girl, half-asleep upon their benches by the King's throne; Ælfberht, the King's scop, word-shaper, idly strumming his harp in harmony with the wind's wild song; our war-leader, Ulle called Ironkeel; and Hund and myself, Ecg, of Ulle's far-famed ship, *Wave-Cutter*. All were quiet. Across the Yule-fire I could see King Godric, leaning upon his massy fist and brooding upon the fire. It danced before us its savage, yellow dance; snapping and waving, writing and leaping toward the smoke-blackened rafters. It cast its witch's spell over us, entranced, as it ate away at the Yule-clog. But scarce half of the great wood was eaten through and it would surely last until the Sun-chariot returned—a good omen. Still, it would be a long Night.

And then a stranger stood at the hall door, making us nine. In the firelight he stood tall and gnarled as a tree; but like a tree, strong to stand the blasts of Winter. Behind him, through the doorway, Winter rampaged over Middle-Earth in shades of deepest blue. Its voice was huge in the hall. Without looking back, the stranger pushed the door shut and began stalking toward us.

As he approached I could see him better, and my wonder increased. He was tall, indeed, as tall as any of the tallest men of Saxonland, and we are not counted a small people. His height was accentuated by his leanness, sensible even under his great gray cloak and travel-stained clothes. He wore a broad-brimmed hat that hid the upper part of his face in deep shadow. Beneath the brim, long, wild gray hair and a beard to match draped over his shoulders, down his chest. I knew not why— I had faced my share of battles—but looking at him I felt the hairs rise upon the back of my neck.

King Godric rose, grim host in the hall, and said, "What do you here, stranger? And why did my guards not stop you, announce you?"

"Blame them not, good king," said the stranger, and his voice was like the coming of Autumn. "They saw me not; or seeing, knew me not." He lifted his head, and one clear eye like a star of ice looked out from under the floppy brim and transfixed the King. "But guards or no," he said, "is this, then the famous hospitality of the Saxon? To interrogate the wayward stranger and leave him standing on a night like this?" And he spread his hands to encompass the Night and all its shadows. As if in answer, the wind thundered past the walls.

The King nodded. "Your pardon, stranger," he said, waving him forward. "You are welcome in my hall. The best seat by the fire awaits you." He scowled at the sleepy thegn, who had not even risen at the outlander's appearance, but who now jumped up and vacated his seat by the fire, and stumbled to an empty bench a few yards away, yet close enough to be of aid to the King should he need it. The King then turned his stern gaze upon the slave-girl, who rose with equal alacrity; and without being bidden, ran to the board by the wall and returned with meat and thick bread and ale for the stranger. The stranger walked to the empty bench, seated himself upon it, and accepted the tray of viands from the slave. He smiled at her, and she beamed; then looked confused; and at last struck with fear. Without a word she backed up to her stool and sat. Her eyes never left the stranger. He, unconcerned, set to with the boar and bread and ale.

"So," said the King, after letting the stranger eat his fill, "what brings you to our hall on such a Night as this, when good folk are keeping the Yule vigil?"

Again that smile like a split in bark.

"I am no 'good folk,'" replied the stranger, and returned to his repast. The King seemed thrown by this answer. The ancient rules of hospitality demand much of the host, but much of the guest as well. One gives a name for a name. For all we knew, he could have been a spy of the Frisians; of the Romans, too, though he looked more a Northman than a southron. What of his flesh we could see—the strong hands, the scant cheek above his beard—was pale as hoar-frost, yet weather-burned and weather-polished. No Roman sun had kissed that cheek.

"Your name, then, good sir," said the King, a little tightly I thought. "And your business this Night."

The stranger stripped a last shred of meat off a bone, tossed it into the fire.

"Call me Harbard," he said, eye glinting.

"'Graybeard,'" grunted King Godric. "A vague enough name, but no matter. Continue."

"And I was upon the hunt this night until separated from my company."

"A poor night to be at the hunt," said Ulle, bold in the word-play.

The stranger turned that one, cold eye toward our bench, and my heart stumbled.

"On the contrary," quoth the stranger. "None better. The game I seek is fleet upon foot in the gale. But we lost him—*it*—in the snow and I became separated from my men. I saw the lights of your hall and—" He spread his hands.

The stranger's tone was even and his words strong; yet there was something about him that I mistrusted; something that he was not telling us. I thought again how his appearance had brought the number of our group to nine, and nine is a sacred number. But it is a magic number as well, and it is widely known that the witches count their charms in nines.

The King, though, seemed unconcerned. "Again, sir," he said graciously, "you are welcome beneath my roof. A warm pallet will be made you, close to the fire."

"Your hospitality is complete," nodded the stranger. "But I must away before dawn paints his pale banners westward."

"Then perhaps you will repay our hospitality with a story," continued the King. "It is custom among our folk to unlock the word-horde, free the long song upon this Night of All Nights."

The stranger considered this. His one eye glittered in the firelight like a chip of ice in a cave. And with a nod and that cryptic smile, he began his tale.

"Once," he said, "there was a man. Call him Reed, as a reed is bent by every wayward breeze. He was a good man but ran with bad company; and he hadn't the heart to say them nay in anything. In the woods, the deep woods, there was robbery; there was rape; and there was murder. No equal meeting of metals, no face-to-face slither of steel upon steel, this; but cold murder, done to the unarmed; done in secret.

"The gold was divided, little payment for low employment, and the robbers disbanded, each to his own mean hovel. But secrets burn bright in the hollows of the night, and Lost's wife asked whence came their new wealth. He told her; and she told their king. And upon a gray, windy day, Lost was made to ride the gallows-horse, danced the wind-dance. They hanged him with strong leather from the oak.

"Nine days and nine nights Reed swayed beneath the oak upon the high hill, a warning to wolf's-heads everywhere. Upon the ninth night the Gray One, Lord of the Gallows, Wodan himself, walked up to the oak-tree and looked upon the man who was Lost. And Wodan said, 'Speak, soul, before you may fly!'

"And the dead man opened his shriveled eyes and his rictus-locked teeth and said, 'I do as you bid, Terrible One. '

"'Then tell me, hanged man, wisdom from the shadow-road. '

"'I would fain tell thee,' said the dead man, and his voice was as the breeze through dead leaves. 'But this leathern cord cuts deeply into my word-box and I cannot. '

"So Wodan, Chooser of the Slain, pulled out his sword and cut the leathern cord which held Reed to the limb. The body dropped, ripe for the harvest. But as soon as his feet struck Middle-Earth, he set to running; and so surprised was Wodan, Father of Gods, that the dead man was away and gone into the tangled woods ere he could grab for him.

"Reed ran and ran. He ran over fields and fens, across mountains and meadows. The wolf saw him pass; the raven croaked his ancient song after him. He longed for the deep bed, the embrace of the grave; but the Earth-mother would not have him. And still he ran. And he howled as he ran, and the children of men lay awake at night and heard him howl; and their dreams were evil dreams.

"And Wodan, Allfather, would not be denied his prey. He gathered his hunting-party, fell souls upon black mounts and stags, and loosed upon the skies his black hounds. They came in full cry; the riders followed and their steeds struck thunder from the sky-vault.

"Yet they caught Reed not, this awful company. His terror lent him wings. In panic he ran from house to house, from hovel to mead-hall, beating at doors with rotted, bony fists for entrance, for sanctuary. But the houses would not hold him either. The folk within threw the bars, huddled together until the dead man and his howling and banging had fled away.

"From land to land he has fled, and ever the wild hunt pursues him in the storm. So it is that the wise man puts prudence before pride, and welcomes not the wanderer without word-trust."

The stranger lowered his head, stopped his tale. Again all was silent save for the wind, the everlasting wind, the wind rushing in torrents of air outside the mead-hall. I pondered the stranger's words. Sage advice, no doubt; but was he warning us of himself? He gave no clue. The firelight shifted and flickered over his wide-brimmed hat and road-worn robes.

Then came a knocking. Faint at first, then louder as if in confidence—or panic. The stranger's head shot up, and his one eye glared out like a dagger of night. He turned toward the knocking—so did we all—the thick mead-hall door. The knocking banged upon the iron-studded oak, made echoes in the rafters. Then it died down, quieted, faded—ceased. We all still stared at the door, but there was nothing now but the wind.

"A shutter," said Ælfberht, "worked loose in the blast. Or a shingle."

"A branch," said I, eager to agree. "Some loose flotsam on the wind."

"Or a reed." The stranger's smile curved beneath his mustache.

We all nodded and laughed empty, ghastly laughs at one another. We raised false faces to each other, daring the fear we saw in each other's eyes. Still the stranger smiled that split-bark smile of his. At last he raised his ale-horn, drank it off, emptied the golden barley-water into his greedy maw.

"Well," he said, setting the ale-horn down upon the bench, "again I must thank you, good King, for your hospitality. But my errand calls and I am away." Then he rose, tall in roof-timber, and strode to the door. None bade him stay this time. We were glad to see the back of him. He opened wide the mead-hall door and wind and wild snow welcomed him. He spread his arms to them, walked out, and the door swung to behind him. Its echoes boomed hollowly in the smoke-blackened rafters.

Ulle, ever first into the fray, was first upon his feet. He ran to the door and we followed. Throwing it wide, he stood in the blast and it flew past him into the hall in a dazzle of snow. But the stranger was gone. The guards, snow-caked and wrapped in their furs, stood upon either side of the door-frame without.

"Where has he gone?" demanded the King of them.

"Where has *who* gone?" said one. "None has passed since the last guest left, O King." The other guard looked confusion at one and all of us.

We looked out into the storm and the wind was like the howl of the lost; like the laughter of the mad. In the distance the storm muttered like the pounding of many hoofs in headlong pursuit of its prey.

Sunderland House

Then said I, O my lord, what *are* they? And the angel that talked with me said unto me, I will show thee what they *be.*

—Zechariah 1:9

I received the message by 'phone," my grandfather said, putting the slightest delay before "'phone" to acknowledge that it was, indeed, part of a longer word. Roy Sunderland was charmingly old-fashioned that way; he was old enough to remember when such things were a novelty, and he never let you forget it. He and I were sitting in the sunny, winterized porch of my grandparents' house on the water in Portsmouth, Rhode Island, one of many such peaceful summer afternoons of my growing-up years. This must have been in the '70s, for he was still alive and I see myself in the thinner and more casual guise of a teenager. My grandmother, mother, and aunts had all disappeared to Newport for the day, and Grandpa had gotten into a confidential mood. I was proud of talking to him "man to man" for once, and listened closely.

Grandpa paused and looked down the blue length of the Sakonnet River toward the distant sea. Gulls keened; a wave broke brittle against the sea-wall.

"It wasn't an easy matter to get down from Providence in those days," he continued. "I had no car—they were still the plaything of the rich, mostly, and even the new Fords were beyond the economy of a student like myself. We were a couple years and an assassination away from the Great War and over ten years shy of the opening of the Mount Hope Bridge; so I had to take the train from Providence to Fall River, change there to the Newport and Fall River Street Railway, and take that as far as Stone Bridge. Then hope for some conveyance to get me down to Pocasset. Oh, there was Frank Pierce's shiny new black Pierce-Arrow five-seater to get you to Little Compton. But Uncle lived out on Grinnell's Point and nothing regular went out there. If it hadn't been Uncle

Perce, I might have begged off, using the perennial student's excuse of homework. But Uncle and I were close, he lived all alone out there, and his call was, well . . ."

As he paused again I could picture the old Sunderland house as it stood upon its storm-watered lawns: a dark, heavy, rambling pile of weathered shingle built by some ancestral Sunderland and added onto by subsequent generations until it dominated the Point and became a landmark for local mariners. In my time it has been joined by houses of lesser bulk and lesser taste. But it is a sad irony that none of my family can now afford to live out there. Some folks from New York now own 'the Sunderland place,' as it is still called. My Yankee ancestors must be spinning in their graves.

Grandpa took a sip of coffee from his heavy white mug and continued.

"I needn't have worried," he said. "When I got off the trolley at Stone Bridge a man approached me and asked my name. When I told it to him, he led me to a Model T delivery-van, saying Uncle Perce had hired him to retrieve me from the trolley. I was more pleased by this than I could say, for the weather had taken a turn for the worse. It was November, that iron-hearted month, already biting cold, and an insistent wind was spitting rain out of the east. The river was choppy and had an ugly, slate color to it. All in all, the first omens of a really good nor'easter.

"Once I and my bag were settled into the van, we bumped off south. You have to picture that drive as it was then, son. Tiverton and Pocasset haven't changed as much as, say, Warwick has, but Main Road was still a longer, muddier, more winding drive then than it is now. The bare trees along the road thrashed in the storm to beat the band, and the rain reduced the road to mud and pools in many places. Darkness was falling, too. I'd left Providence at a decent hour, but night came quickly, as it does that time of year. You couldn't picture a lonelier sight than that long road. The Ford's headlamps could only pick out a few yards of wet dirt ahead, and we crawled down through the blast.

"And that wind—you could feel the whole van rock when a good gust hit it. Still, I was out of the wet and the driver kept up a good prattle as he drove. Far be it from Percival Sunderland to leave his great-nephew out in the elements.

"Well, we got down past Four Corners and into Pocasset, and then cut off Main Road onto the Grinnell's Point Road where it splits off.

Did I say Main Road was lonely? Well, this was lonelier still. Just those swamp-maples and holly-trees and bushes, all shaking as if possessed, and not one light of a house since the Tiverton line. You could feel the land peel away on either side of you, too. The trees were shorter, the woods thinner, a suggestion of more sky, the ocean nearer—the land was falling away and getting narrower and narrower.

"'Briggs Pond back o' there,' said the driver, nodding toward the left side of the road. Nothing but the passing black woods, but I could picture the pond lying beyond them: a broad, shallow plate of silver water amongst the swamps that fed it. Local legend peopled it with ghosts of the drowned. I was surprised and ashamed that I, twentieth-century man that I styled myself, should be glad when we got past it.

"'Ya hear 'em?'

"I started, thinking he meant the ghosts. Then I could hear them too, a high, faint moaning sound.

"'The wind in yer uncle's wires,' added the driver. Above the black woods passing I could now discern the new wires and the lonely poles from which they hung, as black as cut out paper against the dim sky. They carried electricity to Sunderland House.

"'Not for me, nossuh,' said the driver. 'Likely sut yer house on fire. 'And he shook his head sagely, proud not to partake of modern convenience.

"Finally we came clear of the woods, right about where the Whitmores' house is now, and I could just see a dim, yellow light through the rain up ahead. Then the angled bulk of Sunderland House solidified around the light. We took the road to its very end, then turned into the drive that curved around close to the house's front door. Funny what you remember at such a remove—the drive was paved in crushed quahog shells and glowed white in the dark. It crunched under the Ford's wheels. This close I could see that the lone light came from the ground-floor windows of the east wing, on the right now as we faced the house. There was a yellow, wavering quality to it that hinted of a fire in the fireplace—a welcome thought as I thanked the driver and got out of the van into the driving rain.

"I clamped my cloth cap to my head and ran for the shelter of the front door stoop. You might think it silly, me standing out there getting soaking wet, but I couldn't just barge in. You just didn't do that back then, not even with family. Instead I rapped upon the old door with my knuckles and waited. I looked around as the seconds passed. Already the delivery-van was only a tiny, squarish black silhouette, tinier and tinier against the pale glow of its headlamps. The Atlantic was hurling itself on the rocks below the lawn, throwing up explosions of foam as if some wizardry were happening just out of sight. Each wave came in with a boom. The rain slashed down in fits and starts and ran in freshets from the house's gutters. Altogether I felt as if I had come to the very ends of the Earth.

"Then the door swung open and Uncle Perce, tall and big-boned as an old oak, was smiling at me.

"'Roy!' he said, waving me in. 'For Pete's sake, lad, come in out of that damp!'"

(I reflected to myself on Great-Great-Uncle Perce's idea of "damp." We Yankees have a gift for understatement.)

"I hustled in" (continued Grandpa) "and Uncle pushed shut the door. He was a strong man even at his age, which must have been close to ninety then. But it looked as though he had to struggle to keep the storm outside. Finally he got it closed and latched it—a precaution I thought odd, way out there on the Point in those days when most folks didn't lock their doors at all. Even in town.

"I took off my cap and streaming coat. Uncle took them and hung them on the pegs by the door, then grasped my hand in both of his big mitts.

"'Good to see you, my boy,' he said, and from the way his smile folded back the wrinkles on his face I knew he really meant it. More than that, though. There was a look of relief, almost of pleading, in his old face that struck me as both sad and alarming. We don't like to see our heroes weak—it's disorienting, a violation of natural order—and Percival Sunderland was certainly a hero to me. Civil War veteran, founder and chief officer of a successful fishing and fish-meal fertilizer business with his brothers; a man who had wrestled with the terrors of Cape Horn in a clipper-ship and won, not once but four times—no, Percival Sunderland was not someone you took lightly. Locally they called him 'the Captain,' not for any real rank he might have held but just out of respect.

"And here he was in his old robe, clinging to the hand of his callow, twenty-year-old great-nephew as if to a lifeline. For a terrible moment I was at sea. Then instinct or affection must have taken over, for I put my other hand over his cold, gnarled one and smiled back at him.

"'Good to see you too, Uncle,' I said. 'And good to see a fire burning on a night like this. '

"His own grin took on a more genuine aspect then. He ushered me into the room to the right of the hall. This was his library and had always been a favorite room of mine. The east wall was dominated by a huge, tiled fireplace in which now blazed a merry fire. On either side of the fireplace and covering the walls were bookshelves, well laden with everything from the odes of Horace to the adventure tales of Morgan Robertson. Tall windows, hung with heavy brown drapes done in arabesques I could never quite untangle, interrupted the shelves at infrequent intervals. On a sunny day they gave bright prospects of green, expansive lawn, the sea to east and south, and the tangled swampy forests and blue expanse of Briggs Pond to the north. Tonight all they let in was darkness.

"Uncle settled me in his own voluptuous leather chair before the fire and pulled up another chair for himself. In the firelight I was able to take a fuller account of my uncle, and I didn't like what I saw. Under his robe he still wore his daytime shirt and trousers. Now, the wealthy can get away with all sorts of fashion gaffes—it is their prerogative. I've seen some perfectly hideous clothes—orange corduroys with ducks printed on them, elegant women in hats that would have made poor cheese-boxes—on people who could clearly afford to wear anything they liked.

"But Uncle Perce was different. Even in the privacy of his home, in the company of his adoring nephew, he would have been dressed for the day. There was something slipshod and uncaring in what he wore now. His shirt was buttoned askew. That, his pitiful reception of me, and the white frost of stubble on his cheek that the firelight picked out: all combined to give the image of a man under some dire stress.

"Then it was, too, that I realized that the fire was the only light in the house. As isolated as Uncle Perce's house was, it was still one of the few in Pocasset that could boast electricity in that period. Such was the influence of 'the Captain. 'And I certainly didn't expect the place to be lit up like a Christmas tree just for the two of us. Still, it seemed to be taking Yankee frugality to an extreme to sit in the near-dark like that.

"As if reading my mind, Uncle Perce said, 'I find this light preferable to those garish bulbs on such a night. Cozier, don't you think?' I nodded agreement, unsure of what to make of it all.

"'You sounded agitated on the telephone,' I said suddenly to break the quiet. 'What's this about, Uncle?'

"Uncle Perce stared into the fire with an expression equal parts astonishment and resolution.

"'Did you hear them, driving in?' he asked, apropos of nothing.

"'Hear who, Uncle?'

"One of his big hands came up off the armrest and motioned vaguely toward the north wall.

"'They come out on nights like this,' he said. 'I expect the storm churns up the water, makes for an unquiet . . .' Those blue eyes that had seen so much still stared uncomprehendingly into the fire.

"Now I became really alarmed. Was my uncle going insane? Had his isolation out on this spit of land in the Atlantic finally worn down that strong soul? I had no idea how to handle this. I gripped the arms of my own chair as if it would keep me anchored in a sane world, a world in which your elders were confident and strong and didn't hear voices in the wind.

"Again, as if reading my thoughts, he turned to me and said, 'You must think me addled, Roy.' He tried a smile that was ghastly. 'I'm not— or not any more than usual. But that's why I invited you down tonight, you see. I needed a sharp, objective ear to hear—what I've been hearing. I think I'm still pretty sharp for an old coot; but you live alone and you can fool yourself into believing all sorts of things. You're a smart boy and my favorite great-nephew to boot, and frankly I also just craved the company.'

"This non-explanation set me somewhat at ease. But the source of Uncle's distress was still a mystery.

"'You mentioned "voices,"' I tried.

"'You've heard the stories about Briggs Pond, no doubt,' he said with a deep sigh. 'How the souls of those drowned in the quicksand in the pond rise up and sing on stormy nights? A pretty tale, something for the swamp-Yankees to scare each other with on nights like this. Like something beldames told back in Merry Olde England. ' Here he leaned toward me and looked out at me from beneath those impressive brows of his. 'But,' he whispered, 'What if there were a—a *basis* for such tales?'

"'I'm sure there is, Uncle,' I said, assuming my best scholarly airs.

'Race-memory, common myth-patterns . . . There's talk these days of a subconscious—'

"He gave a quick, irritable wave of his hand.

"'You're just saying I'm crazy in nicer terms,' he said. 'I'm not talking about moonbeams and nightmares, lad. I'm talking about flesh and blood. Or what once was flesh and blood. '

"Again I found myself unable to speak, but this time less out of fear for my uncle's sanity than from what he said. That was the rub. I could see now that Uncle Perce was not only sane but earnest; but what he was telling me was incredible.

"'But Uncle,' I said, fumbling for words. 'Here? Now? In the twentieth century?'

"He sighed again and sat back. 'Well, that's the funny part of it, Roy. I am no electrical engineer by any stretch of the imagination, but I have my own theories about the ability of these . . . to communicate. It's dark now, but can you picture the electrical lines leading to this house?'

"'Yes, of course, we—' And I stopped. In my mind's eye I clearly saw them strung between those gaunt poles that marched up from Main Road and all along Briggs Pond. I must have gaped, for Uncle said, 'You begin to see. They tell us that the brain is largely electrical in nature, so—'

"So that was why the lights were out. We were both silent then, letting the night fill in the gaps in our conversation. The rain slapped against the east windows and streamed down them. Under it the surf boomed and boomed its ancient chant against the land.

"'There is . . . another thing,' Uncle said after several minutes. His voice was so low that I had to lean forward to hear him. 'Have you ever considered how perfect a piece of land this is?'

"'Ideal,' I said, hoping my enthusiasm would direct the conversation into more cheery channels.

"'Ideal,' echoed Uncle in more somber tones. ''Tis now. But wasn't always. The views, the location, of course. But once it was hummock and dale, a succession of boulders and pits. My own grandfather, Grand Peleg Sunderland, made it perfect. Amazing what he and his sons could do with just shovels and barrows. Fill? Neighbors wouldn't hear of it— jealous of the old bastard's luck with land. But there was that pond, just sitting there, swampier then than now, no good to anyone, neither water nor land . . . '

"He trailed off, staring into the depths of the fire again. I thought of Briggs Pond in the sunshine, bright and blue and clear. And twice a day the tides drained it off. Who would miss some dirt off the bottom of a pond?

"Who?

"We sat thus for what seemed a long time. The waning fire threw its yellow, flickering light over our faces; I hugged my sweater close around me. Despite the blaze, a chill had seeped into the room, and I wasn't sorry when Uncle Perce rose and announced that it was time for bed.

"'Good to have you here, lad,' he repeated and clutched my hand again. It was like being gripped by a skeleton. 'Hope you can stay a day or two?'

"'I'd be glad to, Uncle,' I said, extricating my hand from his. Fortunately I had thought to pack my textbooks in my grip. I thought again of his wanting an objective ear to hear whatever he had been hearing; but at that point I didn't feel up to any more of what had turned into a very unsettling evening. If he had chosen to avoid it, then I would as well. Instead I waited silently while he lit a couple candles from the mantel and kicked down the fire for the night. Then I followed him out into the hall, where I retrieved my bag, and up the stairs to the second floor.

"'You've got your cousin Joseph's room,' he said, motioning with the candle down the upstairs hall to the left. 'If you need, me, I'll be in my usual haunt at the end of the hall. 'And he turned and walked down toward his bedroom at the other end of the hall.

"I went into my designated bedroom and set the candle down on the bedside table and my bag upon the bed. I sat down beside it and stared at the candle. It was all too fantastic. Away from his presence, I again wondered: Was the old man losing his grip? Since Aunt May had died three years back, Uncle Perce had had the house to himself. I mentioned the way the rich can get away with clothes the rest of us wouldn't be caught dead in. Well, this goes for behavior, too. What might get the rest of us labeled as 'queer' and a trip to Butler Hospital is winked at as 'eccentricity' in the wealthy. I seriously began to wonder whether my uncle, untrammeled by the norms of society, had slipped into 'eccentric.'

"The long trip down from Providence and the weight of the night's conversation bore me down. The darkness of the old house made my eyes weary. I was tired and longed for normalcy and rest. From within the bag I pulled out my toothbrush and tooth powder. Then I went into the bathroom adjoining the bedroom to prepare for bed.

"As I stepped into the bathroom, without thinking I felt for the Bakelite switch to the right of the door and snapped it on."

Grandpa paused.

"'Without thinking,'" he said. "How many disasters, catastrophes, and tragedies begin with those two words? The bathroom jumped ablaze in white light from the fixture in the ceiling. I blinked stupidly at it, not realizing what I had done. I went to the sink and ran water while I put powder on my toothbrush and began brushing my teeth. Still I didn't know what I had done. Even when the singing began, I just thought, 'Uncle must be running his Victrola before bed.' And I brushed away.

"The music was getting louder, a weird singing of many voices, winding in and out of each other in alien harmonies. It got louder still, as if getting closer; and that was when it finally got through my thick, imbecile head. I stopped brushing. I stared at my idiot stare in the mirror. And I looked up at the light, at all that electricity flooding into the house.

"I don't think I had ever moved as fast as I did then. I crossed the space from the sink to the switch in one bound and twisted it off. The room disappeared in inky blackness. My eyes, adjusted to the glare, couldn't see the softer candlelight coming from the bedroom at first and I just stood there, hand still on the switch, waiting for my pupils to open.

"And then I realized that the singing was still going on. It was so close—how can I tell you? *It was in the walls.* Whatever circuit I had closed by turning on the light had let something—some *things*—into my uncle's house, and they were running riot in the wiring. The voices rose and fell and wove and paralleled; crawled, growled, soared. Sometimes one would sail up alone and end on a note like a lone bird, high in the heavens. These had the quality of a cry or a scream. One of these shocked me out of the paralysis I was in. I thought of Uncle Perce—Percival Stanton Sunderland, Civil War hero, sailor, businessman, rock of Yankee fortitude and sense. Percival Sunderland, ninety-year-old man.

"I dodged out of the bathroom and around the corner through the doorway into the hall. Here there was not even the candlelight but an almost invisible, diffuse blue glow from the storm outside. I could make out the long hallway stretching out before me, the banister running alongside it and dipping down the stairs; the orange glow of the fire throwing a carpet of light out the library door across the front hallway floor. All this I could see and did see, lad, which is important to remember, because I never saw those *others*. *I* felt them, to be sure—bumped into them, careened off of them, was slowed and grabbed by them. But I never, ever saw them. And they were cold and wet, and *soft*.

"You will find, son, in circumstances of great stress that a lower part of the brain takes over. I saw it in the war, when things got so awful and confused that you couldn't think about it. You just had to act, trust your body to do what it was supposed to do. It's like letting a horse take its lead, if you follow me. That's what happened to me now. Ghosts or spirits or whatnot, I had to get to my uncle. That damned hallway seemed to stretch itself out like a cat. I thought I'd never reach his bedroom door.

"I finally did, though, ploughing through the unseen souls still jostling around me, and threw myself upon the door. Uncle had not yet blown out his candle—maybe he forgot or wished to read in bed a little. At any rate, it lighted up the side of his bed where he lay, and it—"

My grandfather stopped here. His voice had locked up as if in a vise, and he wiped a shaking hand across his eyes.

"It lighted up his face," he began again. "And his staring eyes. I knew then, I'd never seen death before but you know, but you have to check, you have to make sure.

"He was stone dead. That proud visage that had faced down the worst that man and nature could throw at him was cold as marble. I stayed thus, my hand on that cold cheek, for a good minute or so, until the complete horror of my situation recurred to me. It was as if that dreadful singing were soaking through my consciousness, closer and closer . . .

"And I ran. I was down the stairs and out into the blast before I even knew it. I was running headlong down the drive, down the road, past those mad, thrashing woods, past those hideously still poles and the wires hung between them that sang and sang and sang. The rain dashed cold against my face. It plastered my pants and shirt to me. Somewhere far below a pair of legs was churning, a pair of feet was hammering the hard dirt. Somewhere, I didn't know where, I didn't know whose.

"But they brought me finally to a house, another house, a house where people slept untroubled and read by candlelight only because they weren't connected to that newfangled power yet. There was a pair of yellow windows, a black roofline against the restless sky, a walkway of slate stones, one, two, three, four, five . . . I still remember the beat of them under my heels. Then a door, and the door opened, and more of that good, honest light poured out onto me, and two strong hands held me by the arms and pulled me in.

"I was at the house of Jacob and Maria Wordell on Main Road, about a mile and a half from Uncle's. Do you know it? Well, I expect you never knew them. They were old then, and shocked to see me, believe me. I must have been a sight—Lord! Wet as a drowned rat, wild-eyed, and smears of tooth-powder still around my mouth. They thought at first I'd had a fit, then that I might be rabid! After Maria wiped off my face they realized what it was; but it was still a while before they could get an intelligent word out of me.

"Good old Jacob and Maria. They tended to me patiently, got me calmed down and finally to bed. Many years later Maria told me how she did it. 'Portuguese medicine,' she said with a wink. 'I put the whiskey in your tea.' May she rest in peace, she and Jacob.

"And Uncle Perce, too, hopefully far from where those other lost souls are. I was still half gibbering the next day when the police came, which was a good thing, really. My explanations would have only muddied the waters. They went to Uncle's and found the door still swinging open in the fresh, westerly breeze—funny how a nor'easter will blow itself out and bring sunny skies behind it—and they found Uncle, too, as dead as I left him. They assumed he had had a heart attack—he probably did at that—and that dumb boy (me) had found him and panicked. True enough, as far as it goes. No need to tell them more than that. In a small town like Pocasset, by lunchtime everybody would have known that the captain's great-nephew was cracked. None of their business what really happened.

"The spirits? I guess they're still down to the Pond. I haven't heard anything bad about the house. Perhaps modern wiring blocks unwanted signals. Of course, Sunderlands don't live there anymore. Not that we'd *want* to."

And he sat back and looked way down the River toward Pocasset in silence.

That Certain Slant of Light

It's pretty funny, really, when you think of it. I didn't believe in ghosts. Not really at all. Oh, it was an entertaining concept on cold, wet nights; something that you could wish were true, if only for something really unusual in your life. But not real beliefs, not the inarguable, inescapable presence of a fact. Funny.

But then there were the signs. Not being a believer, I found it easy at first to discount them and assign them to other, more plausible causes. That shadow out of the corner of my eye was merely that—a trick of the light. Those noises, so like footsteps dragging slowly upon the stairs or turning the pages of a book I would never read, were the settling of the house. And the smell . . .

I can't remember exactly where or when I first saw it; for it was visually that I first detected it, just as you may see something in the distance long before you can pick it up by the other senses. I have my own theory about that, but let it wait until a little later. It was that shadow on the periphery of my vision, lurking in corners where honest shadows shouldn't be. If so, then how did I know that it wasn't just that, just a shadow? I simply *knew*. Now I begin to sound like those crank psychics and mediums whose evidence is so flimsy and subjective. If you say you "just know," who is to argue with it? It's like faith in a god or in an afterlife. There are no tangible facts to which you can grab hold and shake until a truth falls out of them. And I am embarrassed to present such a statement, yet such was the fact of it. I knew. Do you need more proof? It didn't react the way normal shadows would. It didn't fall the way a shadow should, given the light and its angle of fall. "There's a certain Slant of light," Emily Dickinson wrote, "Winter Afternoons—/ That oppresses, like the Heft / Of Cathedral Tunes . . ." Dear old Emily, sweet, lonely visionary. Maybe that is the key; maybe the light that cast such a shadow was from another Where and When.

Regardless. There it was. And at first it vanished under a direct stare. Stuck in the knowable, I told myself that I should have my eyes checked. The fear of blindness came to me. Would that I *had* been blind to it. Would that it were that minor a matter.

So my pet shadow increased in substance and refused to disperse when I looked at it. It became more mobile, too, no longer restricted by whatever laws it must obey to keeping to the corners. Now I would watch it crossing rooms, entering through doorways, sitting down. But still so vague, undefined. About this time I began to hear it as well. I mentioned those steps upon the stairs, so slow, so heavy, as if bearing an insupportable weight. I could also hear it approaching me across the level floor. That was the most disconcerting manifestation so far. To be seated, reading or writing, and hear those footsteps, freighted with some Message I did not want to hear; and to turn, the words "Oh, it's you" on my lips, only to have them evaporate because it wasn't "you." There was no "you" at all. Each time I heard the steps approach they ended closer to me. At first they stopped upon the threshold of the room where I sat. Later they crossed just into the room, and later still halfway across. Finally they came to within an arm's length of me. How unnerving this was, to know from one sense that something was there, yet to have another sense tell you that nothing was.

Nothing was.

Later still, shadow and steps meshed somehow in the logic of whatever world the ghost had wandered out of. "Wandered" isn't really the proper word, though. It had purpose; it had a destination, and that destination was I.

But it was as yet still just a shadow. Amorphous and gray, like something you could blink away, but stubbornly refusing to do so. It would stand near me as if waiting for acknowledgment—for the ability to import that Message it brought with it. Then it would fade so gradually that you couldn't say when it was there and when it was not. Once I had deigned to look right at it, it would last no more than a minute—more or less. Again, it was hard at the end to say when it was there and when not.

Then it began to become more defined, as if becoming more real. A pale patch developed where a face would be, and then two smaller spots corresponding to hands hanging at the figure's sides. Darkness gathered at the face's top and side as of hair, short hair, perhaps that of a man.

And those shoulders, surely they were a man's. It was about my height, approximately my build, too, perhaps a trifle thinner.

Then came the smell. Just as with the sight and sound of it, at first it was so faint as to be something that might not be there. A deeper breath would make it vanish. But as with the thing's visual and auditory presence, this too grew. And its nature was such that even its first, faint manifestations were memorable. It was not a good smell. If I say that my first thoughts about it were that a drain had backed up somewhere, near, I should be understating it. I would be offering you the excuse I told myself. As the smell grew its awfulness grew with it. Disease and decay. Yet it was one and the same smell, indivisible. It was the smell of death.

These visits now were accompanied with feelings of discomfort as well. I knew even before the sound of its footsteps that it drew near, for I found I could not sit still. I was uncomfortable in my own skin. From alarm to curiosity my mood about the ghost now turned to dismay. I began to dread its appearance, not as from something inimical to me, but more as of an annoyance.

And still it continued to evolve and define itself. Shadows of eyes darkened, and of nose and of mouth. It had the proportions of a face I knew, if only I could focus it.

Finally came the cold. One terrible day, when that "certain Slant of light" poured in my west window and spread a pale yellow rectangle— the ghost of a window—upon my library floor, the ghost walked in and across the light, crossing it without obscuring it, walked up to me and sat down in the chair opposite to me. My discomfort had grown to actual pain as I turned to face it. The smell contaminated the air; the chill went through my skin; and I looked into the ghost's eyes and knew them.

Now I may indulge my theories. I still do not believe in ghosts per se. Funny to write that, after all the foregoing, but let me explain. I don't believe in spirits that "wander the Earth" in expiation of some crime or regret imposed by a greater being. Materialist to the end, I rather believe in the possible ability of lives to project themselves in time. Perhaps, just perhaps, that "certain Slant of light" throws our shadows not only across the three visible dimensions, but down time as well. Perhaps the density of our lives blocks the light of Time and throws these paths of darkness down the years from our absence. Perhaps.

But this only partly explains my ghost. For him (for so he is) I offer a further explanation. Our lives are mapped out as we walk them. To use a popular and hackneyed term, they are a "journey." And as with any other path, you can walk in one direction—or another. Not everyone, and not in just any circumstance, of course. Else we'd be more crowded on this Earth than we are, the billions of the future jostling with the billions of the present.

For that is where my ghost came from—the future. He found the way to follow his shadow back upon his life-path, and the strength of message to enable him to do it. Once freed from these fleshly shackles and charged with his Message, it must have been an easy thing, really, to retrace his steps along that path to me.

And the Message? Why, I had it already without understanding it; the discomfort and pain that has grown inside my body with each passing week, and that threatens to turn me into the sad-eyed figure that looks at me from across the room.

The Norther

Gonna be a norther."

"You reckon?"

Burnett Jones and his hired man Riley squinted together at the sky. Burn knew it was the day. There was a feel to it, a color to it. The bluebell skies of November were gone, replaced by the dull, heavy blue of gunmetal. You couldn't spend hours, days, years on the prairie and not recognize the signs.

"Best get the herd back to the house," Burn said, turning his horse's head back to the west and not waiting for a reply.

"Right, boss."

It wasn't a large herd, nothing like the rolling tides of longhorns up in the Panhandle. But it was enough for Burnett Jones. He did a modest business raising and selling the wild-eyed cattle to markets in Austin and Waco, and filled the larder with the proceeds. A kitchen garden Susannah had planted provided the rest.

As the two men and their ambling herd topped a rise, the Jones homestead, neat and fresh-painted white in its gentle valley, spread out before them. A creek, bordered by cottonwoods nodding lazily in the heat, wandered across the valley to find its way eventually to the Colorado and the Gulf. On its journey it provided precious fresh water to the Jones land and its occupants. What a pretty spot, Burn thought for the hundredth time. How Susannah had loved it. How she had made it into the Eden it was. Almost perfect.

Except for the serpents.

Down in the little valley, Burn and Riley secured the herd in the corral. Riley was already leading his horse to the barn when Burn called out after him, "See the place is secure, would you, Rile? I've got an errand to see to."

Something in boss's voice made Riley stop and turn.

"You sure, boss?" he said, frowning at the sky. "You ain't got much time, way I see it."

"Enough," Burn said, and cantered his horse to the farmhouse.

Once inside, Burnett Jones set a fire in the stove—not the big, fancy rig he'd bought Susannah the Christmas before, but the little pot-bellied fellow who squatted in the corner of the parlor. He put the enamel coffee-pot on to boil and went to the bedroom. There he stripped off his outer clothes and pulled on long underwear, still smelling of camphor from the winter chest. Just the effort of re-dressing made the sweat pimple on his brow and run tickling down his face. Must be ninety in the shade, he thought, and buckled his gun-belt back over his pants. Lastly he reached into the wardrobe he once shared with Susannah and brought out his heavy buffalo coat. This he didn't put on but rolled tightly in a blanket and tied with twine.

By the time he was finished the water was boiling. Burn found his canteen in the kitchen and emptied it in the soapstone sink.

Mind you don't chip my plates in that sink, Burnett Jones.

Burn smiled at the memory of her voice. He spooned grounds from the coffee tin on the table into his canteen; sifted a ghost of sugar in after it, and lastly a swallow of whole milk from their one cow. Then, hand wrapped in a towel, he picked up the coffee-pot and poured steaming water into the mix in the canteen. He screwed the top on to the canteen and swirled it around some. He almost poured the last of the hot water onto the fire in the stove—there were plenty of stories about untended fires burning down houses while the owners were off doing something else—but then thought Riley might appreciate some warmth in a while. Lastly he hoisted the blanket-roll to his shoulder, looped the canteen's strap around his neck, and opened the back door. Burn looked around the kitchen—the neat, simple table, the dishes stacked on the shelves, the grand stove, the empty sink. He looked a long minute at it all. Then he pulled the door shut behind him.

Riley was coming out of the barn as Burn exited the house.

"Hot water on the stove," Burn called, and Riley raised a hand in thanks. Burn tied the blanket-roll behind the saddle of his horse and swung up. He paused to take another look, this time around the homestead, his homestead, their homestead. Then he wheeled his horse north and west and out of the cozy valley.

You would think there was room enough for everybody in this big land. Texas was big, damned big, and a decent part of its bigness was spread on these grassy, rolling lands north and east of the capital. A little farther up were the Blacklands, land so rich it was the color of night. There the free grandsons and granddaughters of slaves still worked the long rows of cotton. This time of year the cotton leavings huddled in the dusky furrows like the rare snows that graced the land—a puzzling sight on a hot afternoon, snow that didn't melt.

But down this way was cattle country. You needed a sight of land to graze the beasts, but there was still plenty of it, and not many used that newfangled barbed wire as yet. You wouldn't think you'd chafe against a neighbor with all that elbow-room, now, would you?

Burn glanced at the flat, darkening sky once again and urged his horse into a run. No barbed wire here yet, but you knew when you got to Creech land. From this big live oak to that swale, down to the arroyo, everybody knew where their land began and ended. Plus it was easy to tell Creech land—worn, picked over, unloved. Burn didn't pause when he reached it. Nobody stopped him when he crossed onto it, but it seemed as if Nature herself had taken note of it. The grass was patchy and burned, and the rare oaks and pecans drooped in the heat. A breath of welcome cool kissed Burn's cheek, though. It picked up, growing from causal breezes to a steady flow from the north. Here we go, Burn thought, and pulled his collar up.

He had to go a quarter-mile onto the Creech property before one of the hired hands spotted him. By then Burn was passing the outliers of the Creech herd—big, stupid beasts, ragged-coated, nervous and mean. The great horns on Burn's own cattle looked elegant, almost comical. The horns on these critters looked plain dangerous.

Burn picked out the biggest, meanest-looking steer and cantered over toward him. He could see the hand was watching him, and was riding closer to see what Burn was about. Good. Burn got to within twenty feet of the steer—he dared not get any closer, his mount was already beginning to shy—drew his rifle from his saddle-scabbard, sighted it just behind the steer's front leg, and fired. The shot split the air and ran echoing over the plains. The steer, without a sound, collapsed to the ground like a bag of rocks.

"Hey!"

Alarmed now, the hand put his horse into a gallop.

"The *hell* you doin'?" he yelled as he came.

Burn calmly slid his rifle back into its scabbard and turned his horse back east again. Clear of the herd, he urged the horse into a run, then a full gallop. Still within Creech land, he pulled up and looked back. The hand had dismounted and was squatting by the dead steer. Another mounted hand had materialized out of somewhere and was sitting his horse nearby. He had field-glasses trained on Burn; Burn could see the sky reflected off of the lenses. He waved. Hi, neighbor. Burn made sure the mounted man was headed back toward the Creech ranch, then nudged his own horse into an easy walk in the other direction.

Burn hated to kill the steer. Besides being cruel, it was just plain wasteful. He hoped somebody got some good steaks off of it, but then again, hopefully not either of the Creech boys.

They had come out of the piney woods of East Texas two years before. Stableford and Chuse Creech, raw and ready, trouble on the hoof. They had enough sense to set up their spread and make it a go, if not enough to care for it properly. You knew a man by how well he took care of his own. By that standard Stableford and Chuse Creech were not whole men. Oh, they'd debate that with you readily enough with fists, knives, guns even, if they felt the need. But meanwhile half their land was overgrazed and half their herd was underfed. How any man could manage that in the midst of such bounty amazed Burnett Jones.

But little else about the Creeches, or their raggedy-ass ranch-hands, impressed him. Still, if they'd kept to their own he wouldn't have cared. Burn had enough to do taking care of his own. Let 'em run their spread into the ground. Other, better men would replace them.

And to their minimal credit, they weren't cattle thieves. Burn was pretty sure about that; cattle thieves didn't last long in this country. Everything they'd gotten they'd gotten legal. Why, they hadn't done anything illegal—that you could prove. Even Sheriff McCallister could tell you that.

"Nothin' I can do about it," was what he'd actually said. "Sorry, Burn."

McCallister had done his best, looked over the whole Jones spread thoroughly with those bleach-blue eyes of his. The tracks in the yard were too muddled, he said, nothing peculiar to i-dent-i-fy the shoes, he said. He stood in the dusty yard, the shattered kitchen, the nightmare bedroom, chewing his quid, taking in everything but seeing nothing.

But Burn saw. Problem was, you can't convict a man on a look, a leer, a snicker. Not in court, anyway.

Behind him now there were distant noises of commotion. Burn turned in his saddle and saw several mounted men—six, if his eyes were still good—gathered around the dead steer. They assembled there only briefly, though, and as Burn watched they kicked their mounts into a hard gallop toward him.

"Gee-yup," he said to this horse, and put the spurs to it. No real need to stick the poor animal, or use a quirt as he heard the Creeches did. The horse, a big chestnut named Thunder that Burn had had for years, lunged forward readily.

The land was rolling but not abrupt. Burn easily stretched the distance between himself and the pursuing cowboys. Each time he crested a rise he looked back, and each time he was gratified to see how far they still were from him. He let them get a little closer, but not much. Just enough to keep their blood up.

Meanwhile the temperature had commenced its descent. The sweat cooled and dried on Burn's face, and the blue overhead deepened to a grim purple. Burn was grateful for the coolness but knew it was just the start. Look back—they were still two hills back. Burn leaned into the chase and turned his horse a little more to the north, where the far hills stood in still and eerie clarity. The only sounds were the hard tattoo of Thunder's hooves and the wind soughing by Burn's ears.

Another look back: Burn's change of direction had split his pursuers into two groups, one still directly on his trail and the other swinging wide to the left to cut him off. What was it Caesar said? Burn's schooldays Latin was rusty, but he dredged it up: *Divide et impera.* Divide and conquer.

A headlong plunge into a dale, then the breathless lift as the horse swept him up and over a ridge. A quick look—the men to the left were closer now, only one hill back, close enough to distinguish them separately. Three of them; the lanky one in the center with the red vest had to be Chuse Creech. The other two were in shirtsleeves. Not a one had on a coat. Dang fools.

They were all armed, though, and just as Burn reached the highest point of the rise Chuse drew and banged off a shot at him. It went wild—the man was no Sam Bass, and shooting a pistol from a galloping horse almost guaranteed it wouldn't hit what it was aimed at. Still, it made its point. Burn crouched low over his horse's neck and urged it into a flat charge down the farther slope.

A creek cut a lonely line down the middle of the dale below. Burn's horse cleared it easily. But when Burn looked back from the top of the next rise he saw one of Creech's men and horse cartwheel ass over tea-kettle into the creek. Hard to get good help these days. Burn knew just what had happened. The man hadn't committed to the jump; he faltered and the horse had picked it up. You had to commit to a plan and stick to it. It was either yea or nay. Some folks just didn't get that.

When he topped the rise the wind hit Burn like a slap in the face. Definitely colder, like throwing spring-water on your face in the morning. Colder on the hands, too. Burn tugged his gloves from his belt and pulled them on. The land was flattening out now, and what with the wind rushing straight out of the north and the extra speed Burn coaxed from Thunder, he felt as if he were flying. The low hills dead ahead had a vague look now, sunny and hazy at the same time; a pale blue-green that faded to nothing as Burn looked.

And then the snow hit. A few flakes, streaking by like shooting-stars, then a volley, then a blinding cloud. Burn pulled his hat down and his kerchief up until only his gray-blue eyes showed. Going straight into it, the snow looked like a flower continually, furiously blooming.

The things you think of, Burn.

Her voice was low and close to his ear. He remembered that sleepy closeness as they lay their bed together, and he smiled.

"Got a few ideas, don't I, girl?"

The cold wind tore the words from his mouth in a swirl of mist, and brought tears that ran streaming back into his hair.

bam

Another shot, muffled and dull in the snow. Burn glanced back: there were Chuse Creech and his one remaining hired man. Chuse was leaning into the chase, but even as Burn watched the hired man peeled off and turned for home. Within seconds he was a ghost, then nothing. Creech himself was only a gaunt shadow in the storm, gun hand still raised, coming on like some Blacklands angel of death. Burn dared a look over his right shoulder and there were the other two riders, maybe fifty feet back of Chuse. The stocky one had to be Stableford, the other one another hired man. Just the two—so he'd lost a rider somewhere, too. Fine. The Creeches were the only ones he wanted anyway.

Burn could feel his horse getting winded—hell, he was getting tired just from riding the poor beast—and he looked into the blizzard for ideas. He was pretty sure the next gulley was about a quarter mile off. If memory served, it was fairly deep and crowded with stands of cottonwood and pecan. If Burn could get to it, he could cut down the creek and maybe put some more distance between him and his pursuers.

If he could make it. The chestnut was blowing hard, the clouds of breath gusting by Burn's face like the breath of a locomotive, and the horse's formerly solid pace was starting to falter.

crack

A bullet slashed the air by Burn's right ear. *Durned Creech is a better shot than I thought.* Burn put his head down and his spurs in and yelled to his horse to come on, come on a little further, git up, old Thunder. He pulled the horse to the right to put some distance between himself and the shooter; and there, like the charge of the Light Brigade, came Stableford and the remaining hand straight at him at a gallop. Burn shot across their path just as Chuse banged off another shot at him. Someone yelled. Turning, Burn saw the hired hand pitch off his mount. He must have gotten between Burn and Chuse just as the latter fired. Now it was just the Creech brothers and they almost collided on their headlong charges. The storm and distance silenced their voices and the thickening snow bleached them to nothing in seconds; but Burn saw enough to know they had stopped and were having words and waving arms at each other. They were still flailing the air when the snow swept over them.

Easy, Burn. That ravine comes up fast.

Burn eased his horse back to a canter, a walk, a halt.

"Easy, fella," he said, and patted the long, moist arc of Thunder's neck. Snow caked the left side of its long head where the storm hit it. Burn wiped the snow away from the horse's eye, then palmed a handful off the kerchief over his own face. They hadn't stopped too soon; the horse was still blowing like a bellows and its legs shook with fatigue, cold, and fear. How Burn hated to run Thunder like this. The horse had seen him through more than its share of storms, floods, and maddened cattle. It deserved better from him than this. He hoped the Creeches were still after him, but maybe not just yet.

The cold had seeped right through the leather of Burn's gloves. He beat his hands together, slapped them on his thighs and chest until some feeling came tingling back. Dang cold was getting deeper by the minute. Burn reached back and pulled the coat free of the blanket-roll behind him, shook snow off it and shrugged it on. That helped some. How much colder had it gotten? Fifty degrees in maybe the past half hour? The hot, sunny morning seemed years ago now.

Burn looked around him. There was little to see: the tired horse he rode, the patch of grassland on which they stood, swept flat by the wind, and the flying snow. Nothing else. He could be sitting at the bottom of a hole at the end of the world for all he knew. The trail of his horse's hooves was being erased even as he watched, but the wind still blew straight out of the north, and with the snow hitting him on the left side of his face, that put him facing east. Given the time spent racing across the big ground, Burn guessed the ravine was not too far off.

"... where ... dang fool, I tole ... back ...."

Voices. Burn jerked his head around. Voices, pieces of words flew on the howling wind. *They must be upwind,* Burn thought, *heading north of my path.* He listened some more, caught fragments:

"... ing ... bout to ... give up."

Now, now, boys, can't have that. Burn unsheathed his rifle, wiped the snow from the action, and raised it toward the wind. He fired. The shot sounded flat and abbreviated by the wind, but it did the trick.

"... was that?" came down the wind in a high, shocked voice. Chuse, probably. Stableford was the more level-headed of the two, if you could use that term for a pair of blockheads. Burn gave it a minute, then urged Thunder forward at a walk.

The ravine came up quickly. Burn thanked God he hadn't pushed Thunder into a gallop, else they'd be in a heap at the bottom of the ravine by now. He eased the big chestnut down the slope, not too steep here but slick with snow and dotted with clumps of prickly pear. He kept it to an easy, steady pace even when he heard the hoofbeats behind him. They were coming on fast, both of them by the sound of it. Wouldn't do to get caught in that parade. Burn pulled the horse to the left up the ravine, keeping on a steady descent towards the creek.

They were almost in it before they saw it, a mere trickle among it rocky bed, fringed with fans of ice. Burn swore he could see the ice grow as he watched. The same time they reached the creek Burn heard the commotion up and behind him. A man's high-pitched yell, then another in a lower register. Then a horse screaming and heavy bodies thudding into the ground in an avalanche of concussions. Burn could feel them in the ground right up through his horse's body. Nothing to see back there but more snow and the creek winding away into nothing.

At least the wind was less in the shelter of the ravine. The snow still fell, but less in a torrent here than in a cloud. The cleft in the ground muddled the wind so that the snow flew this way and that, a dizzying swirl and flutter before the eyes.

". . . get you, Jones! You're . . . dead, man, you hear me?"

Stableford sounded riled. Burn could picture Chuse lying in a broken tangle with his horse at the bottom of the pitch, and Stableford standing above him with vengeance on his red face. If the man needed any more incentive to keep following Burn, he had it now.

Burn didn't wait to see what happened next. He urged Thunder on up the creek a ways, then onto the south slope again. A strange, confused sound came up quick behind them. It wasn't hoofbeats, more a stumbling clatter of stones and raw, hurried panting. Burn looked back from near the top of the slope and saw a lone figure of a man afoot come lurching out of the storm below him. It was little more than a gray silhouette; but that heavy upper body atop the bandy legs—a farmer's body, Burn had always thought, not the lean, economical figure of a rancher—could not be mistaken. The shadow-arm of the figure ended in a long, pointed extension that Burn recognized as Stableford Creech's old Colt Navy revolver. Creech had a gun, but, Jones noted, no hat.

Burn looked long enough to register the shadow's identity and lone condition before urging his horse up the last of the slope. If he could see Creech, then Creech could dang sure see him. Wouldn't do to get skylighted on the crest and give Creech a good target. He pushed Thunder up and over the crest as fast as he dared.

The storm hit Burn like a volley of buckshot. It was colder still, and the snow was tiny and hard as pebbles, and it stung as it struck the exposed flesh on Burn's cheek. Amazing to think of all that land out there, and nothing to see. The wind yanked his buffalo coat up over his head before he wrestled it back down and buttoned it. Still, the going was easier now because the wind was at his back. There was that, anyway. Not much more to do about the cold but pull the blanket free and wrap it around his shoulders.

Through the screaming of the wind came strange, errant sounds. There was that puffing breathing again, hoarser and raw-edged; and words flew past like wild birds:

". . . get . . . once more, you . . . not done . . ."

Burn rode downwind a way before turning in a slow arc to his left. Heading back into the wind was hard, brutal to both horse and rider. But they put their heads down and pushed on. Burn rode all the way back until the ravine opened dark before him again, then turned harder left. Following the edge of the ravine, he rode until he found the trough torn in the snow at the edge of the ravine by his horse, and by Stableford Creech after him.

Now came the tricky part. Just as he had been downwind of his pursuer, so Creech was now downwind of him. Burn hoped the wind would cover any sounds of jingling harness. The storm was rapidly filling Creech's stumbling trace through the snow and sculpting it into softer, liquid shapes. Enough of it remained, though, for Burn to follow it easily. He was not far now. Almost there.

Was that talk again, now? Hard to tell; it was downwind this time, soft, coaxing, pleading. Burn drew his rifle and pushed Thunder on into the storm. Something ahead—a figure, no two. *Two?* No, a trick of the wind, a dust-devil of snow that flew apart as Burn came up. But the other figure was real.

Creech had found Burn's trail, too. The two men had been following each other in a snowswept do-si-do, and Creech had made it a quarter-way around Burn's big circle. Burn found him sitting on his heels in the snow. His Colt was frozen to his hand, his face locked forever in a red mask of terror. Burn had been right; Creech hadn't even bothered to put on a coat or a duster. His hat was long gone and snow and dried sweat painted his lank, red hair to his head. The flying wrack had already thoroughly plastered the man's side and back. He was a snowman made by devils. It wouldn't be long before he was covered completely. Burn sat his horse and looked long at the frozen man—rigid, dogged, dead, and alone. Then he put the wind to his back and began the long ride home.

Dry Spell

(for A. B.)

It was August 1870, a time of drought. Ephraim Cornell, veteran of the Civil War, stood leaning upon a scythe in his upland field. He was a tall man and lean, whittled down to bare necessities by work and worry. In his gauntness he resembled the late lamented President Lincoln, even down to the Quaker chinstrap whiskers he wore. But there the resemblance ended. His eyes held none of the humor Lincoln's had; in fact, they held nothing at all. His three-button shirt and overalls hung on him like rags on a dead tree; but there was a rigidity to his frame that bespoke great strength. Summer lay heavy and hot and still upon the dense greens of Rhode Island that year. The field of long grass Cornell stood in glowed silver yellow to the woods' edge. From Ephraim's scarecrow figure to the road below and back to the household garden the grass was hewn down and lay a thatched carpet at his feet. Beyond him and to the dark woods the uncut grass rose in a wall to the height of Cornell's chest. The woods loomed in gigantic quiet.

In the quiet a lone bird tweed; hoofbeats came slowly, impressively up to Cornell from his road below. The beats slowed and stopped, and were followed by leather creaking as of a person dismounting. Up over the near horizon of the hill rose two figures; men in the wide-brimmed hats, black coat, trousers, and boots dictated by fashion and in spite of the heat. One wore large black moustaches, and a gun-belt that dangled a heavy revolver against the owner's right hip. The men were crossing the field against the grain of the windrows and stepped carefully. Still Cornell leaned upon his scythe. He stood a silhouette cut from iron on the field's highest point.

When the two men were within speaking distance, the one with the moustache raised his right hand.

"Eff."

Cornell nodded once. The men came on and stopped three respectful rows away from him. Cornell had the sun at his back and the advantage of home-ground, and he waited for the men to state their business. Moustache made a show of looking up and down the long rows.

"Summer's most gone," he said softly.

"Most," allowed Cornell.

A cicada zinged. The sun glared down.

"Been three months since your May vanished," moustache said.

"I know how long it's been, Sergeant."

"Then why aren't you looking for her?"

This last was from the other man who had accompanied the sergeant. The town sergeant was the law in Rhode Island towns at this period, which made the other man his deputy. He was slightly shorter than the sergeant (who, in turn, was shorter than Ephraim Cornell's long six feet), squarely built with the thick upper body of a farmer's son. The wide brim of his hat put his face in shadow, but light reflected up from the shorn grass showed a round, genial face framed by reddish curls. The flesh of his face was pinked by too much sun. He wore no vest but, oddly, a black preacher's tie over his white shirt. He looked as little like a deputy as the sergeant did a sergeant.

Ephraim turned slightly to bring this man straight into his gaze and stared.

"Correct me if I err, Hiram," he said evenly, "but I believe that's the job of this gentleman here." And he raised a finger from the scythe to indicate the sheriff.

The red-headed man bunched his lips as if about to reply. Then he looked past Ephraim and smiled a broad smile full of round, white teeth.

"Well," he said, "if it isn't 'The Last of the Pocassets.'"

Ephraim turned his head and saw another man trudging up from the slope behind him. He was nearly as tall as Cornell but heavier built. Where Cornell was spare, almost wasted-looking, this man was solid. His arms were dark-skinned emerging from rolled-up sleeves of a dirt-stained gray ticking shirt. Galluses stretched taut across his chest to hold up his trousers, and when he brushed dirt from his hands against his pants legs, muscles in his shoulders balled up into hard lines. He waded through the tall grass as through the surf. As he came up he removed the shapeless brown hat he wore, produced a red kerchief from his pocket, and mopped a bronzed face that would have been at home in the longhouses of the Iroquois or the hogans of the Navajo. He smiled and nodded to the other men. Though only slightly taller than they, he seemed to look down on them from a great height.

"This my hired man," Cornell said. "John Annawan."

"I know John," the sergeant said, and extended his hand. He and Annawan shook hands and, after an awkward moment, so did Annawan and Hiram.

"And what have *you* been up to, John?" Hiram asked him of a sudden.

The sergeant turned on him.

"D'you mind if *I* ask the questions, Mr. Peckham?" Hiram stepped back a pace, his face reddening more.

"I was just wondering—" he began.

"Well, *I* was just wondering what our horses were about," interrupted the sergeant. "Why don't you go find out until I call you?"

Peckham waited a second more, looking from face to face of the other three men. Then, with a huff, he turned and stalked back down the slope.

"Mind that hay," Cornell called after him.

When Peckham had gone beyond the slope the sergeant shook his head and turned back to Cornell.

"I'm sorry about that," he said, chuckling. "Town says I got to pay deputies out of my own pocket. Been a lean year—guess you get what you pay for."

"'S all right," said Cornell. He shifted his weight so that he leaned the scythe with his elbow—more genuinely relaxed. "I 'spect Hiram was up here hoping you'd drag me away in chains so's he could snatch up my farm."

"Those Peckhams are a land-hungry race," agreed the sergeant. "Said he just wanted to come in case I needed 'help.' I imagine you're closer to the truth."

"So what can I do for you, Sergeant Snell?"

Snell put his fists to his hips and took a deep breath.

"It's like I said, Eff," he started, almost apologetically. "No one's seen your May and I was wondering if you had heard anything."

"Nothing," Cornell shook his head. "Not since Adoniram saw her in Fall River in the spring."

The mill-town of Fall River, Massachusetts, was just ten miles north of where these men stood in a field in Pocasset, Rhode Island. Since the end of the war five years before, the mills had been gorged on southern cotton and ran day and night. They drew the wayward and the ambitious from towns for miles around; many of them were the young women who tended the looms in the mills.

"That's another thing, Eff," said the sergeant. "Your cousin Adoniram has gone missing as well. I've put the Fall River police on May's scent, but without Adoniram's testimony they're shooting in the dark."

He paused, waiting for some confirmation or refutation from Cornell. When none came he added, "So have you seen ought of Adoniram Cornell of late, Eff?"

"Nossuh," said Cornell. Which was, strictly speaking, true.

"You don't seem surprised he's gone."

"Young fella like that, town like this couldn't hold him for long. 'Sides, he and May allus did foller each other like kids."

Snell stood looking down at the hay, thinking. Then he looked up at Cornell.

"Take a look at your house, Eff?"

Cornell shrugged.

"Barn and ice-house too, if you've a mind," he said, and turned to lead the sergeant down to the farmhouse.

Cornell was silent as they walked. His silence weighed on the sergeant, and to break it he said, "Lookin' peaked these days, Ephraim."

"Missin' your wife'll do that to you." Cornell didn't look at him.

"Got a gun, Eff?"

This brought Cornell up short. He turned to the sergeant.

"'Course I got a gun," he said. "Fought for the Grand Army of the Republic for three years, didn't I? Kilt nine rebs with it, too, if you're keeping a tally."

"Just asking, Eff."

The sergeant searched the house from cellar to attic. Then he did search the barn and ice-house. For good measure Ephraim even led him to the old root-cellar as well, overgrown with grass and thistle as it was. When Snell was done they returned to where John Annawan still stood in the field.

"I hate to ask it, John," the sergeant said, "but what *were* you up to before we got here?"

"Buildin' stone wall," Annawan answered, jerking his thumb over his shoulder. "Wanna see?"

"Yeah."

John led them down the far slope toward the trees.

"Got a cow-pond down there," Cornell said as they walked. "This dry-spell's drained a lot of it off and I don't want them cows follering Hardscrabble Creek back into the swamp."

At the bottom of the slope they stopped and looked down. A wide, oval-shaped patch of mud lay open to the sky there, bordered by dead or dying cattails. Down the middle of the mud wound a thread of brownish water. The mud around it was cracked into crazy tiles.

"There's my wall," said Annawan, and pointed to the far end of the wallow. Between the mud and the forest's edge a stone wall ran. The section at the end of the wallow had been built up so that though its foundation dipped with the land, its top was even with the wall on either hand. It stood about seven feet tall at that point. Gaps had been left at the base of it to allow water through. It was monumental.

"Stake fence would've done as well," Snell mused as he looked it over.

"Stakes don't last in water," Cornell said, shifting on his feet. "'Sides, ain't like we lack for stones in this state."

The sergeant nodded and began stumping toward the wall.

"Good wall," Cornell said after him. "Keeps cows in, rattlesnakes out."

The sergeant paused mid-step and glanced back. Cornell leaned his scythe; Annawan stood with arms crossed. Their hats made their faces blue-black columns of shadow. The sergeant let his foot down and looked to his pistol. He removed it from his holster, peered into the chambers to check his loads, and put it back in the holster. Then he stood and stared at the wall for a long, hot minute. Finally he turned around and began walking back toward the other men.

"I don't know what I'm thinking, Eff," he said as he approached them. "Just doing my job, you understand."

"I understand," Cornell said.

They crossed the field again and accompanied the sergeant down to his horse. Hiram Peckham squatted on the ground near the horses. He was breaking a twig into smaller and smaller lengths.

"You will tell me if you hear anything," the sergeant said after he and Peckham had remounted.

"I surely will, Sergeant," said Cornell, nodding.

The sergeant nodded back and he and Peckham rode off down the road. A cloud of white dust rose after them and hung in the sweltering air for long moments after the riders had gone.

"Think we will hear anything?" Annawan said, staring at the dispersing dust.

"More'n likely," said Cornell. They waited another half a minute. Then he said, "Come on, John. Things to do before nightfall."

Ephraim Marcus Cornell had a horse he named Hoppy. Once he had had a friend named Robert Hopkins, but Robert Hopkins had gone to war with his friend Eff Cornell and hadn't come back. In a field in Virginia one day, part of a projectile with the innocuous name of "canister"—a large tin can filled with iron balls that acted like a giant shotgun charge when shot from a cannon—clipped the side of Bob Hopkins's head. Eff had been there and held his friend while he died. The shot had disarranged the right side of Bob's head, but his left eye still turned this way and that with a fading spark of intelligence that brightened when it lit upon his friend's face. Neither said a word. Bob's eye blinked once, and tears cut through the black-powder grime on Eff's face. A month later a Rebel Minié ball cut into Eff's left arm and shattered the bone. As a matter of course the company surgeon prepared to cut off the arm, but he recked not with Yankee stubbornness. So he cut the ball out instead and left Eff with a white zigzag scar down his forearm and a deep ache there every April when the wind came cold and dank off Narragansett Bay. He was bandaged and put on the next train north.

Back at his family's farm in Pocasset he bought a horse and named it after his best friend, and prepared to marry the proverbial "Girl I Left Behind Me." Mary Elizabeth Gray was a Tiverton Gray, a family that had produced the discoverer of the Columbia River, not to mention several generations of industrious Yankee farmers, fishermen, and whalemen. Ephraim Cornell just liked her blue eyes and the way the shadows of apple blossoms slid over her trim hips. Having no immediate family, he had left her in the care of his younger cousin Adoniram, a boy whose sprightly enthusiasm contrasted with his older cousin's sometimes dour determination. Talk had gone 'round Pocasset and nearby Tiverton about May Gray and "that young Cornell," as talk will in rural towns. But when the returning hero arrived Adoniram led May to his side with grace and happiness. May and Eff were married in June 1865. Adoniram Cornell stood up for his cousin.

But a marriage that had sprouted in so much joy blossomed with pain and difficulties. No children came to cheer the young couple. In the place of babies' cries the screams of ghostly legions in gray tore into Ephraim Cornell's sleep. He awoke in shaking sweats, and May, for all her love, was unable to stop the charges of those demons. The strain began to tell on both of them.

Adoniram helped with the farm. Eff was grateful for the help, especially with his half-useless left arm, and May seemed to bloom again when the younger Cornell stayed for dinner. But their laughter and their shared memories of the years Eff had been away began to grate on him; and one day he asked Adoniram not to come back. The youth, now grown into a handsome buck, smiled with his usual grace and left.

In the summer of 1869, with no prospect of children to help run the farm, Eff hired John Annawan. John was, to use Hiram Peckham's colorful, literate phrase, "the Last of the Pocassets," the native tribe that had once ruled the land from modern Fall River south to the Little Compton line. Their name had been used by the whites at different times for parts of the towns of Portsmouth, Tiverton, and Pocasset; this last finally sticking into perpetuity. In his more philosophical moments John allowed as how this was a "fair trade" for the tribe's near extermination by the whites during King Philip's War.

Like many surviving Rhode Island Indians, John made stone walls, and he made them well. Stone walls had, of course, existed for many years. But New England weather was "somethin' cruel" to anything built upon the land, and John and his brethren were kept busy repairing the stones dislodged by frost and storm.

John Annawan did more than just repair Eff Cornell's stone walls. He was the strong back that loaded the wagon to bring the corn down to Crandallville for grinding; he was the pair of arms that slung the hay up into the loft; and overall he was the good left arm that Eff no longer had and needed for so many chores.

More, John Annawan became Ephraim Cornell's good friend.

John's easy way suited Eff's sometimes exacting disposition. When John saw a better way of doing something, he knew how to phrase it such that it seemed to Eff more like a cooperation than a correction. And Eff found he could talk of the war to John in detail that would have terrified May. Many nights the two men sat their rockers and smoked their pipes and spoke of this or that until all the lamps in the county were out, and the stars glittered in silent glory above. John had the gift of listening, and Eff was grateful.

And then May had gone missing. Things between the Cornells had not improved much over the years, and deteriorated further when Eff learned that Adoniram had been by to "look in" on May while he had been away at market several times. From his bedroom in the house's ell, John Annawan lay and listened to the couple shouting, and stared and stared up at the dark ceiling.

In the morning Eff was worthless.

"Got any of your Indian weeds or something to help me out?" he asked John with a crooked smile.

"B'lieve I do," said John.

After May disappeared Eff did all the right things—rode to the town sergeant, told him, told the Gray family, hunted up his cousin and had a very public discussion with him on Pocasset Commons. Still, some had their doubts. It was no secret that "the milk's gone sour up t' Cornell's," and many remembered Eff's grim moods since his return from the war. But there was no proof—nothing the sergeant could find, anyway.

Then came Adoniram's statement that he had seen May on South Main Street in Fall River in June. Or rather, Ephraim's statement that he had heard his cousin say he had seen May. Adoniram had been headed out of town that day, off to see family in New Hampshire. No one thought to ask about *his* whereabouts for weeks—why would they? Then when they did, it took some hunting just to find his family in the north. Sergeant Snell went to Fall River and sent a telegram to the sheriff of Hillsborough County, New Hampshire; but that worthy wasn't even in the same town as the Cornell kin. Not even close. Day's ride, at least, and for what? Can't you flatlanders keep track of your own family? Not that it came out that way in the spare language of the telegraph, but to that effect.

Anyway, word finally got back that no, Adoniram Cornell had never arrived at his relative's house. Where could he have gotten to? The woods beside Main Road as far as Fall River were scoured, tramps arrested and questioned, and finally came that visit to Ephraim's farm.

Once the town sergeant was gone Eff and John resumed their chores. Ephraim finished another several rows in his field; John went back to check on his new wall.

When the sun went down that evening they hung up their tools for the day and shuffled into the house. Neither was a devoted cook, and without May's presence in the kitchen meals had become simple affairs. Eff hauled a ham out of the ice-house, knife already stuck in it, and slung it onto the butcher's block in the kitchen. John cut four thick slabs of bread from the loaf on the table. Somewhere they hunted up a jar of good horseradish and they spread it thick upon the bread. Then they cut ham and when it was slapped between the bread they took their sandwiches back outside. Neither said a word.

Anyone watching would have thought it strange that the two men, having given over the chores of the day, wouldn't sit to enjoy their meal. Instead they ate as they walked around the house, touching a shingle here, testing a doorframe there. A more curious soul would have noticed that there were stones placed on every windowsill and threshold; gray and black stones, pebbles worn smooth in the tides and each girdled by a white stripe. "Lucky-stones," the folk called them. Why anyone should need so much luck would have been the next question one asked.

Finished with this, they went inside and shut and bolted all the doors—another oddity on an evening just made for a smoke on the porch. Even odder, they closed all the windows as well. The air in the house quickly became close.

Ephraim went to the mantle over the kitchen fireplace—exactly four and a half steps in the dark—and located a hurricane lantern and a tinder-box by feel. He removed the lamp's glass chimney and struck a spark from the flint from the tinder-box onto a wood splinter. This he applied to the wick of the lamp and light swelled out from it. When he was sure the flame was secure he replaced the chimney and turned to carry the lamp to the table where John Annawan was already seated as if he had always been there. Eff's shadow swung huge and black around him as he turned. John produced a bunch of shore-grass bound up with twine. He put the end of the bunch to the lamp's flame, and after letting it catch for a few seconds he blew out the burning grass. Then he got up and walked around the house. As he walked he waved the smoking weeds to spread their fumes all around. He took especial care around the doors and windows. He muttered as he went in a chanting way.

While he was thus employed Cornell turned again to the mantel. From wooden hooks on the wall above the mantel he took down the Enfield rifle he had carried to war. He also took down a military-style leather pouch stamped U.S., and from a drawer in the wall opposite the fireplace, a brass powder-horn. Across the embossed surface of the horn mounted Union cavalry dispersed Confederate infantry in perpetual, frozen fight. The lamplight sparked red fire off the miniature figures' raised sabres.

When John was through with his mysterious rounds he came back to the kitchen and doused his bundle in a bucket of water. Cornell had removed twenty bullets from the leather pouch and was arranging them in neat rows upon the table—one, two, three, and so on, up through twenty. In the lamplight each one sat in a puddle of its own shadow.

"I heard what you said to the sergeant," said Annawan, as Cornell began the routine of loading the rifle. "'Bout May."

Cornell continued the drill—swab, powder, wadding, ball, a twirl of the ramrod and down the throat of the rifle with a shove. Cornell lifted his head to respond when a sound came to them through the walls. Stones knocked and klocked against each other and echoed softly a short distance away. Not that far away at all. In another circumstance you would have thought of someone playing bowls or croquet in the field. The two men sat stock still for long minutes, listening. When nothing broke the quiet, Cornell bent back to his business.

"What about her?" he asked softly. His hands shook.

"Said you missed her," Annawan went on. He paused.

Klock.

"You still miss her?"

"Not if'n I can help it," Ephraim Cornell said, and lifted the loaded rifle to his lap.

The Silent Garden

It was a quiet spring evening when I received one of the usual cards requesting my presence at the Chelsea home of my friend Carnacki. As the mellow warmth of day faded long and gently into evening, I could think of a dozen other delightful ways to while away my time in the Great Metropolis of London; but none, I knew, would be as fascinating.

Therefore dusk found me upon the doorstep of Cheyne Walk, Chelsea, where I rang the bell and was ushered into the scents of a more than superb dinner. Carnacki himself greeted me at the door and laughed as he swept me in.

"Ah," he said. "The errant schoolboy, home at last! The others have preceded you—no, not a word about my recent travels until we do justice to this excellent squab and trout."

Intrigued as I always was by Carnacki's accounts of his adventures, I had to admit that the dinner was worth the time spent to consume it. Afterwards, sleek and content as hounds at King Harry's table, we retired to our usual seats and nooks. Carnacki, as was his wont, settled into his great armchair that cupped his frame like a huge hand. He loaded and fired up his pipe, and ordered his man to set a fire, for the teasing warmth of the May evening had given way to a chill. The rest of us were fairly champing at the bit by this time, eager beyond words to hear what latest wonders our mutual friend had encountered. But he would not be rushed. We knew this, and he knew that we knew, and so all waited as patiently as was humanly possible.

Finally, when the fire was crackling foolishly to itself, Carnacki removed his pipe from his mouth and spoke.

"A casual listener to my tales," he began, staring into the flames, "might be tempted to say that I conveniently find my—what would you call them, Dodgson? 'Horrors'?—in out-of-the-way places, difficult to pin down and verify. Such a sceptic—and I must say that I would be one myself—would doubtless add that such inaccessibility throws doubt upon the reality of my experiences. Understandable. Yet I have just returned from an ordeal of an intensity comparable to any other I have undergone, and all within the limits of this creaking old city of ours. I could, in fact, take you to the scene of it in twenty minutes by hansom—but I shan't. There is nothing to see there now, anyway.

"It came about thus. Bartely—you know Bartely? he is a regular at the Club—came to me a month ago with a request for my unique talents. It seems a maiden aunt of his was having some undefined difficulty with her property. Her sleep was suffering badly and she was at her wits' end. Would I be so good as to pop over there and talk with the old girl? Well, neither my professional curiosity nor my ingrained chivalry would allow me to refuse such a request; so one day I rode to the aunt's house in Bartely's carriage, and spoke to the troubled dame.

"It was, as I have indicated, not much of a ride. The house was—*is*—situated in one of the newer neighbourhoods of the city to the northwest, although I gathered from my host's prattle on the way out there that the house and property antedated most of the *maisons nouvelles* that surround it. In fine, the metropolis had swallowed it. I had hoped to divine more about the problem with the property while we rode in the carriage; but although Bartely ran on at the mouth in a most garrulous and nervous manner, he was little more forthcoming than at the club.

"'Auntie says that it's the garden,' Bartely said with a helpless sort of a shrug. 'Says it's *wrong*, that she can't stand it.'

"'Is it in the nature of spectral noises?' I pressed, eager to get some sort of handle on the problem, if you see what I mean. Then he gave me a queer look, part perplexity, part caution.

"'No,' he said, slowly. 'No noises at all. In fact, that seems to be the rub, Carnacki.'

"We rode the rest of the short voyage in silence. When at last we stopped and alighted, it was in front of one of the most unprepossessing houses you can imagine. It had two stories and an attic beneath a peaked roof. It was narrow and brick—Georgian, I should think, although I'm sure Jessop here would correct me. It was crowded by edifices of clearly a more recent vintage, the inhabitants of which bustled hither and thither along the street and sidewalks with not a glance to the older house. It had a *sad* look—do you get me? As if it had been abandoned by its fellows and contemporaries and left to fend for itself amongst these flashy tyros.

"And when Bartely had knocked upon the front door of this lonely house, the aged mistress who answered proved to be its human double. The curse of a long life, I believe, is that we so often share it with so few of our contemporaries. Towards the end, there we are, still upon the stage; but the rest of the cast has fled, the audience has sought newer and more novel entertainments, and the lights are going out one by one. Such was my gloomy impression of Bartely's maiden Aunt Althea on that brisk, early spring afternoon. In form she was of middling height, thin to gauntness, and draped in the most obfuscating array of antique dress that could be imagined. If there was a flesh-and-blood woman in all that crinoline and dimity, she was well hidden! Only her two veined and birdlike hands, clutching each other as if for safety, and a sagging, lined face that bore a perpetual expression of pleading, emerged to prove her humanity. She looked old enough to have remembered the Queen's coronation (which, I later learned, she had and did), and I wondered at a soul who had seen the advent of steamships and locomotives, telegraphs and all the other churning, charging advances of our modern world.

"But she welcomed us graciously and effusively, as the last defender of a fort might welcome relief troops. As she walked us through the house, I looked over the rooms with both my outward and inward eyes. But besides the dizzying clutter of eight decades of womanly collecting, I could detect nothing. Nothing but the benign 'ghosts' of memory ruled this place.

"'Oh, no,' said Aunt Althea when I put the question to her. 'There's naught amiss with the house, Mr. Carnedy. As I told young Davey here [our well-respected comrade Bartely], the problem is out back. In the *garden.*'

"By now we had traversed the length of the central hall and had arrived at the kitchen. Aunt Althea's steps slowed as she led us past the stacked bowls and cupboards gay with antique china; and she came to an utter and final stop just short of the back door, which opened out onto a narrow garden.

"'There,' she said, one shaking claw pointing through the curtains in the door's window. 'There's the garden, sir.'

"I stepped forward and parted the curtains. Beyond them lay a modest expanse of garden bounden on three sides by a high brick wall and on the fourth by the house itself. Whatever may have been the ancestral demesne of Family Bartely, it had shrunk to a patch the width of a house and a depth a boy could have thrown a rock across. But it was as neat—and as cluttered—as the house itself, and it was clearly dear to this old woman's heart.

"From within the house, however, I could tell nothing. I turned to where Bartely was comforting his aged aunt and said, 'Miss Bartely, perhaps it would be best if you told me something of the problem you have had with your garden.'

"'Well, sir,' she said, 'it's hard to explain, quite. It's a feeling, like, as if someone didn't want me in there.' At this point her face collapsed in tears and she paused to produce a lace hanky from somewhere in her plumage of ruffles with which to wipe her eyes. Bartely, stout fellow, put his arm around her shoulders. When she had collected herself, she continued.

"'Then there's the birds, Mr. Carnedy. The birds! I've awakened to my dear birds singing all my life, sweet as angels, they were. And now they're gone! The garden is *silent!*'

"She leant back upon Bartely's strong arm and gave herself over to more weeping. I saw that further interrogation would be worse than useless, positively cruel, so decided instead upon action. I turned to the door, took one last look through the curtains, then grasped the knob and pulled the door open."

Carnacki paused in his narrative to take a long draw off his pipe. He took it from his mouth and breathed forth a cascade of smoke that ascended into the darkened heights of the room.

"Nothing against you fellows," he said at last. "But you will concede that I have something of an edge on you, as on the mass of humanity, when it comes to psychical sensitivity. Your senses in this arena are gross and ill-defined, whilst mine, a natural gift of heredity, honed by years of study and practice, are as keen as any samurai's sword. Still, what I encountered when I walked out that door was of such a magnitude that I doubt not but that even the dullest, most earthbound chimney-sweep would have stopped in shock before it. It wasn't exactly when I opened the door, nor even when I stepped from the threshold down onto the stone step. But the moment I set foot upon that cursed ground—and there could be no doubt but that it *was* cursed—I was met with a wall of PRESENCE that few other manifestations I have known could equal. This was a trifle more than something just 'not wanting' Aunt Althea to work in her garden, believe me! It was comprised of sheer, vacuous, solid *Silence,* and it met me like a strong wind. No—that is not entirely accurate. For a wind is in constant motion, while this energy was stubbornly immobile. As I took my first tentative steps into the garden, the PRESENCE hit me with unrelenting pressure. It felt as tight and full as an enormous, invisible wen—can you conceive of it? Stretched to transparency by the venomous pus within it, I felt that if I moved too quickly the horrid thing would *burst,* spraying me with its awfulness. And I knew that if that happened that I could never wash my soul clean of its stain— at best. At worst, it would kill me utterly, eradicating me body and soul.

"So I gingerly proceeded into the garden. And all the while the garden itself sat placidly amongst its yews and fruit-trees, its quaint pebbled paths leading nowhere, its fussy beds just breaking with spring's new growth, all in bright April sunshine. Then I thought of Aunt Althea's words, and *listened.* Not a bird sang. Not a cricket sawed. Not even the careless song of the breeze penetrated that unnatural SILENCE that gripped the little grounds. My ears strained to catch a whisper of the world, of the sane and healthy world, but could detect nothing.

"I proceeded in this manner for perhaps ten steps, the pressure of the unseen PRESENCE growing with every step, until I could take it no more. By the time I reached the limit of my penetration, it felt as if the unseen membrane must explode with my least forward movement. The very ground trembled beneath my feet with the tension—do you get me? Now, you fellows know from my other accounts that I am no yellow stripling to run at the first hint of danger. So you can appreciate the gravity of my situation in that silent garden that made me retrace my steps to the stone by the house's back door, up and into the kitchen itself, never turning my back on that silent scene. I have never effected a retreat with more reluctance, nor yet with more mincing care.

"One more detail I will leave you with: As I reached the edge of the garden by the house, I chanced to look down to watch my footing up to the threshold; and there, and all around the edge of the garden, was a border of dead birds. They looked as if they had all flown into an invisible wall and fallen, broken and dead, just outside it.

"I must have been a sight, for even before I had come all the way through the kitchen door Bartely had released his aunt and run to support me. I took the help gladly, suddenly aware of how drained I was from the experience. I paused only long enough to say, 'Close that door, for God's sake,' before allowing Bartely to lead me back to one of his aunt's seemingly countless parlours.

"There he deposited me on a love-seat and brought me a glass of fine brandy (for what maiden lady's house would be complete without a little something to fight the chill?) I drank it greedily down with one gulp, then handed the glass out for more. Bartely refilled it and gave it back to me. This time I savoured it and let it salve my frayed nerves.

"When I was composed again, I spoke with Bartely and his Aunt Althea. I told them nothing of what I had felt in the garden—they were worried enough, from the look of them—but quizzed them upon the history of house and grounds.

"That history proved prosy enough. The first Bartely, or Bertely, had settled there sometime in the sixteenth century, and a descendant of his had built the present house in the reign of the second George. Bartelys of one sort or another—tillers of the soil until recently, I gathered—had inhabited the land ever since with no trace of murder or madness. The most shocking episode of the family history, admitted with a dainty reluctance and sniff of disapproval by Aunt Althea, had been the marriage of an unnamed relation to 'a Scotsman,' and that misguided soul's consequent damnation by way of the Presbyterian Church. I assured her that even that blasphemous alliance could not account for the nameless evil in her property—but what then? Where *did* it come from? And what could I do about it?

"The brandy had done me wondrous good, and in my most professional manner I assured the pair that I would do my best to cleanse their land of this curse. How, exactly, I was to do this, I did not know; but I had a notion.

"I returned to Cheyne Walk and immediately set my mind to the task. First of all I must ask myself what was the nature of the infestation. Linked to this seemed to be the question, 'Why *now?*' If the family had lived there in uninterrupted bliss (barring randy 'Scotsmen') for generations, what had changed to bring this horror forth now? I considered the history of the region. Consulting maps going back centuries seemed to tell me nothing. Since time immemorial the land had been tilled land, giving untainted produce to century after century of rural folk. It was as typical a patch of southern English dirt as could be imagined.

"Then inspiration hit me. I thought again of the nature of that PRESENCE that had met me in the silent garden—of the colossal, bestial rage within it; a rage more than human in its strength. This was no psychical stain of some sordid suburban murder, no clinging, vengeful wraith anchored to forgotten bones. It had that awful, awesome quality of *otherness* that I had encountered before, as in the case of the Hog.

"Do you get me? It was not human; it was un-human; it was *pre*-human. And with that realization the pieces began to fall into place. How long had men been working that land? How long had they been wearing away the soil, ever deeper? Two thousand years? Three? Briton, Roman, Saxon, Norman, ploughs of bronze and iron, gouging, tearing . . . And the final uncovering, perhaps just Bartely's Aunt Althea raking up the litter of last fall and winter. Why, you can't turn over a spadeful of earth in this country without running into some Saxon bier or Roman pergola! 'Oh, sorry, Verus, just dropped in for a visit from the future . . .'

"But this time humanity had uncovered something far older—and more terrible. Imagine, if you will, the Earth as it was countless ages past. Men of science have pushed the age of the Earth far, far back into the shadows of Time, much further than our ancestors could even imagine. Now imagine in one of those far off chambers of Time, an age before the chatter of people or their ape-like forbears; an age before the twitter of birds or the howl of the uncouth beast of the forest; an age before *sound*. Those same men of science have told us that meteorites bombarded the infant Earth—who is to say what they carried? And whence? I have told you before of the Outer Bands that surround our planet. Perhaps one of these acrolites picked up Something on its passage through those Bands and deposited it in the ground that would one day become 'England's mountains green,' Something that thrived upon the unfathomable silences of Space itself. And there it lay, buried and re-buried by the ages until the repeated scraping of our rural swains uncovered it. No wonder even the birds couldn't live there.

"So much for the source of the thing. I had no proof, nothing material, that is. But I have learned to trust my feelings on such matters, and I have rarely been proven wrong. My continued existence is proof of their accuracy. And my theory fit what I had encountered. As for what to do about it, I secluded myself with my most esoteric books, especially with the papyri of the Egyptians. Those Egyptians knew a thing or two about the other worlds that border our own, I can tell you, and I sought their wisdom. Then, too, they were that much closer to the ancient Mysteries such as this one. Finally, after days locked away with my grim books, I felt I had found what I sought. It was deep within the Sag'yaa Manuscript, in a chapter dealing with the Songs of the Gods. The author had not given the thing a name, but his description could not be mistaken. I cleaned myself up enough to be presentable to the public and dashed off a telegram to an old friend of mine, Dr. Anis of the Egyptian Polytechnic College of Antiquities and Architecture in Alexandria, and called in a favour I had done him some years past. The return telegram stated that he would be glad to do me the return favour, but that the item I needed must be returned. I responded that it would be, and far away I could feel the wheels of my plan begin to turn.

"Next I must return to the silent garden. I would have avoided this if I could, but I could not. However, it did not mean that I should go unprotected. From amongst my chest of amulets I chose the K'noth amulet, whose protections are valued among those who must face aberrations of the senses—sight and sounds and the like. I had no illusions that it would protect me completely from What lurked beneath that garden, but hoped it would at least allow me to work there for a short time. I looped the amulet's chain over my head, and tucking the medallion into my shirt left for my next errand.

"Later that day I sent a note to Bartely telling him that I needed to return to his aunt's garden the following day. I would have gone then, but the day was far advanced and my own state was still less than optimal. Meanwhile I assembled all I would need on the morrow in a large portfolio; and at last, collapsed into bed.

"The following day I gathered up my books and portfolio and took a cab to the Bartely house. Bartely himself, alerted to my visit, answered my knock and led me inside. His Aunt Althea was seated in one of her parlours and nodded a greeting as I passed the door. But she did not rise, and I did not bid her approach. There was no need to involve her in this any more than necessary. Bartely and I could undertake the next step ourselves.

"We went back through the kitchen as on that day a couple weeks before. There I stopped him and set down my burdens. I opened the portfolio I had with me and withdrew a sheaf of Japanese rice-paper in sheets approximately two feet square. These I had treated at home with a mixture of ingredients—oil of jaguar, reduced essence of certain leaves from Java—the exact contents of which needn't concern you chaps. Suffice it to say that, applied to a sheet of paper, it renders it sensitive to some of the more vile emanations that can be encountered by the un-wary. It is the same basic theory as governs photographic plates, if you follow me. 'Psychographic plates,' as it were. I divided the sheets be-tween Bartely and myself, and we emerged into the garden.

"I still felt the PRESENCE—for who could not?—but its effect upon me was dulled, impotent, such was the effectiveness of the K'noth amulet. It was no more than a discomfort now, no more than one might feel from an excess of caffeine—a jitteriness, an exaggerated awareness of one's own skin. I felt as I am sure any one of you might have felt in that situation, and I assure you that I did not enjoy it! For me it was as if I had been given a strong anaesthetic; my sharpened senses were muted and only half aware. Bartely felt the PRESENCE too, bland man of business though he is. He faltered upon the edge of the garden and looked around him, frowning, as if someone had uttered something of-fensive.

"'Come, old man,' I said, clapping him on the shoulder. 'Aunt Al-thea is counting on us!' I instructed him to lay the rice-paper sheets in regular intervals upon the ground across the garden. I did the same, and at the end of ten tense but uneventful minutes we had thoroughly pa-pered the entire plot. Then, silently sending a prayer that it neither rain now blow, I led Bartely back into the house.

"There I explained that what we had just done would serve to define the extent of the horror in the garden, in order that we might know where best to attack it. Bartely was all for action immediately, to beard this unknown lion in its den and destroy it. But I counseled patience. We could do nothing until we knew the focus of the PRESENCE any-way. And even then I was still waiting upon my shipment from Dr. Anis.

"As luck would have it, both conditions were met the following day. I was just preparing to return to the Bartely house when my man came to tell me that a package had arrived for me. He looked less than pleased, and when I came to the front door I discovered why. A drayman, a splendid specimen of Cockney strength in dirty coveralls and boots, stood upon the doorstep. But he held his cap in his hand and politely asked where he should put 'that reekin' pot, Guv'nor.' I looked past him and saw my shipment from Dr. Anis on the man's dray—an enormous earthen jar, half-obscured by the wooden crate protecting it. And the man was right; even from my doorway I could smell the strange, exotic, just this side of noxious mix of spices it contained. I'm sure this, as much as the drayman's presence, had served to put my man in his sour temper. Reassuring him that yes, I had ordered this package and must deliver it to another address, I gathered up the paraphernalia of my peculiar trade and joined the drayman up on the seat of his conveyance. I gave him the address of Bartely's aunt's house; and if he at first harboured some doubt about conveying his cargo thither, it was nothing that could not be countered by the judicious application of a 'fiver.'

"So we set off, the prim streets of Chelsea echoing to the clomp-clomp of the dray's big horses. When we got to the Bartely house, I leapt down and helped the drayman lift the crated vessel down to the ground. It wouldn't do to pay the expense of shipping it all the way from Egypt, just to have it shatter upon a London pavement! Besides, more than mere money was at stake here. I had the powerful feeling that, were this horror not addressed, sooner rather than later—perhaps set free by no more than the scuff of a shoe—it would break free of its earthly bonds and we would be faced with much more than just a silent garden.

"Wilfred, the drayman, and I wrestled the crate up into the house and thence back into the garden. I was right about the power of the PRESENCE to affect even the most thick-fibred among us. Wilfred shivered after we had set down our burden and muttered something about 'bleedin' chills' before he stomped off on his way.

Alone in the garden, I surveyed my circumstances. It was one of those changeable days we get in May. The whole month is, of course, subject to the most extreme changes of character. Mother Earth is rousing herself after her winter's rest, neither fully awake nor asleep, and the weather reflects her moods. This day the clouds were piling up black to the north and I anticipated rain ere long. But the papers I had laid the day before were still dry and intact, for which I was thankful.

"And even the most cursory glance at them painted a shocking picture. Those sheets towards the outer edges of the garden were largely as I had left them, with a few streaks of brown on them as if they had been passed over a candle flame. But as the eye moved over the sheets towards the centre of the garden the streaks and discolourations increased both in frequency and contrast; a winding, tangled confusion of bifurcating branches; darkening from brown to burgundy to an angry purple, until those sheets at the middle of the garden were almost solid colour. Taken as a whole the image they presented reminded me of a tree seen from above; microscopic images of nerve ganglia; or one of those many-armed sea-baskets of the deep. Or an octopus. The arms or branches or tentacles of the Thing sprawled in all directions to grasp the whole of the garden. Here and there among them were bulges or polyps in the branches that reminded me disquietingly of seed-pods.

"I knew from this that I was not a second too early with my preparations. I dragged the crate across the garden to the epicenter of this network of horror, and even through the numbing protection of my amulet I could feel the awful PRESENCE pressing in upon me. Taking a pry-bar from my satchel, I attacked the crate. From out the splintered boards and a thick packing of straw I carefully withdrew the large, earthenware jar—much like an old Grecian amphora, if you see what I mean, but larger still. Its every surface was incised with hieroglyphs telling a story I feared to read. There was a wooden cap to it, sealed with black wax; and when I removed this, the full, overpowering reek of herbs gushed forth. It was immensely old and immensely heavy, and I was sweating freely by the time I had it positioned *upside down* upon the tainted earth at the centre of the garden. Making my task harder still was that I had to keep most of the herbs contained in the jar from spilling willy-nilly all over the garden. But it was a duty that I would not have imposed upon any other. The dangers were too great.

"That done, I retired to the house to 'catch my breath,' if you get me. I was in for an ordeal and no mistake, and I must needs gather my strengths. I sat upon the threshold of the kitchen door and gazed out, panting from my exertions. The garden glowed in new green in its utter silence. Above the leafing trees, the sky had gone an ominous purple—

a purple that recalled the stains on the inmost sheets of rice-paper. Even as I sat thus, the whole scene flickered, and thunder tumbled down the sky. The air was heavy with in-held energy.

"Once I felt revived, I picked up my satchel and strode to the middle of the garden without hesitation. 'If it were done when 'tis done, then 'twere well it were done quickly'—*Macbeth,* eh? I walked right to the middle of the web of tentacles by the amphora, knelt down, and opened my satchel. From it I withdrew the parts of my electric pentagram. The ground would not take chalk; but pushing aside my psychographic 'plates,' I drew a circle in the dirt with sprinkled marble-dust, ground from funerary monuments whose original occupants I dare not name. Within this I spread a pentagram; and upon this I assembled my electric pentagram. All the time I was thus employed the terrible silence of the garden crowded upon my eardrums. I strained to listen until it *hurt,* but even the sounds of my own movements sounded tiny and far away. Of the sounds of living things there were none. The air was hot and pregnant with moisture and a strong smell of rain. A dropper-full or water would have set it off.

"Only the thunder came through the overpowering quiet, and this more and more frequently. A sense of urgency invested my actions. I connected the galvanic battery to my electric pentangle, stationed myself in the middle of its calming blue glare, and immediately felt better. I was not quite at the very centre—the *epicentre*—of the web of evil—that is, where I had positioned the ancient urn; but I was near enough that I could be in extreme danger if anything went awry. It did not reassure me to think, either, that what I feared lurked *below* me; for with as much faith as I put in my 'defences,' as it were, I knew that they extended in a horizontal plane and not a *vertical* one. You will recall, I have no doubt, that nasty episode of the Hog, when the gaping pit opened up *within* the precincts of my 'defences.'

"But fortune favours the bold, wot? Satisfied that I had done all that I might, I reached once more into my satchel and drew forth a tuning fork. But not one of your tuning forks of usual design, mind. This fork had *three* tines versus the usual two, and was as long as my forearm. Incised upon its tines were symbols of great potency, incantations in the lost language of Lomar, chosen as much for the rhythm and music of their syllables as for the inherent power of their message. This curious instrument I struck upon my knee, producing a keening vibration in three harmonised tones that penetrated both the silence of the place and my amulet-borne protection. If I tell you the chord pulsing out from that tuning-fork suggested at the same time the singing of angels and the cry of sea-birds, I will not be unfaithful to the *timbre* of the thing. Do you get me?

"While the fork still hummed in my hand, I reached over my 'defences' to the rim of the inverted amphora; lifted it up, and struck the tuning-fork into the ground beneath it by its handle. Then I lowered the jar back over it—and waited.

"To be perfectly honest with you chaps, I did not really know what to expect. When dealing with the Outer Monstrosities one must maintain a guarded mind—yet an open one, too. For there is often no telling what form these Monstrosities may take, and one must be flexible enough to meet them in all their infinite variety. But I was guided, as I often am, by the Sigsand Manuscript. I knew at least that this PRESENCE manifested itself in a crushing silence, and the Manuscript has this to say about such things:

"'As certain Metalls do flock towards the Magnet, so too doth certain of the Outer Things flock unto their opposite Entity. Like calls unto Unlike in this Manner; for the Unholy Stink will be drawn by the sweetest Perfume, and the Foulest Darknesse unto the Purest Light. So, too, will the most Awfull Quiet, such as may be found amongst the wand'ring Bodies of Heaven, be drawn towards divers Noyses and Tones, seeking to consume them in the Terryble Emptiness of their Essence.'

"And so I waited. But I did not have to wait long. The very ground beneath me began to hum, just as the tuning-fork had before; and as I squatted thus, hands and knees pressed to the dirt, the humming grew to a vibration, the vibration to a quiver, the quiver to a shaking. You may glean some idea of what I felt if you have ever stood in a cellar room and felt the approach of one of London's subterrene trains through the walls. In fact, several of the Bartclys' neighbours were later heard to complain of 'Tube rumblings' felt that day—this regardless of the fact that no Underground has yet reached that corner of the metrop'!"

Carnacki paused here to chuckle and shake his head. He also glanced at his forgotten pipe, now cold, and refilled it from the tobacco pouch kept ever handy on his side-table. When he had it filled and lit he took a long, luxurious drag upon it. He expelled an equally languorous cloud of smoke into the still air of the room, and looked at us. And I recoiled. As many times as we had convened to hear Carnacki's outlandish tales, as many times as he had cheated death and his "Outer Monstrosities," yet had I never seen his eyes look so grave. It was as if dark clouds had gathered behind them.

"Now," he continued, "now I truly began to feel the dread PRESENCE. The shaking beneath me settled into a sub-audible *moan* that numbed me throughthrough the palms of my hands, through my pantslegs—anywhere that I touched that cursed ground. I also had the curious but undeniable feeling that the *Earth itself* was being numbed—do I make myself clear? It was as if the unnoticed but constant buzz of every molecule of Creation were being stilled. I was once speaking to a musician who played cornet in a dance-hall orchestra, and following one of their performances I complained to him that I hadn't heard his playing. He responded that, no, perhaps I had not, 'but you would have noticed if I hadn't been playing.' It was the same now in that silent garden, under those purple, beetling skies: the very music of Creation was being snuffed out. I reached a tentative hand to the amphora, and was reassured to feel it still vibrating from the tuning-fork beneath it. Looking around the garden I noticed the queerest *change* come over everything. How can I put it? From the roots up, all the plants, trees, rocks, and brick walls, even, were *fading slightly*. It wasn't that they were becoming transparent, but more that their colours were becoming dull and less vibrant. Men of science tell us that all is energy, energy that reaches us through the senses in waves. I felt that I was witnessing the cessation of these waves, and it made my heart cold.

"All this time I had regarded these phenomena as though through a filtre, the filtre of the K'noth amulet around my neck. If I have a failing (and the gods know there must be more than one!), it is my curiosity; and this time, as with the cat, it nearly cost me my very life. Here all about me were the signs of this terrible PRESENCE—terrible, yes, but awesome, too, in its power and unknown provenance. And here I sat like a spectator to it rather than a participant in its destruction. I could stand it no more—I reached up and pulled the loop of the amulet's chain over my head.

"Not Achilles himself and his famous heel suffered more than I at the dropping of that protection. Immediately the ancient *Silence* flooded into my head and body and soul. My skin went dead-numb; thick fingers of Silence pulsed through my ears into the sides of my head and into the very hemispheres of my cerebrum, blotting out thought and memory. I clapped my hands to my head and screamed, screamed with all my heart—but not a whisper could I hear. You know how it is when you cover your ears and say something? Even in the faintest breath of a voice, you can always hear yourself. Well, not in this hellish, enveloping cloud of Silence. It flowed in rushing streams through my brain, eradicating everything in its path. I could feel all my memories, all my life, all my *self,* being drowned out in that murdering Quiet. I fell to my side, writhing on the ground, screaming my silent scream. All consciousness was shrinking to a point—here, now, me. In panic I sought to push the crushing, smothering Silence out, to reclaim my silenced mind. But at best I could only keep it at bay, a strenuous status quo that took every ounce of my strength, concentration, and experience. And ever I felt that Silence pressing upon the outer walls of my reduced consciousness. More than anything, some primitive instinct of self-preservation must have arisen within me to combat that PRESENCE, for certainly I was no longer capable of more than the simplest effort. Blindly I grasped for my amulet, for the Silence had half numbed my eyes, making my vision milky. But all my questing fingers felt was the stilly earth. I felt the great sadness of total loss overwhelm me.

"And then, miracle of miracles, the Silence began to recede. No earthly tide ever withdrew from sandy shores with more slowness—but it *did* recede. I opened my eyes to renewed sight. Not five inches from my outstretched hand lay the amulet on its chain. I grabbed it up and yanked it over my head with enough force to cut my ear. But no time for such trifles now. My mind was clearing, the lights coming on again in the many chambers of my brain. The thick fingers of Silence slipped out of them, palpably weakened, reluctantly but unmistakably sliding out of my head like some tribe of slimy slugs. I sat up. My head cleared, my hearing opened. Feeling returned to my limbs with the 'pins and needles' of returning circulation. Now the nature of the ground altered, too. Once again it felt whole, *alive,* if you get me. The growths of the garden, too, were flushing with renewed colour. The dullness flowed back out through the trunks and stones, roots, dirt. Gone. I blinked away tears of pain and stumbled to my feet. In the spaces between my psychographic 'plates' of paper, I could see the dullness of the Silence shrinking, its edges drawing inwards towards the centre.

"And at that centre stood my Egyptian urn. Its countless hieroglyphs were glowing; and as I stared open-mouthed at it, I realised that they were *singing,* too. A thread of tiny voices rose in ineffably sweet tones; a choir of more than earthly beauty, weaving and soaring through each other, higher and higher. Against this magical chorus the Silence withered, cringed, shrank. It was pulling in faster now, tightly around the base of the urn, drawn in by the vibrations of my wondrous tuning-fork. It was flowing in like water around a drain—can you conceive it? I could not see this, and yet I *did.* Perhaps it was with my Inner Eye— or just a visual manifestation of an aural experience. I don't know. All I know is that the PRESENCE and its awful Silence were being sucked into that ancient jar, and I rejoiced at it. At last, as the singing hieroglyphs attained a ringing, triumphant chord of more than perfect, almost transcendent harmony, the last of the Silence disappeared under the earthen lip of the amphora—and was gone. The choir ceased—and a peal of thunder pounded the air directly above me like a great gun. The tension of the day had reached its breaking-point, and the rain poured down in a sweet, sweet flood. I dropped to my knees, spread my arms and turned my grateful face up towards the heavens. The rain washed the last vile traces of the PRESENCE from me and from the garden.

"Well, after a few minutes of this I began to get chilled. I picked myself up and staggered to the Bartelys' house. The PRESENCE was gone—even Wilfred the drayman could have told you that now. The quiet in the little yard was natural now, the small quiet of out of the way places and of unhurried hours of contemplation. And even as I pulled myself up the back steps of the house the first trills of bird-song sweetened the rainy air. I smiled to think of the querulous note in that song, as if the little bird were complaining of the rain that had cleansed its home.

"The rest is quickly told. Aunt Althea Bartely was completely scandalised by this grown man too dim-witted to have come in out of the rain, and bustled me into a blanket and easy-chair and plied me with hot tea and scones.

"'Catch your death out there,' she fussed as I sipped my tea. If only she knew . . . ! But she never shall; and besides you fellows the mass of Britons will never know how close they came to obliteration. I sent a note to the shipping company to retrieve the Egyptian urn; and when we set it upright again, a curious thing came to light. All the herbs that had filled the urn were crisp and sere, burned as if by a thousand autumns. They were little more than ashes as they spilled out onto the ground. Such was the power of that PRESENCE, even within the confines of that ancient urn.

"The spot upon which the urn had sat—the very centre of the infestation—never grew another blade of grass, nor do I expect it ever to. Aunt Althea, thrilled to have her birds again, promptly set a bird-bath to cover the bare spot; and I trust that the cheering nonsense of robins and wrens and sparrows will sanctify the spot more effectively than any thaumaturgy of mine."

Carnacki smiled and rose. "And out you go, my own little birds!" he said, shooing us along. And we severally went out into the cool London night, and to our homes.

Niddy-Noddy

The woods rose tall and the pond lay still, and the road crawled on between them. *Like betwixt Scylla and Charybdis,* thought Abra'm Symmes as he walked the road. He was no scholar, but he would have had to have been a far more lubberly sailor than he was not to know about the ocean-going adventures of that great mariner, Odysseus. For Symmes—a sailor without a ship—the analogy was especially poignant. All his adventures these days were landlocked; and the road was long and lonely that would lead him back to his Mother Ocean.

Just now Abra'm's lookout was for shelter. There was still an hour of light left on this October evening, but he did not care to be caught in the open on a landsman's night. This was Massachusetts in the cold, gray dawn of the eighteenth century, and no one doubted that the Devil and his train rode free over the countryside in the dark.

Upon the pond leaves of yellow, bronze and crimson hung above deep, dark reflections of the trees—spots of color dropped on a black mirror. Overhead these same trees thrashed their limbs in the cold autumn wind like the legs of some gigantic insect, scrabbling to right itself. *I am losing even that little water,* Abra'm thought as the road carried him leftward and away from the pond and into the woods. Soon the stilly waters were lost his sight; the wind did not even stir the dead leaves upon them.

As Abra'm walked on he felt the restless woods close in upon him. He sometimes felt this stricture, almost a panic, so far from the ocean. *Oh, for the vast blue expanses of sea and sky!* he thought, eyeing the crowding trees. *For a clean wind to fill the sails and sweep away the filth of living.* Yet he was not so hidebound as to be blind to the charms of the land when he found them. The road, after testing a few shallow dales, climbed to a peak. At the peak the granite that underlay the hill tore free of the loam and rose, five fathoms of stern, gray granite against the sky. Abra'm paused in its presence and admired it. On the descent beyond, too, he breathed in with delight deep draughts of the forest air. It was not yet cold enough to lock away scents, and he savored the ancient spice of the fallen leaves; the rich incense of earthy decay; the sharp cleanness of pine.

And fast upon them, the reek of corruption. *Something dead,* he thought, wrinkling his nose and looking around him, *and recent dead.* His affection for the land evaporated. Upon the ocean when something died (and how many of his shipmates had he helped sew up in their hammocks and tip over the gunwales?), the sea folded it to its bosom, and it was gone. Here on the land, though, the dead lingered and rotted and stank. Abra'm pulled his collar up about his ears, clamped his cocked hat more firmly upon his head, and strode more quickly to escape the stench. Somewhere something cried out in a long, hollow wail that cracked on its last note. It soared up through the incessant roar of the wind and died away again.

In another couple of minutes he was rewarded with the pale yellow of open land beyond the tree trunks ahead of him. He came out into a field of half-shorn cornstalks. Many still stood or leaned or hunched over the earth like a beaten army, too weak to leave the field of battle. In the wind the cornstalks' sere leaves rattled like pennants of the dead. The field looked not so much harvested as thrashed into submission. Beyond this grew fields of unmown grass, long and dun in the failing light, and hissing in the wind. The woods had pulled away but hunched on every horizon, dark and forbidding and unknowable.

Long before he reached the next belt of woods Abra'm came upon a house. It squatted to the right of the road, and he did not even recognize it as a house until he was almost upon it. It was low, a story and a half, little more than a cottage clapped around a thunderous great central chimney, and it lurked in blacker darkness amongst its weeds. The inner shutters were all pulled to. As he got closer to it he could see gaps in the clapboards through which light leaked, and dark patches on the roof where shingles had been blown away and not been replaced. The door, when he reached it, sat its frame slightly askew; and the stone doorstep looked as if it had been pried up from a field by a passing plough. The house was, in a word, mean.

But shelter it was, and Abra'm approached it up a dirt path almost invisible between grass and small trees let go wild, and rapped upon the door.

He waited. In the pauses of the wind he thought he could hear a low, rhythmic singing from within. Light grew upon his cheek, and he turned to see the inner shutters of the right-hand window cracked open. He was being observed. He could almost feel the warmth of the yellow candlelight—and someone's curious gaze—upon his face.

The shutter snapped closed and there was a rattling from the other side of the door. Abruptly it was yanked open—although only a couple inches.

"What do you want?"

Abra'm was confronted with a visage so wild that he took a step back. Through the opening of the doorway glared a man slightly taller than Abra'm's tall frame, with a wilderness of wiry gray hair that had only partially been captured by a string in back. From within this tangle the man's eyes, of some indeterminate color, stared out from under thick black brows. The brows were pinched together in such a fierce and determined manner as to look permanently so. *I wager I could stand a shilling up in one of those wrinkles,* Abra'm thought. From the eyes the face dwindled away in less impressive features. A long, pointed nose, lipless mouth, and doughty ball of a chin, looking as if it had been stuck on as an afterthought to differentiate wrinkled cheeks from wrinkled neck, completed the portrait. Below that the figure was clad in a dingy white blouse that hung off his spare frame; knee-breeches, stockings, and shoes.

But it was the eyes that arrested Abra'm. They looked past him rather than at him, and Abra'm wondered whether they ever blinked. He collected himself and doffed his tricorn.

"Your pardon," he said in as forthrightly a manner as he could manage. "I merely beg shelter for the night."

The stare remained.

"I can pay you," Abra'm added hopefully. The wind gusted and tossed his own hair about his face. Borne upon it was the same distant howl he had heard in the woods. Abra'm could scarce credit it, but the other man's brows tightened a smidgeon more.

"Best get out of the cold, then," the man said suddenly, as if chiding Abra'm for being abroad, and swung wide the door.

Abra'm stepped in and the other shut the door with a scrape and a thud behind him. The interior, though as mean as the exterior, was a welcome surprise. The place smelled of dry-rot and old meals, but was not unhealthy. Neglect rather than barbarism reigned here. A fire in the fireplace's great, sooty maw dominated the scene, and sent flickering light and shadow over all the furnishings. Here and there the fire was augmented by candles; but these were of poor quality and their flames jerked and danced in sickly rhythms. A table, little more than two planks nailed to kindling legs, stood close at hand. A straight-backed chair, blackened with age and looking as if it had been salvaged from a wealthier man's trash-heap, stood at the table's side. For all the chair's misplaced grandeur, Abra'm noticed that one of the legs was bound with rag, and that a couple of its upright supports had disappeared. A knife and a pile of shavings and sticks lay upon the table opposite the chair— evidently the late chore of the master of the house. Boxes and bundles crowded the corners of the room. A hoe, startled at its own incongruity, stood against the wall.

The only other chair in evidence was pulled close to the hearth's right hand, and it was occupied. A woman as wild-looking as her mate sat there, bone and sinew lost in the stormy faded folds of her dress, rocking back and forth in her seat. The chair was not a rocking-chair. It was, however, the better made if not the more imperial of the two chairs. Mistress had a claim upon some respect, Abra'm mused. He might have used the word "affection," but that emotion would have been alien to his host's hard features.

The woman worked as she rocked. In her left hand was a strange device, an I-shaped assembly of wooden rods constructed such that the end-pieces stuck out at right angles to each other. The woman twisted and swooped it through the air before her in a weird motion, gathering to it the yarn she pulled from a basked at her right side. Abra'm recognized the device as a "niddy-noddy." It was the alternative for households too poor to afford a spinning-wheel. This niddy-noddy was already freighted with a graceful figure-eight of yarn. The yarn was gray.

As she performed her wizard motions before the fire, the woman hummed or sang:

"Mm hm-hmm,

Mmm hm-hm hmm.”

Abra’m recognized this as the low singing or chanting he had heard from without. He turned and found his host still staring at him.

“I am in your debt, friend,” Abra’m said. “As I said, I can pay you.”

“No debt of mine, neither, friend,” the other said. “And I’ll take none of Caesar’s coin.” He looked Abra’m over with his unblinking stare. “Are ye good with them hands?”

“Aye,” Abra’m said, looking at his hands as if to make sure he still had them. “I’ve wielded fid, marlinspike. and hatchet with ’em in my time.”

The other nodded—a quick jerk of his leonine head—and motioned Abra’m toward the table. Then he walked to the fireplace and took an earthen bowl from the mantle. He also took down a dipper from where it hung on the mantle’s edge, dipped it into an iron pot suspended above the fire, and ladled steaming broth from it into the bowl.

“Mmm hm-hm hmm,” hummed the woman. “Two heads, hm-hm hmm.”

Abra’m flinched when the broth splashed onto the man’s hand, but the man seemed not to notice. He set the bowl on the table with a dull *thunk* and produced a spoon from a tangle of tools at the table’s other end. Then he turned to the shadow-haunted corners of the room and pulled a long-legged stool out as if by magic. This he clattered down by Abra’m.

“Sit.”

The hospitality was crude but sufficient. Abra’m sat and set to. The broth, little more than water, occasional disks of carrot, gelatinous-looking potato, and some less recognizable plants, was plain but good. Abra’m scooped it up with relish—his walk in the cold has sharpened his appetite.

“Meat’s scarce,” the host interjected. “Expect some soon.”

Abra’m nodded and spooned more soup into his mouth. The host seated himself upon the rickety throne opposite him.

“Whence came you?”

“To west’ard.” Abra’m waved his spoon the way he had come.

“’Cross Mount Misery, then.” It was a statement, and the host pronounced the word *mizzry*.

"Curious name for so humble an eminence," Abra'm ruminated aloud, returning to his soup.

"Comes from that damned fool Israel Coffin, losing his cow up there. You could hear it bawling for weeks afterward."

"Yes, I heard it."

"No, you didn't."

Abra'm looked up; the other's gaze still held somewhere two inches above and several miles beyond Abra'm's head.

"That was nine year ago," added the host. "Cow's long gone."

"Niddy-noddy,
"Two heads an' one body."

The wind shook the house like someone trying to awaken a sleeper.

Abra'm looked at the woman in her faded dress. The hand and its device continued to weave the air, dipping, turning, dipping. For something to say, Abra'm said, "You keep cattle? I saw none without."

"No," said the host. "Beasts eat more'n they're worth. I work this land."

Abra'm considered this, remembering the battered cornfield and grass gone to seed; but said nothing.

"Niddy-noddy,
Hm-hm hm hmm."

The host rose (he seemed to do everything abruptly, as if remembering his next move at the last moment) and turned again to the shadows. When he turned back he held another stool, the legs of which were broken.

"Fix this," he said, dropping the stool on the table by Abra'm's bowl. "When you're finished, there's a bed in the attic."

Abra'm quit his greatcoat (it was, despite the wind keening through the chinks in the wall, too warm) and took his clasp-knife from the pouch he carried. He downed another spoonful of soup, pushed the bowl aside, and picked up the ruined stool.

It was far stouter than what Abra'm sat upon, being made from a disk of solid tree-trunk and three thick, oaken legs. Yet the legs had been snapped off near the seat. *Must've been one well-ballasted mate what sat here,*

Abra'm thought, and began to dig out the stumps of the stool's legs with his knife. His host sat back down opposite him and stared into the faraway.

"Late," he muttered. "Gettin' late."

The knifepoint punched into the splintered wood and turned. Bits and chunks of it fell into Abra'm's lap, from which he flicked them toward the snapping fire.

> "Hmm hm-hm hmm
> Hmm hm-hm body."

The niddy-noddy wove the air; its shadows snaked across the woman's face. As Abra'm glanced at her he realized that she wore the same stare as her husband, her eyes glaring out like the twin heads of leaden spikes from the same tangle of gray hair. They seemed to look into worlds where Abra'm had no business. He turned back to his chore.

From the pile of shavings on the table the host picked up a stick and a knife of his own. With a look of intense concentration, he leaned forward and began whittling the stick. Abra'm wondered why he was doing that while Abra'm repaired the man's own stool. It seemed a pointless industry.

"Always something to do," the man said, staring and staring at his knife slashing through the wood. Blond curls of it fell onto the hearth.

> "Niddy-noddy,
> Hmm hm hm-hm hmm."

"Quiet, woman!" The host shot to his feet, scattering splinters. "Like to drive a man to the Devil with all your noise."

The woman did not even look up. In a softer voice she continued:

> "Hm hm-hm hmmm,
> Two heads, hm-hm hmm."

Abra'm's host sat back down and picked resumed his whittling. Abra'm noticed that the woman's coil of yarn was almost complete. He again took up one of the broken stool legs. The sockets the legs fit into were clear now and he set the disk-seat onto the floor at his side. With care he began paring the leg's end to fit one of the sockets. At one side of him gloomed the man; at the other, the woman. He had the absurd image of himself at the middle of some bizarre family group, and it unsettled him. He felt as if he were usurping someone else's place.

". . . knows how long it takes to do a thing," the man grumbled.

"Pardon?" Abra'm looked at him.

"Said, 'Who knows how long it takes to do a thing?'" The wide stare rose to meet Abra'm's gaze. "Should have been back ages ago."

"Niddy-noddy . . ."

Abra'm pushed the leg into one of the holes in the seat and thumped it home with the ball of his palm. The leg fit snugly—it didn't wiggle at all when Abra'm tried it.

"'Tisn't *that* far." The host's knife slashed through the stick he was whittling. When he had reduced that one to shavings he took another one from the pile on the table. Without a pause he cut into the new piece, and his knife hissed *sshuk, sshuk* through the wood.

". . . two heads and one body."

Outside the wind rose and galloped over the roof. The gaps in the walls sang in soprano harmony to it, reminding Abra'm of the lost animal sound he had heard in the woods. The host suddenly tossed his knife and stick to the table, levered himself to his feet and stalked to one of the windows.

> "Hmm hm-hm hmm,
> Hmm hm-hm hm-hm."

With a final twist the woman completed her spinning. The hand with the wool-heavy niddy-noddy dropped to her lap and she stared into the fire with a heavy resignation.

At the window, the host unlatched the shutter and prised it open a crack. Abra'm had the strange notion that a deep blue light—that the darkness itself—shone in upon the host's avid face. His stare had at last become focused upon something.

"No," the host said, "Won't be long now. Think I see him coming."

The Music of Your Life

It looked like the end of the storm, but it wasn't. An unexperienced observer—someone "from away," as they say—would say it was the eye of the storm, but it wasn't that, either. This wasn't that major a storm to have an eye, just one of your November nor'easters, buzz-sawing its way up the coast. This dry-stretch was a gap between bands of rain, nothing more, just enough time for Emery to take a quick walk. All day he had hidden away in his study, reading local history, as the rain pattered and pelted and slashed at the windows, and now that the rain had stopped he'd be damned if he didn't have his daily stroll on the beach. Why, the sun was even trying to come out now. A furnace glow spread from just over the land to westward (Indian Point that was) and across the underside of the storm's gray and tumorous belly: fiery orange to tangerine, goldenrod to butter, thence back to gray. Emery stopped by the edge of Second Creek to admire Indian Point's treeline cut sharp and black against the dying glow until the renewed rain splashed his face. He turned back toward home.

His eyes must have been dazzled by the sunset (yes, that must have been it), because he didn't even see the rock until his toe hit it. He lurched forward and performed a brief, awkward, stuttering dance upon the sand to balance himself (thank God no one was around to see it, and thank God he hadn't broken anything either, because, well, no one was around). Then he turned to confront whatever it was that had tripped him. It was black and angled like a small pyramid, and it was a rock, wasn't it? No. Shielding his face against the rain and the spray from the surf exploding nearby, Emery bent over to look more closely at the thing. Nature did not usually create edges so neat and square, he thought. At least not out of plastic. He pushed his fingers down into the cold, damp sand on either side of the object and began working it back and forth. Rain dashed teasing under his collar; the ocean growled. He pushed his fingers deeper into the sand and found the object's bottom edge, just as square and slippery as its upper edge. Emery squatted down and, bracing his right foot in front of him, pulled at the thing. The sand gave it up reluctantly, with a sucking, retching sound. It came free—a heavy, black, rectangular box, maybe ten inches by six by eight. He turned it over. Rain washed sand from its gleaming face. It was as black and slick as a whale's skin. Emery nearly dropped it back into its quondam grave (already filling with water from ground seepage) before he had turned it completely over in his hands. It wasn't all oily plastic. The back was sodden, rotted cardboard, pierced with round, regular machined holes. Another side (the bottom?) was flatter and had round stubs for legs at each corner; and the last side featured a pair of knobs and, when he dug the sand from between three decorative chrome strips, the circular mesh of a speaker.

It was a radio.

Emery marveled at it, turning it over and over in his hands. Where had it come from? How long had it been there? Emery knew his history—if nothing else, retired professor or no, he knew that—and he knew all about the enormous "summer cottages" that the rich had once built all along this section of Rhode Island coastline. A succession of hurricanes, beginning with "the big one" in 1938 and proceeding through Diane and Carol in the '50s and culminating with Gloria, Bob, and Irene, had erased those grand homes from the earth. One sometimes came upon shards of crockery or pipes jutting from the sand, or clumps of bricks still adhering to each other as if to the long-gone wall they were once part of, emerging from the beach like ancient reefs called forth by the storms. Was this another relic of that ruined age of luxury? Had its original owners (for Emery already thought of the radio as his) listened to the forecast on this very device, the day the winds came to devour their house?

Spray, salt, and chill dashed into Emery's face, and he blinked as if waking up. Time to go. The rain was back in force and the tide was coming in. In fifteen minutes the spot upon which he stood would be under water.

Emery tucked the radio under his arm and straightened up. He began to walk back toward the dunes, toward the pond and his cozy house. But three steps on he was brought up short with a jolt. Looking back he saw a long, thin, red-and-black-striped tentacle stretching from the sand to the back of the radio. A closer look showed it was an electrical cord, as miraculously intact as the radio itself. Emery stooped again and carefully pulled at the cord. It ripped open a jagged scar in the sand as it came up, ending with a sudden spray of sand as the plug popped free.

Emery walked through the gap in the dunes beside Second Creek. Its rain-deranged waters rushed furious to the sea. Then behind the dunes to the left, and up the pond's muddy edge to the snug home of Emery Brooks, M.A., Ph.D., etc. He kept as close to the dry land as the thick breaks of phragmites would allow; Quicksand Pond had not been named on a whim, and local lore was replete with tales of those lost in the damp sands. Local legend also said that such nights as this called the drowned dead from their clammy graves to rise and sing in the storm. Comforting thought, Emery mused. The wind tore the waters of the big pond into foamy tatters and hurled them seaward.

Once inside Emery shed coat, boots, and hat, and pushed his feet into his fur-lined slippers. Cozy already. Put the pot on to boil for tea, and the scene was almost complete. Emery carried the radio into his study while waiting for the water to boil, and, clearing a space among the books and papers, set the radio down on his desk. In the pool of light from the desk-lamp he examined the radio more closely. Remarkably intact—a few crazed cracks in the black Bakelite cover, but nothing serious. Emery sat and began wiping the remaining sand and wet off the box with a handkerchief. A name, written in the long, stylized chrome font he thought of as "Refrigerator Bold," emerged across the radio's lower edge—*Chama*. Never heard of it. He'd have to call Joe to ask about it. Joe would know. Then he turned the radio over and removed the cardboard backing. It was little more than pulp anyway; it folded and melted around his fingers as he prized it out and dropped with a sodden *plop* into the wastebasket. Within the dark interior of the radio was mystery—more sand and the labyrinth of wires that pulled voices out of the air. Now he'd really have to call Joe. Emery knew history; his brother knew machines.

But Emery could at least clear the thing out before calling his brother. Then he might have something concrete to tell him. Emery opened his desk's center drawer and took out a letter-opener. He hoped the point wouldn't damage any of the old electronics. Carefully he began digging sand out of the radio's back. It fell in damp clumps and grains on the blotter. There was seaweed as well, twisted and dry and crackling, and an odd shell or two. Emery had dug out all he could when he remembered watching his brother work on a similar radio once. He turned the box over, bottom up. Sure enough, the heads of a pair of screws stared dully at him from out the black plastic. Another reach into the drawer and a screwdriver appeared. *Let's hope they're not rusted solid,* Emery thought. He set the screwdriver's flat end into the slot of one screw and twisted. A little resistance and some grinding, and it came loose. Emery unscrewed it completely, set it aside, undid the other as well, and set that aside in the same place. The radio still wouldn't come apart. Then Emery remembered the tuning-knobs on the front of the thing. A quick pry from the screwdriver, the knobs fell away, and the whole guts of the radio now slid smoothly out of its shell. As he pulled the mechanism clear of the case, more sand pattered down. For all that, though, the inside was pretty clean. He twisted his handkerchief into a point and began nosing out the intimate spaces between the wires and tubes.

And wedged between two metal plates, a bone. Age and salt-water had stained it a pale brown, and it was as out of place as it was possible to imagine; but it was definitely a bone. Animal? Human? He was no biologist, but years of beachcombing had taught him the airy look of fish-bone and bird-bones, and this was neither. A mammal's bone, he guessed, a digit from a paw or finger. The old Atlantic was the grave of multitudes; there was no guessing where the thing came from.

A scream rose into the stillness of the house. Emery started; then, smiling at his own nervousness, he rose to shut off the teapot's banshee wail. He poured himself a cup over a bag of Earl Grey and a tot of whiskey, and brought the heady-smelling brew back into his study.

Eviscerated—the word came to him as he beheld anew the dismantled radio lying on his desk. It lay like a shelled creature of the deep, a horse-shoe crab or something, smooth exterior and baroque tangle of hidden limbs and organs within. He'd finish clearing out all the sand and sea-weed—and that odd bone, too—and then give Joe a call. Who knows? Maybe he could even get the thing working again.

Emery sat back down and continued his cleaning. Rain played a staccato against the window and he looked up to see the world disappearing into the deep indigo of twilight. Beyond the fringe of lawn, Quicksand

Pond tossed restless in its muddy bed. A couple lights from windows across the pond, the angled white shape of a lone seagull running down the wind added to the loneliness of the scene, and with a shiver Emery drew the curtains across it. He loved the view in the daytime, but at night he felt like a specimen on display in his lighted cage. The night blinded you to who or what might be looking in.

Back to the radio. He took a sip of his toddy and stared at the thing. He had cleaned most of the sand from it, but that only renewed the mystery. There were tubes, probably long blown, dark brown wires and magnets and coils and contacts . . . and that damned bone. He picked up the letter-opener, and inserting the tip under the bone, tried to pry it from its metal bed. No good—it would not be dislodged. Whoever or whatever had jammed it in there had done a good job. It fit neatly into the space between two metal contacts as if it were meant to be there. Emery dared not put too much force into it for fear of breaking the radio. Time to call Joe.

He picked up his cell phone from the desk and touched the speed-dial number for his brother. While he listened to the dial tone, he looked over the radio once again for any detail that might be important. There was a logic to it, he knew: electricity ran in a circuit, and did things along the way. Joe had explained it to him a dozen times, but it still baffled him. It was a physical version of that cardinal rule of history, "Cause leads to Effect," but for the life of him he couldn't—

"Hello?"

"Hi, Joe? It's your brother, Emery. How're things in Maine?"

"Hey, Em. Cold 'n' snowy. How about scenic Rhode Island?"

"Cold and wet, just what you'd expect. We had snow but it's all long gone. A real blinder of a storm tonight, though. The Pond's up on its hind legs."

"No doubt. Remember that time we walked all the way around the pond?"

"Of course. And that abandoned shack? Too creepy."

"Yeah. So what's happening in Pocasset?"

"Well, I found a radio—"

"Oh, cool! At the flea market?"

Emery smiled at the memory. It was one of those touch-points that linked the brothers so closely: Emery and his younger brother had spent many a happy Sunday pawing through the junk at the flea market in nearby Tiverton.

"No, actually I found it on the beach—*in* the beach, to be exact."

"No way. It must be fried!"

"I'm not sure, Joe. It looks pretty intact to me."

"Well, how old is it? What's the brand?"

"It's a"—Emery clamped the phone between ear and shoulder while he turned the radio's case over—"it's a Chama."

"Yama? Like Yamaha?"

"No. Chama—C-H-A-M-A. Ring a bell?"

"No, that's a new one on me. Fada, Philco, RCA, sure, but Chama? Does it have tubes?"

"Yes, two of them."

"Then it's probably pre-1960."

"Older'n that, I'd say, judging from the design. I'd put it at the '30s."

"Fire it up—see if it works."

Emery picked up the radio's cord and leaned down to push the rusted prongs into the wall outlet behind his desk. When he sat back up he could see the vacuum-tubes beginning to glow a strange shade of green. It reminded him of the color of fresh kelp on the beach, saturated and almost too bright.

"It's on," he said.

"Wow. Now, how about the workings? Which way does the current run?"

Emery laughed. "That's why I called *you,* brother! I'm at sea. It's just all wires and gizmos to me. Oh, and a bone."

Static crackled through the phone.

". . . tone?" came Joe's voice between gasps of static.

Emery said, "No, *bone,* not tone. It's a bone, and it's wedged between two small plates of metal."

"That . . . right. Pretty . . . up, if you ask . . ."

Damn the phone. Hoping to regain the signal, Emery stood up and walked across the room.

"Joe?" he said. "You're breaking up. You know how crummy the phone signals are down here."

"Yeah, a pain in the ne . . . 'bout that bone?"

"Well, it's—"

And the phone went dead in his hand. No Joe, no static, nothing. Emery held it in front of him and stared at the screen—JOE CALL ENDED.

"Blast," he muttered. He tried calling his brother back, but the signal cut out before it went through. In disgust, he threw the phone onto the couch and stalked back to his desk. The radio's tubes were now slowly pulsing with green light. At its brightest it was hard to look at. And there was the noise. Static, or was it the rain on the roof? Emery took the black housing and placed it back over the radio's working, tapping the tuning-knobs back onto their spindles. He sat before the radio and listed to the static, swelling and fading just as the light of the tubes had done, but getting steadily louder as if rising from a depth. After a minute the sound leveled out into a low, steady buzz. He turned the volume knob up and twisted the tuning-knob to the right. That was when he noticed that there was no dial to the radio. *How was one to find a station?* he thought.

"'Don't touch that dial,'" Emery quoted from some long-forgotten program of his youth, and turned the tuning-knob anyway onward on its journey through the electrical waves. Horns rose golden and happy out of the static. After three notes Emery recognized "In the Mood," by Glen Miller. *Wasn't WALE somewhere in the 90s?* he thought. "The Music of Your Life," twenty-four hours a day from downtown New Bedford. His parents had listened to it in the car when Emery and Joe were teenagers. Nice to know something had survived on the air that long.

Then he remembered: "The Music of Your Life" had been off the air for years. A revival? An announcer came on: "You're listening to the Music o—" Then static flooded over that, too, just as Emery was thinking that the voice sounded a lot like the old announcer. What was his name? Dead these thirty years, at least.

He tuned the knob slowly, leaning close to the speaker to catch the faintest signal. On through the crackling silences, the lonely wastes of empty air . . . The hum rose to a growl, and Emery stopped the knob. Nothing—just more static. A little further on and a man's voice foundered out of the noise:

". . . Kavaju. Repeat after me: Kavaju."

"Kavaju," Emery said without thinking.

"Iyento ch'ch. Repeat after me: Iyento ch'ch."

"Iyento ch'ch," Emery faithfully repeated. What was this, a language program?

"Repeat after me," said the voice again, flat and implacable. "Oyentu voolomus."

"Oyen—" began Emery, but caught himself. This was silly. He listened for more instructions from the voice. But it never came back. There was stillness for almost a minute; then the static rose up and washed over it.

Emery had almost reached the end of the "dial" (even without a dial, he could feel the knob grating to a stop) when he heard a low whine. The teapot again. No, he had shut the burner off. He was sure of it. Gone now. Turning the knob back with painful slowness, he recovered the sound. Not a wail, exactly; there was too much focus to it, too much . . . music. *The Music of Your Life*. A high, lone voice, uncurling up into the rain-shot air and drawn into this ancient radio set. After a few moments a second voice joined in, lower but in sad, minor harmony. Then a third, winding between the two. A fourth—No, that was just the wind, fluting through the eaves. When Emery listened back to the radio, though, there *were* more voices. A chorus rose and fell in interlacing harmonies; no words, just pure voice. It was sweet to Emery's ears, but sweet in the way a sunset is, or sweet as flowers growing upon a grave; the bittersweet of things lost and gone. Like the light in the radio's tubes, the singing grew. What station *was* this, anyway? Now the voices veered and slanted away from one another in a mockery of their former harmony. Some of the lower voices pushed to the fore like the deep notes of an organ, carrying the music on to darker paths, unknown ways. The higher voices, unlocked from the melody, wandered into sickening, stratospheric curves.

It was getting to be too much. Emery turned the volume knob to the left, but the voices kept on rising. In one of the quiet moments of the song, coinciding with a lull in the storm, he heard a soft crunch outside his window. He knew that noise; he had made it himself numerous times—a foot pressing down on the mat of dead reeds by the edge of the pond. And a muted splash, the sound of feet coming out of water. Then the voices surged up again. Behind them Emery thought he could hear another crunch outside; but the wind was back and the rain whipping across the walls of the house, and the wind rising with the nameless song. Emery, his hand now trembling, turned the volume knob all the way to the left until it clicked off. But the voices kept pouring from the rusted mesh of the radio's speaker, and the wind rose shrieking with them. And now the wind was all around the house, and with it the voices, so many voices, cold and somehow each alone in their multitude, called through the rain-drear night to this one house, alone by a pond by the sea.

And the Sea Gave Up the Dead

In 2004 historians and naturalists alike were galvanized by the news of the discovery of the sea-journals of British naturalist Margate Townshend. The small, sharkskin-bound octavo volumes came to light during an auction of an anonymous lot at the London auction house of Berkley and Dighton that year and were subsequently purchased by representatives of the Miskatonic University School of Natural History. As a first-hand account of Captain James Cook's second great voyage of exploration (1771–75), by an aide to the ship's official "natural historians," Johann Reinhold Forster and his son George, the value of this document is unquestioned. The wealth of data on the flora, fauna, and native customs of the Pacific will be of inestimable worth to future scholars of history, anthropology, and biology.

But the journal's importance transcends even these great boons. Specifically, it may settle for once and for all the long debate as to why Cook, retreating from the Antarctic pack in January 1774, abruptly came about in Latitude 47 degrees south to make his famous run to 71 degrees, 10 minutes south, "as far as I think it possible for man to go."

The period in question in Townshend's journals is January 5–11, 1774. Scholars will be struck immediately with the many discrepancies between Townshend's account and those of other diarists aboard the *Resolution* (the redoubtable Cook among them). But certain internal evidences in Townshend's text, coupled with its virtual agreement with other shipboard chronicles on all other aspects of the voyage, have led many to the conclusion that Townshend's account is the more reliable; and, conversely, that there was a conspiracy of silence among the rest of the explorers over what they found during those lost days. The reasons for this will become obvious upon reading. It is with the intention of inspiring further debate and intellectual inquiry that the following text is now published and submitted to the public for the first time, through a grant from the Francis Wayland Thurston Research Fund.

———

1774 Jan'ry 5.

This morn the wind calm, the sky clear—a Blessing to be free of the wicked Cold and Ice-mountains of the extreme South. Quantities of Sea-Birds encounter'd, incl. Albatrtoss, Sheerwaters, the *Puffinus* of Linnaeus, &c. Flying Fisshe too, flockes of them such that the Deck was littered all about with them, shining like Bars of Silver. They flew head on into our Ship as if driven by a Blast. Later encounter'd Several of Squidd of unknown species, swimming S.S. W. These we saw off and on until the Duske descended, after which Time these fishe were visible by the bright Maculations of Colour upon their long and many Armes.

1774 Jan'ry 6.

Clear and the Wind continues astern, warmer every Day, tho' while the weather stays amenable the Crewmen appear restless. One or two complain of the Squid, which Creture we have seen in increasing Shoals of hundreds, nay, thousands. Their Peculiarity evaded me untill one of the seamen caught one up with his fizgig [i.e., harpoon]. He landed the Squid upon the deck for our Inspection. It proved a large (15 feet) variant of *Teuthis* Linn[aeus], but in place of the usual Finns imployed in moving them thro' the water these have large Wings of a membraneous Aspect much like to Bats wings. A set of segmented Fingers sprout from either side of the Squids head and it is upon these that the Wings are spread as Sails are set upon Spars. I made bold to christen it my self, calling it *Teuthis megaptera* after its great Wings (*pace* Linnaeus).

Beyond this, tho', we did not have time sufficient thoroughly to examine this Specimin, for the Sailors did not like the look of its Eyes, saying It gives us the Evill Eye. Forster, eager to dissect the animal, attempted to assuage their Fears, reminding them that onlie a Man can possess a Soul & a Consciousness & Will. But they are a superstitious Lot and to ease them we threw the Thing back into the Sea.

1774 Jan'ry 7.

The wind that had blowne us clear of the Antarctic regions now abates somewhat, the sky still clear but temperature hot. More squid pass on, flights of many Birds, too—Albatross, Tropick birds, & the Great Petrel *Micronectes giganteus* Linn., all in a South by Southwesterly fashion. Their Shadowes make a pattern on the deck like a moving lattice, so Numerous are they, and the sound they made was as the whistling of a Great Gale. Whither they go I cannot say, as we found no Land in that Direction.

At mid day the lookout espied a Cloud of prodigious Size on the horizon N.N. E. This bespoke volcanic Activitie and thus an island where Island was not recorded to be. So the *Resolution* was steered towards this cloud, the Crewe being on short Commons of mouldy bread and foul Water, and nothing loth to find fresh, but the Clowd provd to be of mighty Size and Distance, and by the setting of the Sunne with the wind slackening we had not raisd this land.

To night the schools of Squidd continue by us. Their glowing Spots were so many that we saild thro' a River of Jewells, as it were. The Seaman Isaac Gillis join'd me at the rail to admire this Spectacle, and even claim'd to see a Patterne or Message spelt in the arrangement of the Spots. But this I could not credit, and later some of his fellow Sailors told me O don't mind him, Sir, Gillis is just an ignorant old son of a Pagan Scotchman. He comes from the Western Isles of that Nation (so they informed me) and believes in Selkies and the Like.

But I am arrous'd to Inquiry at this Gillis, for the Patterns he claimed to see were not the same Markings that I could make out. On an Inspiration I later tested him with Mr Hodges paints [William Hodges, expedition artist aboard the *Resolution*—Ed.] and discovered him to be colour-blind in the Redd spectrum. Thus his Worde is doubly suspect, and I will in future guard myself against his Deceptions.

1774 Janu'ry 8.

Hot and increasingly stille, but we raisd the Island whose Smoke we espied yesterday, in approx. 50 S., 135 W. It is indeed a volcanic Formation, compriz'd of basalt, pumice, & granite, and rises in black & shere Cliffes on 3 sides, viz S., W., & E. Upon its Crest wave a forest of Palms and Cycads *cycan circilanus* Linn., and it is from the midst of these that the great Cloud tumbles upwrd into the Sky. The soil eroded from the volcanic Ejecta must have been sown with the above Verdure by passing Birds, yet no birds did we see upon this Day. In contrast to the past two Days not a bird was in evidence neither upon the Land nor upon the Sea. They all had fled.

As we approach'd the Island a Wind freshened from the North and blew upon us a Reek such as few of us can have ever known. It was blended of Sulphur from the smoking, thundering Caldera above, but also of a Stench of Corruption so strong as to send some of our stoutest Mariners to the rail. Upon rounding the Island to its North side we discovered the Source of this hellish Smell. Here the Land shelved down more gently than the other Sides, and met the muttering Surf in a Beach of black Sande. Strewn as far as Eye could see upon this Strand were thousands of the Bodies of *Teuthis megaptera* I have described before, all beached and rotting in the Tropick Sun. What can have driven them so to maroon themselves I cannot imagine.

30 yards beyond the edge of the water the Forest began; and as anchor was dropped and the *Resolution* came to rest, People emerged from those Trees. At that distance (half a mile) little could be discern'd as to their Nature, but that they were typicall in Colouring to other South Sea Islanders we had seen, being dark of skin with black hair curled like that of a Negroe, and that they were a large People. However I was chosen, along with Mr Forster *père*, and several Seamen to accompany Capt. Cook ashore in one of the boats, and soon had better opportunitie to see them.

Having crosst the water we stepped in amongst the decaying Squids and up the beach, and here I was able to view these Salvages more clearly. They were indeed a large People, the least of whom was not less than six feet in hight, and some of whom loomed over our tallest Sailors. They wore skirts of some woven grass, both Sexes, to cover the Organs of Generation, but chests bare, Females too as in the fashion of the women of Otaheite. But notwithstanding this Boldness of attire there was no attraction to them. Rather, all, Male and Female alike, bore a fierceness of expression which precluded any native Charm. This Fierceness was accentuated by Tattews, on arms, legs, Breasts & especially on the Face. Those on the Face called to mind the *moko* of the Indians of Taika Mowi [the Maori of New Zealand—Ed.], but less individual in character. All the Men before us wore a Tattew design of ropes of vines or tentacles spreading out in curling ramifications from a single Eye imprinted into the forehead. The Skill used in creating these Tattews was impressive, and the Designs might even have been considered beautiful but for the dire Aspect of the Wearers faces. The Men, too, wielded

Swords edged with Sharks teeth such as we had found on other Islands, which added to their Wild apperance.

Captain Cook, ever bold unto the point of Rashness, approached them with open arms and offerd them gifts of Paper [a rare commodity in the Pacific—Ed.], but they would have none. One of the seamen, who knew some of the Ocean dialects, went with him as interpreter. The rest of us stayd back, between the line of menacing Islanders and the line of stinking squid Bodies, and I would be hard prest to say which was worse. It was a tense Situation, made worse by a feeling of Unease that had spread thro' the ship, but the Crew were eager for decent food and the water in the Hold green & foul, so it was deem'd worth the Risk.

The Conversation between the Capt. and the Islanders appeared to be going peacefully. Then Gillis, the same sailor who had spoken with me about the Squids, walked to one of the dead Monsters on the sand and bent down as if to touch it. At this 20 Warriors broke from the line and were running towards us, swinging their Swords and bellowing in an access of rage. Luckilly our Men were arm'd with muskets and raised them to fire. Before they could do so Capt. Cook yelled Shoot over their Heads!, which the men did. The explosion of the muskets checkt the Warriors in their charge, but only just, and not nearly as thoro'ly as we had wished. While they stood thus, weapons raised but irresolute, not 20 Feet away, and our Men frantically reloading their Pieces, I could see Cook and the interpreter in converse earnest and swift with the Islanders. You must not touch the Squidd, the Interpreter calld to us, They are sacred to these people. At this, we moved as one a few feet forward and away from the Squid, keeping our eyes upon the Warriors, who watched us likewise. I put up my hands in a Motion of appeasement, and all relaxed somewhat. At length Cook and his man came back to us, and we were told that we would be allowd to obtain Water & Comestibles but not stay overlong.

We return'd an hour later with 2 boats and 22 Men, and our reception this second time was reserved but not as hostile as before. In fact, as the Day progress'd, our Primitive Hosts became more amicable and aided us in finding the needed Supplies. In the company of one Titan warrior, a hairy Rustum named A'tai, I was allow'd to roam in their Forest to find animal Specimins, but a poor collector did I make. The Island was remarkably free of most of the higher forms of life, altho' I detected the spoor of many Birds, which now seem to have deserted the Isle. I was put in Mind of all the avian Multitudes we had seen winging Southwards the previous Days, and wondered.

With the bipedal Population of the Island I had more success. The Interpreter Sailor joined me & Mr Forster and we were able to interview Several of the Salvages upon divers Subjects, & here my inquiries bore curious Fruit. [He is playing with us here, referring to the fruit gathered by the sailors—Ed.] For it was quickly borne in upon me that every Soul upon the Island was Colour-blind. [This is not as far-fetched as it sounds: Pingelap, also in the Pacific Ocean, is another example of an island where the achromatic mutation spread throughout an entire population.] This explained why some of the Selvages, attempting to help our Men gather Fruit, gathered ripe and unripe alike, unable to tell the colour diferences.

Of material Culture they have precious little, besides their Huts (mean in comparison with other Societies we had encounterd), canoos, & sundry tools. In One greater hut, tho', they kept their religion, and this they explicated with Enthusiasm. They believe in a Great Squid (they told us), named Tlulu, who would one Day rise up out of the sea and raise this Tribe of the Faithful to Mastery of the Earth. The North is said to be Sacred to him, and that region is *tapu* [taboo] to all save the Faithful. To reckon the Time of His rising, they have built Charts of woven sticks & string so contrived to Predict the position of sartain Stars in their Courses. [Townshend may be mistaken—this is very reminiscent of the *mattang* of the Marshall Islands, used for navigation—Ed.] These they hang about the House of Tlulu like so many Snares set to entrap Time it self.

The Southern Summer day was long but by the time sufficient Stores were gathered to the Beach the sunn was westering. Our hosts expressed sadnes (by word if not by expression) at our leaving & urged us to sail South, to other Islands far greater than their own. But this we knew for a Lie as we had but lately traversd these Seas and encounter'd naught save Ocean Ocean & more Ocean. We thanked them, said naught of our true destination, and we prepared to embark.

But as the Sun neared the horizon of a sudden our Hosts all faced North and the Men set up a loud chaunt, viz:

> Tlulu Tlulu
>
> Fan glei Ma-glawa na'
>
> Tlulu R'lai waga-nal fata'n

and the Warriors stamppd their feet in time on the black Sand & beat their Chests with the flat of their Swords. The Women moaned in unison, such a doleful Sound as of the Winds of the World mourning the Last Day. And as they moaned they sank to their Knees & thence lay prone upon the sand. Now the Men made to do the same, until the whole Population was spred upon the beach like a Congregation of Mussulmen facing Mecca. It was a spectacle I expect to see in my Memory the rest of my life, the Island rising high and green behind us, the volumes of Smoke higher still, into the indigo tropick evening, those giant brown bodies laid upon the Sand, glistening in the last Rayes of the setting Sunne, and the putrescent remains of the squid not washed off by the Tides. All grew terribly quiet—only the soft sudden Clap of waves upon the Strand. Of a sudden the ground beneath our feet commenced to vibrate, and from the smoking Mountain at our back came a deep and angry Mutter. It only lasted some seconds, but impressed us again with the Titanic forces intombed beneath these lands of the South Sea. And when the islanders arose we saw that they were all Smiling, and One pointed to the wide Sea and said Tlulu.

1774 Jan'ry 9.

Ill Dreams last night of undefined Horrors—all complain of them. The blue-green Abyss beneath us—too many Monthes at sea. We lay at anchor all night, the Captain and Master not trusting to navigate amongst unknown shoals and Reefs in the dark. A guard was placed on deck against any possible Incursions by the Salvages, and indeed in the morn we found the *Resolution* ringed by canoos. Capt. Cook and Johann Forster spoke the nearest Canoo and were told they were there to protect us, tho' from what they would not say.

Preparations were made to procede Northward, but the Natives would no[t allow it], beseeching us to stay and injoy the Bounty of the Island, though to speak truly those benefits had been scanty Enou[gh]. Cook directed them to move away from the Ship but they would not and brandished their swords & spears. At last the Captain order'd a Cannon fired across their bows, which mighty sound astonisht these Salvages much but dissuaded them not one jot.

Now the brutes paddled towards our ship and showed ev'ry Intention of boarding with consequent Murder & Pillage, but this time it was Captain Cook who would not have it and ordered the cannon loaded with grape[shot] and fired into the midst of them. The discharge made great slaughter amongst the warriors and sank 2 canoes, yet did they come on more Determin'd than ever, blood in their Eyes.

Now it was to be seen that more Islanders, roused by the noise of the Battle, were issuing forth from the island in more canoos. In fact, it seemed the whole population of the Island must be upon the water, so Numerous were they, and armed at all aspects. Our crew was all armed as well and with the Cannon & swivel the Muskets bang'd and clatterd making and ungodly Din in the quiet morning air, yet the Natives came on again and again. Soon it was evident that we must slay All or be born under by their sheer Ferocity and numbers, and this the Capt. was loth to do, so ordered sails set and whilst the Guns kept the most Zealous of the attackers at bay, we made good our escape.

Even as the wind freshened and bore us away to the North the Islanders tried to keep pace with us, paddling furiosly and all the time calling Tlulu Tlulu in Voices made rough by exertion. Now 3 of the Canoos spread Sail also, much like those tall triangular Sails imploy'd by the Indians [i.e., the Maori—Ed.], and bid fair to catch us up, the wind being in their Quarter. And upon these sails we could see an Image of their Great Squidd-God or Tlulu painted in some red pigment, terribel to look at. But for all their paint & Tattews & infernal shouts & armes the gunners made short work of them, spraying them with lethal loads of grape and round-shot & tearing their pretty Sails all to rags & filling their bilges with the Blood of the slain.

In an hour we had left them behind and stood on at a fair pace, some 8 knotts under a cloudles Sky. With the fair weather & Sun and our escape from the islanders our mood should have been lighten'd, yet our Crew were still surly and recalcitrant. As we progressed thro' the foaming Water I felt this choler spreading even to me, and I observ'd Mr Forster *père* more disputatious & ill-favoured than usual. Seaman Gillis is on the edge of Hysteria, and sadly his Mood conveys easily to the other seamen. Many now speak in Low Voices of the Squidds and their possible meaning. They do their chores faithfully but without the Alacrity of former days. There is nothing so plain as Mutinie, but it would be fair to say their hearts are not in their work. We saw few fish and no Birds at all on this day, altho' an occasionall Squid of the ubiquitous *megaptera* species shot past us, ever South. And it was plain to me now that Bird and Beast alike had not been migrating *to* anything, but fleeing *from* Something. And we are ploughing thro' the waves towards that Something.

To night Gillis was clappt in irons and will be flogg'd upon the morrow. He had been becoming more erratick all day, and as Night fell he clamber'd into the shrouds, there to observe the squid beneath the Waters. He began yelling down that now he could see the Patterns intire, he had learnt the cipher of the Squids maculations and it told him we should arrive at our Destination in a day and a nights Time. With the Mens mood already wound to a high pitch the Boatswain called for Gillis to Come down out of there, be a good lad and shut it, but he would not, and finally the Mate and a couple Hands must needs climb the rigging as well and chase him even to the Topsail yards before securing him & returning him to the deck where he was restrain'd. My heart is mov'd to sadness and regret at the Poor man and his plight, yet he seems the most sanguine and Cheerfull of our company anticipating Great Things to come. That he is mad is without a doubt, but I am reminded of his colourblindness and that of the Islanders, and I now ask myself not What is it that they do *not* see, but What is it that they *DO* see?

1774 Jan'ry 10.
Wind constant, nearly a Gale out of the S.S. W. Sun and hotter, the Mood on deck sombre. Gillis brought up to Deck this morning, bound to the shrouds and given 12 lashes. Still he complaind none, and when the doctor applied salves to his Back, and a new sail was spread upon the mainmast, disclosing a gigantick Squidds head and tentacles he had painted in tar upon it, he laughed like to burst his Lungs. The Mate secreted him far below Decks, in hopes that his Laughter will not further annoy the crew, who are become surly for lack of Slepe. All complain of bad dreams, my self included, of the Depths of ocean & of Somthing rising to be seen, a great and awful Revelation. The text

And the Sea gave up the Dead which were in it [Rev. 20:13]

revolves in my mind again and again tho' I try to silence it. There is no wholesome Distraction to put in its place, however, as the Crew are silent, the Forsters are silent, the Captain is silent, and the sea is become a wide and featureless Desertt devoid of Life of any kind. For even the strange squid have quit these Waters, responding to Who knows what Stimulus or warning. Yet our Captain has set his aquiline face and implacable Will towards the Unknown North, as resolute to discover what is undiscover'd as to go where he has been forbidden, *tapu* or no. The Wind seems to manifest his intent, pressing the sails until the Masts creak and groan in a most worrysome Manner. He is, indeed, the Captain of *Resolution*.

As I write this in my berth before a Sleep which I dread, the only sound of Human activitie is the hoarse laugh of Gillis, secured deep in the Hold.

1774 January 11.

In the Latitude of 47 degress 9 minutes South, Longitude of 126 Degrees, 43 minutes West. Sun, hot, the wind dyed in the Night. The Sea the colour of Pewter, the sky a steely blue such as I have never seen—a vast Slate upon which anything may be written. V. early this morn awaked by a shout. As I lay in my berth wondering if it emanated from the Captain's cabin or no, I heard the rapid thumping of bare Feet running upon the deck above my head, and soon divers Yells and Alarms. I rose quickly, glad to be free of the Gripe of unspeakable nightmares, and came up on Deck.

All the Crew were awake and running hither and yon, many crowding along the bow rail and cat heads forward, staring Ahead. I joined them, close by Captain Cook himself. Like his Men, his Countenance was set & grim & intent upon the Sea before Us.

There, several miles distant, the Ocean was heaving up in a wide Circle, a smooth, silvery shield betokening some titan Current upwelling from unguessed Depths. A Hand in the rigging guessed it to be 2 miles in diameter, and contrary to its evident dispersal of water we were being drawn towards It. Still we remain unmoving, fascinated by this Irruption from a World beyond our most acute philosophies. This is What we have been drawn towards, the Captain said quietly at my side, This is What the Salveges tried to discourage us from reaching. And still we drifted towards It, and the only sound on that flat, immeasurable Plain was the gurgling of the uprising waters.

We should have stayd thus and, God help us, have been caught by that unholy Current but that at that moment there was a Commotion aft. Gillis had contrived to escape his bounds, evade his Captors, & run pell mell up onto the Main Deck, calling and screaming in a most hideous Manner, Tlulu! Tlulu! So aghast were we at this apparition, his hair disheveld, his eyes distended, shirt in flying tatters behind him as he ran, that for a moment no one thought to restrain him. In that moment he grabbed up from beside one of the Canon two of the six-pound balls, careen'd to the rail and throwing his Hands holding the shot straight out before him, dove over and down to splash into the Sea. We watched as his body, still clutching the balls, legs kicking, faded and faded into the Green waters, faded, dwindled, and Gone.

Then Consciousness returned to us as with a slap, and the Captain ordered the Boats over the side Immediately. Cables were strung betwixt Ship and boats, and the doughty Sailors manned their oars, bent their backs to the Task, and turned the *Resolution* about and away from that nightmare Fountain in the Middle of the sea. They rowed like men possess'd or reborn, reborn to Sense and Duty, and rowed us until the Upwelling had disappear'd back over the horizon. Then a clean, fresh Breeze arose from the N. W., the boats were pulled in and stowed, and the Captain directed us on a course as near due South as could be attain'd without nearing that Island of Evil People. He speaks now of returning to find the Southern Continent, for which even the most Profane among us praised God Almighty, officer and man.

———

Thus ends the disputed portion of Margate Townshend's manuscript. It should be noted that there is no Able Seaman Isaac Gillis on the ship's list for the *Resolution* for the voyage of 1771–75 (nor for any of Cook's voyages, for that matter), nor is there any island in the location Townshend indicates. However, papers may be recopied or revised during the long, quiet watches at sea (as we know Cook himself did in journal entries dealing with cannibalism); and the unknown island seems to have been an unstable formation of recent origin. Things that have risen may sink, and those that have sunk may rise again.

Acknowledgments

"And the Sea Gave Up the Dead." First published in S. T. Joshi, ed., *Black Wings II: New Tales of Lovecraftian Horror* (PS Publishing, 2012).

"Detachment." First published in *What Is Anything?* (August 1990).

"An Echo of Pipes." First published in *Crypt of Cthulhu* (Michaelmas 1985).

"From the Realms of Glory." First published in *Weird Fiction Review* (Fall 2010).

"The Hollow Sky." First published in S. T. Joshi, ed., *The Madness of Cthulhu: Volume Two* (Titan Books, 2015.).

"A Tale of a Lonely Island." First published in *Spectral Tales* (June 1988).

"The Walker in the Night." First published in S. T. Joshi, ed., *Black Wings V: New Tales of Lovecraftian Horror* (PS Publishing, 2016).

All other stories in this book are previously unpublished.